"This second volume in best-seller Dickerson's Dericott Tales series follows two narrators who overcome self-doubt in accepting their physical differences and gain the confidence to love while finding solace in their Christianity . . . Dickerson writes a well-developed and wholesome romance between pleasant characters whose happy ending readers will easily root for."

—BOOKLIST ON CASTLE OF REFUGE

"Dickerson does a nice job of evoking late-14th-century England and has succeeded in crafting a pair of engaging—if sugary-sweet—characters that romance readers will enjoy following. The Christian flavor of the story feels natural and appropriate to the time period."

—KIRKUS REVIEWS ON CASTLE OF REFUGE

"Court of Swans is a well-crafted escape thriller with plenty of longing glances to break up scenes of sword fighting. Delia is a compelling protagonist because she is able to see the good in people—rarely do you see an obviously wicked stepmother so often given the benefit of the doubt. A perfect pick for fans of period dramas who want a little action mixed into their romance."

—MOLLY HORAN, BOOKLIST

"The Piper's Pursuit is a lovely tale of adventure, romance, and redemption. Kat and Steffan's righteous quest will have you rooting them on until the very satisfying end!"

—LORIE LANGDON, AUTHOR OF OLIVIA TWIST AND THE DOON SERIES

"Christian fiction fans will relish Dickerson's eloquent story."

—SCHOOL LIBRARY JOURNAL ON THE ORPHAN'S WISH

"Dickerson is a masterful storyteller with a carefully crafted plot, richly drawn characters, and a detailed setting. The reader is easily pulled into the story."

—*Christian Library Journal* on *The Noble Servant*

"A terrific YA crossover medieval romance from the author of *The Golden Braid*."

—*Library Journal* on *The Silent Songbird*

"When it comes to happily-ever-afters, Melanie Dickerson is the undisputed queen of fairy-tale romance, and all I can say is—long live the queen! From start to finish *The Beautiful Pretender* is yet another brilliant gem in her crown, spinning a medieval love story that will steal you away—heart, soul, and sleep!"

—Julie Lessman, award-winning author of
the Daughters of Boston, Winds of Change,
and Heart of San Francisco series

"Dickerson breathes life into the age-old story of Rapunzel, blending it seamlessly with the other YA novels she has written in this time and place . . . The character development is solid, and she captures religious medieval life splendidly."

—*Booklist* on *The Golden Braid*

"Readers who love getting lost in a fairy-tale romance will cheer for Rapunzel's courage as she rises above her overwhelming past. The surprising way Dickerson weaves threads of this enchanting companion novel with those of her other Hagenheim stories is simply delightful."

—Jill Williamson, Christy Award–
winning author, on *The Golden Braid*

"Melanie Dickerson does it again! Full of danger, intrigue, and romance, this beautifully crafted story [*The Huntress of Thornbeck Forest*] will transport you to another place and time."

—Sarah E. Ladd, bestselling author
of the Cornwall novels

CLOAK *of*
SCARLET

OTHER BOOKS BY
MELANIE DICKERSON

THE DERICOTT TALES

Court of Swans

Castle of Refuge

Veil of Winter

Fortress of Snow

Cloak of Scarlet

Lady of Disguise

YOUNG ADULT FAIRY TALE ROMANCE SERIES

The Healer's Apprentice

The Merchant's Daughter

The Fairest Beauty

The Captive Maiden

The Princess Spy

The Golden Braid

The Silent Songbird

The Orphan's Wish

The Warrior Maiden

The Piper's Pursuit

The Peasant's Dream

A MEDIEVAL FAIRY TALE SERIES

The Huntress of Thornbeck Forest

The Beautiful Pretender

The Noble Servant

REGENCY SPIES OF LONDON SERIES

A Spy's Devotion

A Viscount's Proposal

A Dangerous Engagement

CLOAK *of* SCARLET

MELANIE DICKERSON

THOMAS NELSON
Since 1798

Cloak of Scarlet

Copyright © 2023 Melanie L. Bedford

Published in Nashville, Tennessee, by Thomas Nelson. Thomas Nelson is a registered trademark of HarperCollins Christian Publishing, Inc.

Thomas Nelson titles may be purchased in bulk for educational, business, fundraising, or sales promotional use. For information, please email SpecialMarkets@ThomasNelson.com.

Publisher's Note: This novel is a work of fiction. Names, characters, places, and incidents are either products of the author's imagination or used fictitiously. All characters are fictional, and any similarity to people living or dead is purely coincidental.

ISBN: 978-0-8407-0819-9 (hardcover)
ISBN: 978-0-8407-0822-9 (e-book)
ISBN: 978-0-8407-0853-3 (audio download)
ISBN 978-0-8407-0883-0 (trade paper)

Library of Congress Cataloging-in-Publication Data

CIP data is available upon request.

ScoutAutomatedPrintCode

To Aaron
The one I love
The one who loves me

ONE

SPRING 1386

VIOLET WORE HER RED CLOAK AND CARRIED HER GRAND-mother's favorite foods—Mother's fresh bread and the apple-cherry cake Violet had made—in a basket in front of her on her mule's saddle. Grandmother had not been feeling well the last time Violet went to visit her, so she said a little prayer under her breath as she went.

"Tread carefully, Mistress Sally," she told her mule, patting her soft gray neck. The road was still muddy after all the rains of the past few days.

Violet's red cloak that her grandmother had given her guarded her against the chill in the early morning air as she traveled in the company of one of their villeins, who was on his way to market in the town of Bilborough.

When they came to the crossroads near her grandmother's village, they parted ways.

"Take heed and be watchful," the man said. "Baron Dunham's men are about."

"I thank you. I will." Violet had heard tales of Baron Dunham's men demanding money from travelers on the road, but she'd never had any dealings with him or his men. Nor did she wish to.

Violet urged her mule into a faster trot, hugging the basket to her stomach.

Two weeks ago she'd met a young man on this same road, just at the crossroads, riding a fine warhorse. He was quite handsome and definitely not from her village.

"Pardon me," he'd said politely. "Can you tell me the way to Bilborough?"

"Yes," Violet said, pointing him in the right direction. "If you stay on this road, you will reach Bilborough in about fifteen miles."

The man nodded to her, his dark blue eyes fastened on her face in a polite but intent way. "I am Sir Merek of Dericott. May I ask your name?"

"Violet of Burwelle." She smiled, hoping she did not seem overly forward. But the man was a knight, so he surely would not mistreat her in any way. It was against his code of chivalry.

"I thank you, Violet of Burwelle. Perhaps I shall see you again."

"Perhaps you shall."

"Fare well."

"Godspeed," Violet said, staring after him as he rode away.

But today she was alone on the road. More's the pity. She

had lain awake the night before imagining what she would say to the polite and handsome Sir Merek if she were to encounter him again. Perhaps that was silly of her, but he was the first handsome knight she had ever met.

The weather was glorious after the rains. Flowers grew along the roadside. It would be a shame not to pick some flowers for Grandmother.

Violet stopped her mule and slid to the ground. She listened for horses' hooves or voices. Hearing only birds singing, she started picking the flowers with the brightest colors—pinks, blues, and purples—along with some white daisies.

She once told her mother, "I like the way the white daisies make the color in the other flowers seem even brighter and prettier."

Her mother gave her a slight smile and shook her head. "You think about the strangest things."

She was very different from her mother, who seemed to think only about things like cooking and cleaning and never about singing or dancing or reading books. "You are like your grandmother," her mother told her once, "always staring at the clouds and memorizing psalms and poetry. Someday you may be a poet yourself."

"Or a troubadour, writing songs?" Violet teased, lifting her eyebrows.

"Oh no, not a troubadour." Her mother scrunched her face in a sour look. "Troubadours are wanderers and thieves. You don't want to be like them."

Mother's dislike of troubadours was well known.

Violet's grandmother, on the other hand, had been known to run out of her house when she heard troubadours passing by and beg them to sing her a song. Grandmother also liked to sing while she worked and picked flowers for every room in her house. Perhaps that was why Violet liked visiting her so much.

She placed the large handful of flowers on top of the cloth-covered food in her basket. When she tried to remount her mule, she nearly spilled everything. She decided to walk the rest of the way and lead the mule by the reins.

Her mind wandered, as it often did, to Mother's expectation that she would marry Robert Mercer, the son of the landowner who lived on the other side of the stream, the boundary between their lands. But Violet didn't like Robert. He never spoke to her directly. If the man wanted to marry her, as he said he did, then he might at least talk to her and find out what she liked and disliked. Besides, two years ago she'd overheard him saying to her brother, "What good is it for a woman to learn to read?"

She hadn't heard the rest of their conversation, but his words made her sure that she would not marry Robert Mercer.

Father had taught her to read when she was very young, before he died of a fever. He'd been the younger son of a knight, and he had inherited the plot of land she and her mother and brother, as well as their villeins and tenants, now farmed.

After she'd indignantly related what Robert had said about women learning to read, her mother said, "Robert may not even know how to read himself. He has no need for reading because he has a goodly amount of land, and he has plenty of people to work the land. He knows how to cipher, does he not?"

At the time Violet had shrugged her shoulders. She didn't know, didn't want to know. Now, as she led her mule toward her grandmother's house, she found herself thinking that if no other offer of marriage came along, she might actually give in and marry him. She hated the thought of disappointing her mother, after all she had done for her, taking her in when she was an orphan with no one to care for her.

But Grandmother thought much differently from Mother. When Violet said that her mother wanted her to marry Robert Mercer, Grandmother had smiled, a wistful look on her face. "Is that what you want?"

"No," Violet answered. She imagined her future love as a handsome man who was brave and capable, who wrote and played songs like David in the Bible, who loved her more than anything. And the man she wanted to marry would never disapprove of her knowing how to read.

"Perhaps it is not likely to happen," Violet told her grandmother, "but I would marry a man who reads and writes, who is noble and good-hearted, and who is in love with me."

"I have faith that you will marry just such a man." Grandmother gave her a mysterious smile. "Do as you wish, my dear, and don't let anyone tell you that love is not important. Love is everything."

As she picked her way down the muddy road, Violet said softly, rubbing Sally's neck, "Love is everything."

She soon arrived at her grandmother's cottage and called out in a singsong voice, "Grandmother! It's me, Violet!" Then she pushed the front door open.

"Oh, my dear! I was just wishing for a visit from you." Grandmother made her way quickly across the room, then hugged her and kissed her cheek. "And what is this you've brought me?"

"Some flowers I picked, and cake, bread, and some cheese."

"Oh, my sweet Violet. How thoughtful you are." She kissed her cheek again. "And how fetching you look, with your red riding cloak against your dark brown hair."

"I love you, Grandmother." Violet gently embraced her frail shoulders. "Let me put the flowers in a vase for you." Violet hurried to get the pottery vase and fill it with water. When she returned, she asked, "How are you feeling? No more headaches, I hope."

"I am well enough, well enough."

"Is something wrong? Are you in pain?"

"No, no, I am well. Just the same few aches that a woman my age can expect to have. No, but I will warn you that there have been some brigands—"

"Brigands, here? Did they harm you?"

"They did not harm me, but they took the money I had planned to use to buy a goose and a pig. You knew that my pigs died, did you not?"

Violet nodded. "I remember. They got the wasting disease."

"The money they stole was what I needed for my winter meat. Without it . . ." Grandmother shook her head.

Violet knew. It meant that she would go hungry.

She longed to assure her grandmother that they would provide her with a pig, but the disease had spread through their herd as well. And even if they had a pig to offer her, Grandmother wouldn't take it.

"Who were these brigands who took your money?" Violet asked.

"Not the usual kind. I would call them liars who rob from the poor to give to the rich. It was Baron Dunham's men."

Violet gasped and covered her mouth.

"He's been sending his men all over the village to steal from the villeins and also the landowners, who then force their villeins to pay for what Baron Dunham's men take from them. His men have been all over in the past week. I'm surprised they didn't accost you on your way here."

"How dare he do such an unlawful thing! He is a baron, so he is wealthy already. Why must he take from the poor?" Her heart ached as she thought of her grandmother being so cruelly treated, as well as other widows who were perhaps even less able to afford what was taken from them. "But what excuse did they give for doing something so dastardly?"

"His men said they are collecting a protection tax, to protect our lives and our property, but there haven't been any brigands around our village—nary a one—in at least ten years." Grandmother's face grew tense as she spoke.

"Did they take all your money?" Violet asked.

"I am afraid so." Grandmother gave a wan smile. Then her eyes narrowed, and she lifted her chin. "I told them they would get nothing from me unless they took it, that they were cowards indeed to threaten and steal from an old woman."

"What happened?"

"They searched the house until they found my coins, and they took them." She said it matter-of-factly, staring placidly back at Violet.

"How dare they?" Violet breathed out the words, drawing her hands into fists. "What were their names? Where are they now?" She was ready to find the men and force them to give her grandmother back her coins.

"Baron Dunham's men—knights, some of them—are well trained and we cannot fight them. There is nothing we can do. Our best hope is that word will reach the king and he will do something to stop the baron."

Violet had heard talk of Baron Dunham taking an unlawful tax from the people who lived near his castle and village of Bilborough. She'd also heard a song the troubadours sang about a robber baron who stole from the people and used his castle as a base for his thieving. She marveled that anyone could dare to offend God in such a way, deliberately violating the Holy Scriptures, which condemned rich men who oppressed the poor, the orphan, and the widow.

"What kind of men would do such a thing?"

"The men were obeying orders from Baron Dunham. He is the one who is most to blame. They were ordinary-looking men, except for the one in charge. He had a scar that went from the bridge of his nose down to the corner of his mouth." She drew a line on her own face with her finger.

"What kind of man, but especially a knight, would obey those kinds of orders? If I were a man, I would—"

"You would get yourself killed, my dear. I am glad you are

not a man." She waved at Violet to sit at the table. "Come, let us not speak of it any further. It will only make us angry. Instead, let us enjoy these beautiful flowers and this delicious cake you made."

Grandmother lifted the dense cake from its cloth wrapping and held it to her nose, closing her eyes and taking a long breath.

"Mmm, it smells so good I can almost taste it."

Violet did her best to push away the feelings that made her chest ache and set about cutting the cake. They both ate a large piece.

"You are a very good cook." Grandmother smiled at her.

"Mother makes better bread. I am apt to forget what I am doing and let things burn."

"Do not be so modest. When someone gives you a compliment, it's all right to believe them. And even if you don't believe them, just say thank you."

Violet smiled and looked into her grandmother's eyes. Even with saggy eyelids and the faded blue, she had the loveliest eyes. "Thank you, Grandmother. I am glad you like the cake, and I'm glad you are well."

But her thoughts drifted to the men who were stealing from her grandmother and everyone else in the region. Even though her grandmother obviously didn't want to spend Violet's visit talking about that, the injustice of it simmered just below the surface of her mind, along with the fear that her grandmother would go hungry this winter, a thought that kept Violet's chest tight.

After a meal of bread, cheese, and cake, her grandmother took her outside to the vegetable patch. They walked around observing the new growth of her plants, and Violet helped her pick the peas and beans that were ready.

Violet's grandfather had been a free man, and as such, he had been called on a few times to fight for the nearest lord, who happened to be Baron Dunham's father. Had he not paid in full everything he owed the baron? Indeed, Violet didn't understand why he owed that man anything. And now the baron's men were raiding the widow of that faithful and loyal man.

"It is so unjust."

Grandmother looked up, the pea pod in her hand half shelled. "What is the matter?"

"Those men took your money."

"They were following the orders of the lord of the land."

"But it was not right. The Holy Writ is very specific about not mistreating and robbing poor widows."

"I am not so very poor." Grandmother went on shelling peas with a small smile on her lips.

Violet huffed out a breath. "You know what I mean. This is an injustice . . ."

Grandmother stopped shelling and gazed straight at Violet. "Is there anything you can do to right the wrong?"

Grandmother was trying to get her to accept it. Instead, Violet said, feeling a bit obstinate, "Perhaps there is something."

"No." Grandmother shook her head. "Baron Dunham is the lord of the land. He may as well be the king, as far as we are concerned. And a king may do as he pleases with his subjects. So why do you fret so?"

"Because it was your money, not theirs."

"You and I do not love money. If money is all they want, then let them have it." She recommenced her pea shelling. "We will never be content, as God intended, if we rage against the things we can do nothing about. It is better to accept them."

"I don't know how to do that." Violet shelled the peas in her lap with a bit too much force, sending a pea flying through the air. "And if we do nothing, then how will anything ever change?"

Grandmother was tucking the shelled hulls in the palm of one hand while her fingers quickly and methodically shelled another and another, finally throwing the empty hulls in a bucket by her feet.

"You are right, Violet."

Uh-oh. Grandmother usually only called her by her name when she was a little annoyed or feeling serious.

"If you are able to meet with the baron someday, then you can complain, if he allows it."

It seemed a strange thing for her grandmother to say. Why would she ever meet with the baron? He lived miles away.

"But in the meantime, what good does it do to upset yourself?"

"It does no good, of course, but I cannot control my feelings the way you do. When I see something happening that is unjust, it makes me so angry. I don't know how not to feel what I feel."

Grandmother slowly nodded her head. "I understand better than you think. I was just like you when I was your age, and for a long time afterward, but I learned, through my many years, that I am only hurting myself by not accepting injustice when I have no power in the situation."

Violet stared hard at the peas as she shelled them, finally saying, "I know you are probably right, but what they did was wrong, and I cannot help but feel angry about it."

"It is all well and good to feel it, but don't let your anger linger, leading you to do something foolish."

They shelled in silence while birds chirped and chittered away through the open windows.

Grandmother pulled her shawl down over her upper arms and pinned it under her chin. "I believe the wind is bringing rain. Will you stay the night and go home tomorrow?"

"I told Mother I'd be home today."

"She will understand, especially if it rains."

"I don't want to worry her."

"Very well." Grandmother placed a portion of the peas in a cloth bag, then quickly stitched the top closed. "Take these to your mother." Then she also tried to give her some apples and a bunch of leeks.

"We have plenty. Keep them." Violet kissed her grandmother's soft, wrinkled cheek. "I love you, Grandmother. Pray for me."

"Of course, my dear flower. I always do."

"And I always pray for you."

She patted Violet's cheek. "I thank you, lovey."

As Violet rode back toward home, she imagined being with her grandmother when Baron Dunham's men came to demand her money. Violet saw herself shaking her finger in their faces, saying, "Shame on you, taking a poor widow's money!"

Depending on what kind of men they were, they might look

ashamed and apologize, then leave without taking the money. Or they might yell back at her and restrain her while they took the money, threatening or even striking her before riding away.

Violet rode along, letting her mule go slowly, ruminating over how difficult it was to fight against injustices when one was neither wealthy nor powerful.

The sound of horses' hooves gradually entered her consciousness. Could it be brigands, or worse yet, the baron's men?

The sound grew louder as she looked over her shoulder. Two men on horseback were bearing down on her. And they wore the colors of Baron Dunham's guards.

Two

Violet moved her mare to the side of the road and waited for the men to pass. She sat straight and tall, with her chin up, to make sure they did not mistake her for a poor villein who would not put up a fight.

The men slowed as they approached. Her stomach sank, but she glared at them as they neared her. It appeared as though they were not going to pass her by without a word, as she'd hoped. But she refused to make it easy for them and urged her mule forward.

Mistress Sally, a bit spooked by the strange men and horses, lurched forward but then fell into a steady trot.

The men followed her.

"Pardon us," one of them said, bringing his horse alongside her mule. "We would like a word with you, if you don't mind."

She turned her head to look at the man speaking to her, recognizing both his voice and his face. It was Sir Merek, the young and handsome knight she'd met two weeks before. He was one of Baron Dunham's men!

"I do mind." Turning forward to face the road, she kept moving. But she'd seen the look of recognition on his face as well.

"Violet, it is Sir Merek. We met on the road a fortnight ago."

She didn't answer him. How dare he seem so polite when he had probably been the one to take Grandmother's money?

"I am a knight in the service of Baron Dunham, and this is Sir Willmer. We only wish to ask for directions. Is this the way to Lappage Valley?"

Her blood boiled inside her as she tried to think of what to say. Should she control her temper, as her grandmother had advised?

"Isn't your name Violet? Did you hear me? I am Sir Merek Raynsford of Dericott, and we are on our way—"

Violet turned and glared. "How dare you go about the countryside stealing from poor widows?"

"What did you say?" Sir Merek squinted at her. "Stealing from widows?"

"Yes. How dare you take money from my grandmother and all the other people of her village? I suppose you also shoot arrows at orphans for sport."

"I haven't taken any money from your grandmother, nor anyone else." He leaned back in the saddle as he stared back at her.

"Do you dare to say that you and the other guards have not been going about demanding money on behalf of Baron Dunham?"

"I dare, for I have done no such thing. I am an honorable

English knight. I do not take money unlawfully from grand-mothers." Again, he had the gall to look affronted, staring right back at her as if he wasn't lying like a common slithering snake.

The frightening part was how sincere he sounded, but how could this knight possibly be ignorant of what the baron was doing? How could a knight in the baron's own guard be unaware of the evil practices of the baron he served under?

"My grandmother's money was stolen, demanded of her, by Baron Dunham's men."

"For what reason?"

"They claimed she must pay a tax to the baron in order to remain under his protection."

"Good maiden, why would you fabricate such an outrageous lie? Baron Dunham's men are doing no such thing. We protect the villagers from brigands and thieves, and we do not take money for our service. It is a lord's duty to protect his people, and Baron Dunham does his duty to his—"

"Me, fabricate outrageous lies? You were born for the task, I see." Violet's breath was coming fast and shallow as she struggled to stay calm enough to speak. "What form of chivalry is it to accuse a lady of lying? Are you saying my grandmother, who is practically a saint, lied and that you did not take money from her?"

"Someone is lying, because neither I nor any of Baron Dunham's men would do such a thing."

He did sound as if he was telling the truth, and his face did not betray any signs that he was lying. But Violet didn't want to be fooled.

"Take us to your grandmother so that we can discover the truth."

"So you can take her food also? Or perhaps you want her firewood so she cannot cook or keep warm?"

She could see her words affected him, as his cheeks were turning red and his jaw twitched. Well, let him stew. Someone had taken the villagers' money, and if he did not do it, then he should take on the task of discovering who did. Besides, there was something suspicious about the other man who hung back and let Sir Merek do all the talking.

Sir Merek took a deep breath and let it out slowly. Then he unclenched his jaw and said, "Neither I nor the baron's other men would ever take money or anything else from a woman, especially a widow. If someone is doing such a dastardly thing, I want to know about it, especially if they are doing it in the name of Baron Dunham."

The way the man behind him was staring uncomfortably from her to the ground and back to her made her wonder . . . Did he know something Sir Merek did not?

"Perhaps we should leave it alone," the man behind him said softly. "The woman is daft. Addled."

Violet glared.

"The only way to settle this," Sir Merek said, "is to talk to the supposed victims and find out if what you say is true."

She had begun to think Sir Merek was telling the truth, and since she didn't want to be guilty of falsely accusing anyone . . .

"Very well, then. I will take you to my grandmother and we shall see if she recognizes you as the ones who took her money.

But if you lay a hand on her or try to take anything that belongs to her—"

"You have my word as a knight, I would never do such things."

Truly, he looked quite earnest.

"Follow me, then." She turned her mule around and the two knights followed suit.

As they drew near the village, Violet grew a bit nervous about leading these strangers to her grandmother's house. Finally, she said, "If you truly wish to discover the truth about Baron Dunham, you could ask any of the villagers. Baron Dunham's men were forcing everyone to pay them for protection from robbers."

It was strange, but as angry as she was with Sir Merek, she couldn't get rid of the feeling that he of all the baron's men might be trustworthy.

Merek followed the young maiden.

Perhaps she was addled, as Sir Willmer had said. Certainly she was full of vinegar and distrust, and she did not treat him as most other maidens did, meekly deferring to everything he said, or flattering and flirting with him.

No, this maiden with the violet eyes and her spirited words was quite different. She must be a landowner's daughter, as no villein would speak to him that way.

He remembered when he first met her how her red cloak had looked against her pale skin and dark hair. She was a beauty.

And he'd never seen anyone with eyes that color before—like the most intensely colored wood violets. Had he imagined that she had told him before that her name was Violet? She had not answered him when he called her Violet or when he asked her if that was her name.

He'd probably never see her again after today, and that was all well and good. Her accusations troubled him, although he knew they must be false.

"Let us be on our way," Sir Willmer said quietly so the maiden wouldn't hear. "We have that letter to deliver for the baron."

"First I want to talk to this woman's grandmother."

Before they reached the village, the maiden turned her mule down a lane that led them past plots of plowed earth on one side and a stand of trees on the other. They came around the bend to a little wattle-and-daub house squatting between two vegetable patches.

"Grandmother!" the young maiden called, dismounting from her mule.

An old woman opened the door of the cottage and stepped out. "Is everything all right?" she asked, looking from the maiden to Merek.

"Grandmother, tell these men what happened to your money," the maiden said, taking her grandmother's arm in one hand and holding her mule's reins in the other.

"Good afternoon," the older woman said, smiling and nodding to Merek as Sir Willmer hung back several feet.

"Good afternoon, madam," Merek said. "Would you be so

kind as to tell us if it is true that the baron's men have been taking money unlawfully?"

"I'm afraid it is true," the woman said. "Are you one of King Richard's knights, come to help us?"

"I am Sir Merek, one of King Richard's knights, and I am now in the service of Baron Dunham, at the king's request."

As soon as he said "Baron Dunham," the woman's expression faltered.

"I will not harm you. Please tell me what happened." There was a patient look on his face.

"Go ahead," the maiden said softly.

"The baron's men came and demanded money. They even searched my house. They took all the money I had."

"And you are certain these were Baron Dunham's men? Can you describe them?"

Her description of two of the men could have fit almost anyone, but when she mentioned the third man had a long scar on his face, from the bridge of his nose to the corner of his mouth, Merek knew exactly whom she was speaking of: Sir Goring.

His blood rose at the injustice, and he understood now why the young maiden was so adamant. Surely the baron was unaware of such things taking place, but Merek would certainly inform him.

"I thank you for explaining what happened," Sir Merek said, "and I shall make sure your money is returned to you. Will you tell me your name?"

"Alina, widow of Thomas Markeley."

Merek nodded to her. "Thank you for trusting me with this information. I shall do my utmost to right this wrong."

Violet no longer looked angry, and she seemed even more fair of face—although she still didn't look as if she completely trusted him.

Merek turned his horse around and Sir Willmer did the same, and they rode away.

"I want to go into the village," Merek said, "and question a few villagers to see if this was an isolated incident or if it is a regular occurrence."

"We don't have time for that fool's errand," Sir Willmer said. "We should do as we were bid by the baron and deliver the letter."

Sir Merek came to the crossroad and turned in the direction of the little village just visible to the right. "We need to find someone to speak to regardless, to learn how to get to Lappage Valley."

When they reached the small cluster of humble houses, Merek hailed the first man he saw, who was carrying a bucket of water in each hand.

"Good sir, can you point me in the direction of Lappage Valley?"

The man, who wore the clothing of a poor villein, barely raised his eyes. He set down his buckets and pointed back the way they had come.

"Go left at the crossroads and then I think it's ten miles or so."

"I thank you. And one more question. Have men come through here claiming to be Baron Dunham's men, demanding money?"

The man clasped his hands together. He glanced at Sir Willmer, then bowed his head, his shoulders stooping even more. "Lord Dunham is our lord, sir, and we all do as we're told."

"Yes, but my question. Have Baron Dunham's men made you pay a tax in return for granting you protection?"

The man once again glanced up, looking past him at Sir Willmer. He looked down again and shook his head. "No, sir," he answered.

"No one has demanded money from you?"

"No, sir."

The man seemed to be trying to shrink himself, folding his arms into his body.

"Thank you. You may go," Merek told him.

"Sir Merek, we should go." Sir Willmer tilted his head in the direction of Lappage Valley. "The baron won't like it if his letter gets there too late."

Something did not seem right in the way the villein had answered his questions. Could it be that what had happened to Violet's grandmother had happened to everyone in the village and they were too afraid to speak up?

Merek and Sir Willmer turned in the direction of Lappage Valley.

Perhaps it had been only the natural meekness and fear that Merek often saw in the poor people who had barely enough food to keep them alive. Having little power over their own lives, they were fearful of anyone in authority, whether it be the Church clergy or the lord of the land, to whom they owed both work—helping in the lord's fields—and a portion of their meager harvests that they were able to glean from the small plot of land in the lord's demesne.

And since Merek was the lord's guard, did his bidding, and bore the sword, the people were just as fearful of him as they were of the lord.

Merek had been in Baron Dunham's service for only two weeks, but he believed Baron Dunham was a good and generous lord who did not overly tax his people. He'd had that discussion with him when he came into the baron's service. He replayed it in his mind as they urged their horses into a fast trot down the road.

Upon his arrival at the castle, Baron Dunham had greeted him with, "Sir Merek. I've heard many good things about you." The baron was smiling as he motioned Merek forward. "King Richard thinks highly of you and your brothers, and I am extremely gratified to have you in my service."

"I thank you, Lord Dunham. The honor and privilege are mine."

"And you are very capable with a sword, I understand. What are your intentions while you are here?"

"My intentions?"

"What do you hope to accomplish?"

"To uphold the peace and security of the people, and to protect the king's interests."

Baron Dunham stared into Merek's eyes. "These are noble goals."

"I strive to be benevolent and to have Christlike character in all I do. It is a knight's duty to be loyal to his king and to enforce what is right and good in the eyes of God."

The baron said, "A true noble knight. I can see why the king is impressed with you. And your brother is the Earl of Dericott?"

"Yes, sir."

"Tell me, what do you imagine will be your duties while you are here?"

"I imagine that I will be protecting the people from brigands and robbers and upholding peace and justice, as well as training young squires in the skills of warfare."

"Very good, very good." Baron Dunham rubbed his chin, then clasped his hands in front of him. "I see we are in agreement that we have an obligation to protect the poor from the brigands."

"Yes, precisely."

"You think as I do, Sir Merek. Righteousness at all costs. Yes, you will be my right hand, to uphold goodness in the land."

Those were the baron's words, and Merek had believed him.

As Merek and Sir Willmer rode side by side toward Lappage Valley, he recalled a feast in the Great Hall that same night. Baron Dunham had toasted Merek, lifting high his goblet of wine.

"To Sir Merek, my newest and noblest knight, devoted to upholding righteousness in our land. All of you," he said, specifically addressing the guards, "shall treat him as one of our own."

The men drank to Merek, and he in turn raised his tankard to all of them.

But Violet, the girl with the red cloak and the violet eyes, had made serious accusations against the baron's men, and he needed to get to the truth of this matter.

They were back on the same road they had been traveling

when they had encountered the girl. Perhaps they would see her again.

As if his thoughts had conjured her up, he saw a flash of scarlet up ahead as Violet and her mule turned off the road into the woods.

Merek started after her, Sir Willmer grumbling but following close behind. Though the forest was fairly dense, the trees couldn't hide the bright red cloak she was wearing.

"Wait!" he called out. "I only wish to ask you a few more questions."

Finally, when they had nearly overtaken her, she turned her mule around to face them. "What is it you want?" The young woman glared at him, as defiant as ever.

He didn't wish to be rude to the woman, but she certainly made it difficult not to be. "As I said, I only wish to bring about justice. If I wished to harm you, I would have done so already. I would like to help."

She narrowed her eyes at him. "The only way you can help me is to force Baron Dunham to give back the money he has stolen." She sighed, her expression softening, her lovely eyes very intent, almost pleading. "I pray you are willing to help. Isn't it enough these people have to pay so much to their lords—boon harvests and boon works, giving a portion of their meager harvests every time there's a holy day, a portion of the food they need, just to line their wealthy lord's storehouses and his pockets? They are also forced, by law, to work a certain number of days in the lord's fields. Then you guards, with your swords and your threats, come and take what little bit of coin they have managed to save."

She blew out an exasperated breath. "I do hope it is true that you want to help, but it is difficult to believe that these things are happening among your fellow guards and you do not know about it."

He'd rarely seen a woman look so passionately earnest, and never on behalf of the poor. But her allegations vexed him. The baron would not condone such things—unless Merek was wrong and the baron had completely fooled him.

"I appreciate your concern. And though it is true that I have not been in Baron Dunham's service very long, only two weeks, I'll have you know that Baron Dunham and I had a conversation about this very thing, and he assured me he is as eager as you are to help the poor and adhere to what is right and just."

"Ha!" The rude sound exploded from her throat. "Are you truly so deluded?"

"Come, Sir Merek," Sir Willmer said in an annoyed voice. "This waspish maiden has hindered us long enough. Let us be off. We have a task and—"

Violet frowned and raised her brows at them.

"Who is your father?" Merek demanded, ignoring Sir Willmer. "He must be a landholding lord. What is his name?"

"He is no one of any importance to you, but yes, his land does have a few villeins."

"How can I tell you what I have discovered if I do not know where to find you?"

"I have not learned if I can trust you yet. But if you promise to help the poor villeins around about this region—"

"Sir Merek, come—" Sir Willmer began.

"I promise I will do my best to help them, but I wish to know your name and where you live."

She clenched her jaw. "My name is Violet Lambton, and I am the adopted daughter of William Lambton. If you ask anyone in the village of Burwelle, they can tell you where I live."

"Adopted?"

She gave him a mistrustful look but then said, "My birth mother died when I was a small child."

Her eyes and her tone were defiant, as if she was daring him to look down on her.

"Now can we go?" Sir Willmer asked.

"Thank you, Violet Lambton, for that information. I shall look into these accusations of yours."

"The people need the help of someone honest, Sir Merek." She said his name for the first time, and she even sounded almost humble. "I hope that person is you. Good day."

She turned her mule around and urged her into a trot.

Sir Merek turned his horse back to the main road so they could continue to do Baron Dunham's bidding in delivering his missive.

What an intriguing young woman.

Lest he become enamored, he reminded himself that Sir Willmer called her waspish, and he was not wrong. She was determined to think ill of Baron Dunham. But was it possible that she was right and Merek was wrong about the baron?

As a knight who very much wished to fight injustice and defend the weak, it was most irritating to be accused of injustice by a young woman who, though she was the daughter of a free landholder, was of no particular status or high birth. Indeed, it was surprising she had the courage to accuse the baron and his men of anything.

He wished to know more about this courageous maiden, Violet Lambton with the bright red cloak and eyes that matched her name.

THREE

VIOLET SAT AT THE LITTLE TABLE IN HER ROOM AND STARED out the window at the wheat waving in the wind. Her cheeks warmed as she remembered how harshly she had spoken to Sir Merek.

Why had she not held her tongue and her temper, as her grandmother had counseled her?

She couldn't help remembering the look of surprise and indignation on the young knight's face when she made her accusations and told him what the baron and his men had been doing. Perhaps he just hadn't been there long enough to untangle the baron's hypocrisy.

Or perhaps, though less likely, the baron didn't know his men were stealing in his name and without his consent.

Either way, Violet wanted to do something to help the people, so she took out a sheet of parchment and her pen and ink and began to write.

"What are you writing there?"

Violet's mother stood in the doorway.

"A letter."

"To whom?"

"King Richard."

"Whatever for?" Mother's mouth hung open and her eyes were round.

"I am informing him that Baron Dunham is stealing from the poor."

"Darling, you mustn't. What if your letter is intercepted by the baron's men? And what if the king tells the baron what you said about him? Things could go very badly for you, for all of us. You mustn't take such a risk." Mother's hand was on her heart, a pained look on her face.

"Why would my letter be intercepted by the baron's men? I think that very unlikely. And why would the king endanger the person who has given him valuable information about the misdeeds of one of his noblemen? He will investigate Baron Dunham and discover that I am telling him the truth and stop him. He will thank me."

"Surely you do not think so. Do you really believe the king of England will thank you for maligning one of his noblemen?" Mother's voice was raspy. She began to look as if she might cry. "You mustn't. Truly, you mustn't."

"Mother, you worry too much. The king will wish to know of the baron's wrongdoings."

"Who will you get to deliver it? That person could be secretly working for the baron. Violet, you mustn't."

Violet should have known her mother would react this way.

"I shall take every precaution, Mother. I will find a courier from another village outside the baron's control."

"The king will probably not even read it. You should not bother with writing it."

Her mother would not stop worrying. Violet knew this. And since she didn't want to bring her mother so much anxiety, she said, "Very well. I won't send it."

"I think that is best." Already her mother looked and sounded happier. "These powerful men have so much to lose, they will crush anyone who stands up against them. You remember what happened to the priest who spoke out against the baron, do you not?"

The priest was found hanging by his neck in the crypt of his own church. People said he'd been tortured, possibly for days, before he was killed. Some said it was the work of the baron, who was angry because the priest had spoken out against him, and others said it was the work of brigands who were passing through and had stolen from the church coffers. No one seemed to know for certain, and people rarely spoke of it anymore.

"I remember, Mother. Don't worry. I won't send the letter." Violet sighed.

Violet's heart was heavy. She wanted so badly to tell the king about Baron Dunham's cruelty. Surely the king would be outraged at such blatant abuse of his subjects. Surely he would at least command the baron to stop taking money from the poor.

But her mother's distress was too great a burden for her, after all her mother and father had done for her, taking her in and caring for her. She could never repay them for their kindness to her, a stranger, a helpless, needy child who could give them nothing in return.

Still, shouldn't she try to send a letter to the king? Even if he did not read it, or it did not reach him, at least she would have made the effort.

She was just a young woman who didn't know anyone in the king's court, and it was true that she was an orphan of no importance. Her adoptive parents were not wealthy, though they always provided plenty of food and clothing for her, and even employed a few servants. But she knew how to read and write, and therefore she had some responsibility to do what she could.

Thinking back on her interaction with Sir Merek, she wasn't sure why she had told him that she was adopted. Her parents never spoke of it, and she knew little more about the woman who birthed her than that she starved to feed her daughter, even unto her own death.

Her parents said they did not know much about Violet's natural mother, just that she was a poor woman living alone outside the village in a tiny hovel that had been abandoned by its previous owner. No one knew her name or who Violet's father may have been. But Violet had often wondered if her parents had concealed information from her. After all, everyone knew everyone. People rarely left the village where they were born. How could they know so little about this woman?

Violet often imagined various things about her birth mother and father. She liked to think they were good people, kind and loving, who were now in heaven with God, Jesus, and the angels.

Sometimes she wondered if her mother was cast out by her

family after becoming pregnant with Violet. Or had her mother lost her husband to the Great Pestilence? Having no one to help her, had she set out on the road and ended up in Violet's little village? Then, having no way to support herself, had she been too proud to beg, giving what she had to her daughter and quietly passing out of this earthly life without anyone knowing who she was?

Violet had been five years old when her mother died. She tried her best to remember her. Mostly she remembered a feeling of sadness, of her mother holding her in her lap and weeping. She recalled asking her mother for some bread once and her mother slowly shaking her head.

"There is none," she had said. A tear fell from her eye, and she wiped her cheek with her finger. Then she gently hugged Violet.

There were other vague images, of purple irises blooming, of a gray stone building, of her mother holding on to her hand, and she remembered often being cold. There was no sunlight in any of her memories, only gray skies.

She also remembered the pain of hunger, a hollow pain, and the dread that it brought with it.

She had an early memory of the man who would become her adoptive father picking her up off the ground. She'd felt overwhelming fear, but then he said, "If you come with me, I'll give you a nice warm apple pasty."

She didn't know what an apple pasty was, but it sounded good. Still, she cried at being in the strange man's arms. And when she saw her older brother, Theo, for the first time, he frowned and made a face, then ran away, causing Violet to cry harder. Everything around her was strange, and she wanted her mother, the one person who had always been with her. But somehow she knew that her mother was gone and she would never see her again.

Her new mother placed her on a low stool in front of a tiny table in her new home and set all kinds of food in front of her. Violet had been able to eat only a small amount before her stomach felt uncomfortably full. And all the while her new mother spoke softly to her, telling her she was safe and well and would never have to be hungry again. She promised to keep her warm and clean and brush her hair and dress her in pretty clothes.

"You will have your own little bed. Your new father is making it for you now, and you will have warm blankets and will sleep close to the fire. You'll like that."

Her mother and father treated her as if she were their own, and Violet loved them for it. Theo had been an ordinary older brother, sometimes treating her harshly, other times playing with her and teaching her the ways of the world.

Violet might not have remembered much about her birth mother, but she did remember the pain of hunger and the kindness of the strangers who took her in. Those memories kept her humble and grateful.

She put away the letter to the king and went for a walk.

The birds were chirping and singing, as the sun had finally come out. Spring crispness kissed her cheeks, but she could almost smell summer as well, with its clover and moist air.

Were the people from the nearby villages starving because

of the greed of Baron Dunham? Like her grandmother, would they have to forgo a bit of pork in their frumenty and eat only vegetables? How many needed warm clothing and shoes for the coming winter and couldn't afford them because of the baron? Were children going to bed hungry?

These thoughts haunted her, whispering to her mind as she tried to enjoy the sunshine.

God, show me what to do.

Should she defy her mother, ignoring her pleas and fears, and send a letter to the king anyway? But the thought of her mother's anxious expression made going against her wishes impossible.

Perhaps there was something else she could do to help the people who were victims of the baron's oppression.

The knight, Sir Merek, had argued that the baron would not unlawfully take money from his villeins. He seemed so sincere in his insistence that he—and the baron's men—had not been stealing from the villagers, and yet she knew it was so.

Was it truly possible that Sir Merek did not know what the baron's men were doing?

At first, she was too angry to think he might be telling the truth and had discounted his assertions of innocence.

She thought again of the priest who had been hanged. Had the baron had him killed because he knew too much? If so, Sir Merek would be in as much danger as that priest if he discovered that the baron was indeed evil.

And now Sir Merek knew her name and knew her father's name too, God rest his soul. How long might it be before the baron knew that Violet was speaking out against what his men were doing?

O God, I beg You not to let anything terrible happen to Mother because of me.

On their way back from delivering the baron's letter, Merek couldn't stop thinking about the girl with the violet eyes. She was so angry, and her eyes had flashed as she accused the baron's men of taking money from the poor—just the sort of thing he would never do.

Was the maiden unhinged? Or was there some truth to her accusations? He had to find out.

He was granted an audience with the baron as soon as he and Sir Willmer returned.

"Did you have any trouble delivering the missive?" Baron Dunham asked.

"No, my lord. All was well. But I did hear something troubling along the way."

"Heard something?"

"Yes, my lord. There is talk that you are taxing the people in exchange for protection from brigands, that your men take money from villeins as well as free men."

The baron stared hard at him without speaking. Then he crossed his arms over his chest and said, "And you believed this talk?"

Merek had expected him to show some surprise, to vehemently protest the accusation. He hesitated a moment before answering. "No, sir. I did not believe it, but I said I would investigate. I also wanted you to know that such things were being spoken—"

"You are one of my men. Are you taking money from the villeins?"

"No, sir, of course not."

"Then obviously it is idle talk."

"Yes, sir."

"I do not appreciate people spreading such lies about me and my men. You are to let these people know that these false accusations will not be tolerated. Remind them that bearing false witness against one's neighbor is a sin against God."

Merek carefully guarded his thoughts and his expression as he listened to the baron and watched his reactions.

"Yes, sir." Merek bowed and backed away.

"You are pleased to serve me, are you not?" Baron Dunham asked. "You are well-known to the king, and your reputation will be even greater after serving me. That pleases you, does it not?"

"Yes, of course."

"Very well. You may go. And, Sir Merek?"

"Yes, my lord?"

"I want to know who it is making these false accusations. I want their names and where they live."

"Yes, sir." Merek bowed again and continued to back away, then turned and left.

His heart was pounding as he exited the castle. Baron Dunham was lying, he was almost certain. How foolish Merek felt, remembering how he had defended the baron, insisting he cared for the poor and would never steal from them.

Did the baron think Merek was some daft boy who knew nothing of life and would believe the man just because he said so? Well, he was not so gullible as the baron thought.

He couldn't say exactly why he was so sure the baron was not being truthful. Perhaps it was because he didn't seem surprised at all by the accusations. Perhaps it was the cold look on his face, or the way he immediately attacked Merek's judgment. Or perhaps it was the baron's expression when he demanded to know who was speaking out against him. His expression reminded Merek too much of other unjust and ruthless men he had known.

Merek strode across the castle bailey, his chest burning with purpose. But he stopped just short of heading to the stable and turned and went to his barracks.

The first thing he needed to do was find more witnesses to the wrongdoing.

Sir Willmer was sitting on the side of his bed taking off his boots when Merek entered their room. Sir Willmer lay down on his bed with a cross between a sigh and a groan.

Merek ignored him and put away his sword. Next, he took off his clothes and dressed in his oldest clothing—a shirt that hung to his thighs and a pair of hose similar to what the villeins wore. Finally, he put a light cloak on over his shirt.

"Where are you going?" Sir Willmer asked from his reclined position.

"Nowhere." Merek hoped his gruff voice would put the knight off from asking more questions.

"Why are you wearing those clothes? You look as if you're going on a pilgrimage to ask forgiveness for your sins." Sir Willmer was smiling, clearly amused.

Merek had known Sir Willmer such a short time, he couldn't know yet if he could trust the man. "Take your ease and I will return soon."

"Are you going to the kitchen for a few cups of ale? Because if you are, I'll go with you."

"I am not. I'm just restless and in need of a walk. Are you in need of a walk around the castle yard and town?"

"I should say not." Sir Willmer lay his head back down and closed his eyes, folding his hands over his chest.

Merek hurried out of the barracks at a fast pace, hoping no one was following him.

When he approached the gatehouse, he pulled the hood of his cloak low over his face, stooping and walking with a slight limp. His ears itched as he walked past the guards, listening, but they said not a word and let him pass.

The town of Bilborough was at the bottom of the castle mount, looking sleepy as the sun sank low in the sky. A few people were moving about, but slowly, as if weighed down by exhaustion. Merek couldn't help but think that as a knight and part of Baron Dunham's guards, he was responsible for these people's welfare. If they were attacked, he was their defender. And one could even argue that he had more of a responsibility to these people than he did to Baron Dunham, especially if the baron was pillaging the people who were entrusted to him by the king.

A woman was drawing water at the well. She looked to be around thirty or forty years old—it was difficult to tell with villagers who had spent so much time in the sun and weather.

She was struggling to pull the heavy bucket of water to the top of the well and barely glanced his way as he approached. But then she looked again, no doubt realizing he was a stranger.

"May I help?"

She shrugged. "If you wish."

He took the rope from her and finished pulling the full bucket of water to the top, then poured its contents into one of her own buckets, which sat on the stone wall around the well. Merek sent the bucket back down to the bottom of the well and drew it up again, filling her other bucket.

"Allow me to carry them for you."

"My husband may not like it," she said, raising an eyebrow at him.

"Do not worry. I will not harm either of you."

She raised her brows warily.

Merek took the two full buckets, one in each hand, and followed her. He kept his head up, trying to make eye contact with anyone who passed, but the people barely glanced at him and hurried on their way.

Several people were sitting outside the alehouse.

"Good evening," Merek said, nodding to the men. They did not return his greeting.

The woman stopped at the baker's shop, which was probably also the baker's home. She turned to look at Merek. "You can set them there. I can bring them inside."

"May I come in and meet your husband?"

She shook her head, obviously waiting for him to put the buckets down.

"I wanted to ask you some questions."

She gave him a square-jawed stare.

"Just one or two questions about whether you have any complaints about Baron Dunham's men."

At those words, she opened the door to the bakery and went inside, slamming and barring the door behind her.

Merek thought about knocking on the door and trying to talk to the woman's husband, but he didn't want to seem as if he was harassing her, so he put the buckets on the step in front of the door and left.

He went back into the town and looked for someone who might talk to him, but the few people he saw—a woman finishing up at the well, a man with a bundle under his arm, an older child carrying a younger one on her hip—all hurried away from him.

He went back to the alehouse. The patrons sitting on their stools outside stopped their conversations as soon as he drew near. Merek nodded to them, and they all just stared. Merek went inside and encountered the alewife dipping ale from a large barrel.

After a quick glance at him, she looked back down at her task. "Ale is a half penny per tankard," she said as if by rote.

"Thank you." Merek held out a silver coin, much more than a half penny.

Her eyes grew big as she stared at the coin. "I cannot make change for that."

"I don't want change. I only want to ask you if the baron's guards have taken money unlawfully from you."

"I don't want your money or your business," she hissed in a low voice. She pointed to the door. "Go. Now."

"Is this man bothering you, Ma?" A big, burly man of about twenty years old came in from outside.

"He was just leaving," the woman said in a taut voice.

Merek considered arguing with the woman and her son, assuring them that he meant them no harm and only wanted information, but he had a feeling that would get him nowhere. So he turned and went back outside.

Surely there were some friendly people in this town.

"Good evening," he said again to the group of men sitting outside.

No one answered him. Finally, an old man said, "Good evening, stranger."

The other men sent him a glare, but he just took another swig of his tankard of ale.

"I'm new to this region. My name is Merek."

The old man nodded to him.

"I've heard tell that there be bandits who take money from people round about, pretending to be Baron Dunham's guards."

He could almost see the men's shoulders stiffen. No one said a word, but the old man stared up at him, as if taking note of his appearance.

"Can anyone tell me if this is so?"

The old man looked down.

"No one will tell me? Are you so afraid of the baron?" Merek realized, a little late, that he had spoken too freely.

One man cleared his throat. Another glared at the road and then spit onto the ground, sending up a puff of dust.

"If you had any sense . . . ," someone said, mumbling something unintelligible.

Another man grunted, then said in a matter-of-fact tone, "You should leave."

Merek's blood was beginning to heat. His temper would get him in a world of trouble, his eldest brother, Edwin, had told him more than once. How could he prove to these men that he meant them no harm?

It seemed as if he had gone about this all wrong.

Merek clenched his jaw tight, nodded to the men, then turned and walked away.

Would he have to befriend someone from the town and gain their trust first before he could ask them anything about the baron? He contemplated going back to get his sword and forcing those men outside the alehouse to tell him what he wanted to know—the truth of what was happening here. Were they so cowardly that they did not wish to stand up to those who were stealing from them, even if it was Baron Dunham? Couldn't they see that he was only trying to help?

Merek forced these wrathful thoughts away as he remembered the wise counsel he'd received first from his brother Edwin and then from his priest. He took deep breaths as he walked through the village once again, passing a few people, though it was growing late and most were probably at home.

He turned down a side road and found himself behind the shops in a field that appeared to be lying fallow. He needed to calm his heated thoughts and formulate a plan, so he walked out into the field and sat down.

The sun had gone down, so he lay on his back and stared at the moon, which was big and bright and just coming up above the horizon.

Merek was not a particularly trusting person, and he believed he had good reason to be so guarded. But the king had sent him to serve under Baron Dunham, and Merek had believed the baron's words about wishing to serve and help the poor. Now, as he looked back on that conversation with the baron, he realized he'd been fooled.

As he gazed at the night sky, Merek decided to pray for wisdom and guidance. But not having slept well the night before, as soon as he started his prayer, he felt himself growing sleepy.

FOUR

MEREK AWOKE TO TWO CHILDREN SQUATTING BESIDE HIM.

Light burst on his eyes as one of the children moved a lantern close to his face. Merek pushed it out of the way and saw that no daylight was left in the sky.

"Why are you sleeping in this field?" the boy child said.

"In the widow Sanderson's field," the girl child added.

Merek sat up partially, propping himself up on his hand. "How old are you?"

"Seven years old," the boy said. "We're twins."

"Why aren't you at home? It's dark."

"Our father lets us play outside." The little girl stood up from her squatting position and stared curiously at him.

"After dark?" Merek asked.

"Our father drinks until he falls asleep," the boy said. "He's usually snoring by the time it gets dark."

"Where is your mother?"

"Our mother is dead." The girl looked as though the information was simply a matter of fact.

"She died when we were born." The boy, along with his twin sister, was still leaning in close and staring curiously at him. "Are you a stranger? You don't look like anyone I know."

"I'm Sir Merek." He stood to his feet.

"If you are a knight, why are you sleeping here on the ground?" The girl started brushing the sticks and leaves from the leg of his breeches.

He wanted to tell them he wasn't accustomed to sleeping on the ground and explain how he'd grown annoyed with the townspeople who wouldn't answer his questions but had done the nobler thing and walked away to cool down. If he hadn't, his thoughts could have led to violence, which would not have been very charitable.

Merek had learned to pay attention when his chest grew tight and his head grew hot. Of all his brothers, he was the one with the hot temper, and that had only become worse after he was imprisoned unjustly and sentenced to death for a crime he hadn't committed, all because of the greed of evil people.

But that was behind him now. He was learning to control his anger, and now he needed to be patient and do whatever it took to discover if the baron was evil too.

He gazed down at the seven-year-old twins, their faces too serious for children their age. He sighed, glad they couldn't detect his angry, vengeful thoughts.

"Where do you live?" Merek asked. "I'll walk you home."

"Our father is the butcher. We live in the butcher shop."

"Let us go, then. You can show me the way. What are your names?"

"I'm Conner and my sister is Sigrid. Are you a drunk?"

He frowned, then reminded himself that they were only children. Besides, he probably looked drunk, falling asleep in a field. "I am not. I am a knight in the service of King Richard."

"Where's your sword?" Conner asked.

"And your armor?" Sigrid added, her voice high with excitement.

"I don't have them with me," Merek explained. "I rarely wear armor, and I wasn't expecting to need my sword tonight."

"Do you have somewhere to sleep?" Sigrid asked. "My father would let you sleep at our house."

"That is very kind of you." Merek was surprised to feel his heart squeezing at the little girl's concern for him. "I have a place to sleep, but I thank you for the offer."

The little girl skipped ahead toward the town and the row of buildings ahead of them. Thankfully, the light of the full moon made it easy to see where they were going.

"Does your father buy ale from the alewife?" Merek asked.

"Yes." Conner looked excited at the prospect of helping him. "Do you want some ale?"

"No, I was only wondering . . ." Whether the alewife and her son were always so uncharitable. But they were probably not bad people, only very averse to answering his questions about Baron Dunham.

"The alewife has a son." Conner led the way to the butcher shop.

"He's too old to play with us." Sigrid hurried beside him on her short legs. "He shot me with a slingshot once, but he said it was an accident."

"And Baron Dunham's men? Do you ever see them?"

Conner looked quite serious. "They pass through the town a lot."

"Have they paid a visit to your father in the last few weeks?"

"They came to our house and took Father's money," Sigrid said in a loud whisper. "But I'm not supposed to talk about that."

Conner hung his head, and when he looked up, he said, "The baron's men take everyone's money. People are sad."

"They take everyone's coins and chickens and goats and give them to the baron," Sigrid said.

"Do the people complain about it?"

"Not very much," Conner said. "They're too afraid of the baron."

Merek's head started to grow hot again. Everything Violet and her grandmother had said was true. And no wonder the people were afraid of his questions. He'd been foolish to speak so plainly to them, to not realize that if the baron was overtaxing and oppressing them, then his questions would not be safe for them to answer. In their eyes, he was behaving suspiciously and putting them in danger. And no wonder Violet had been so angry with him when she found out he was part of the baron's guards.

They were nearly to the road that passed through the town when Conner pointed. "That's Father's butcher shop. He's asleep now, but if you come back tomorrow, I'm sure he would give you some meat if you're hungry."

Merek had to swallow the words that jumped into his throat, protestations that he did not need charity from their father, and said instead, "I thank you. Perhaps I will see you both again. But you really shouldn't be wandering around by yourselves after dark."

"Why not?" Sigrid asked, staring at him with wide blue eyes.

"Because there are wolves about."

"Father says the wolves never come this close to the town, not unless there's been a drought and the wolves get really hungry."

"Well, then, there are other reasons it's not safe to be out after dark alone."

"I can take care of my sister and me," Conner said, tilting his head as he stared back at Merek.

"I'm sure you can. Just be careful." They were standing in the road now, a soft glow coming through the windows of the shop that was their home.

"We will," Sigrid said cheerfully, taking her brother's hand. "Let us check on Father," she said, leading the way to the front door. "Fare well, Sir Knight."

"Fare well, Conner and Sigrid. I shall come back to make certain you are being taken care of," he said softly, more to himself than to them, before throwing his hood over his head and heading back toward the castle.

His mind churned with his every footstep as he tried to think what to do.

He could go to King Richard and tell him what the baron was doing, but the king would probably want proof. It was no small thing to make accusations against a nobleman. Besides,

Merek's only evidence were the words of one young maiden, her grandmother, and two young children. He needed more information and hopefully some kind of proof that he could take to the king.

In the meantime, the people were suffering, and he had to do something about it. He could not stand by, a servant of the king, no less, and allow this unjust treatment to go on.

How dare Baron Dunham lie so blatantly to him? The man was the worst hypocrite, as he professed to desire to do every good and generous deed and yet he was doing just the opposite— stealing from those who could least afford it.

Merek needed a plan. He also needed to discover if there were any other men among the baron's guards who did not agree with what the baron was doing, men he could trust to help him. And he'd have to be extremely careful how he went about discovering who was loyal to Baron Dunham and who was not.

Someone was knocking at the door.

"Violet, will you see who it is?" her mother called from the back room.

Violet, who had been making cakes in the buttery, wiped her floured hands on a cloth and opened the door.

Robert Mercer stood in the doorway. "I picked these flowers for you." He thrust a handful of wildflowers at her.

"Thank you. I love flowers," she said, feeling both his awkwardness and hers. "Would you like to come in?"

She immediately regretted asking him inside. What business

did he have with her? She had no desire to be alone with him, and she knew he wanted her to marry him, and she did not wish to answer him yet. But she couldn't be rude either—her mother would be appalled—so she moved aside and let him in.

He nodded to her as he stepped over the threshold of their stone manor house that easily accommodated Violet, her mother, and her brother, Theo, along with a servant, Ada, who slept in the attic room.

Robert Mercer looked down at the apron tied around her middle.

"Were you cooking?"

"I was making some cakes."

"You cook?"

"Not very often. Mother and Ada do most of the cooking, but I like to make apple and cherry cakes when we have the extra fruit."

"You do not look as if you eat a lot of cake." He glanced down at her figure again.

Violet wasn't sure how to reply to that. Reluctantly, she said, "I give most of the cakes to our neighbors."

"To the neighbors?" He raised his brows.

"Yes, to help them feed themselves and their children." She sighed, wishing again that she had not invited him into the house.

Robert opened his mouth but closed it without saying anything. Then he nodded at the flowers he had brought and that she was still holding. "Wouldn't you like to put those flowers in some water?"

"I shall find a vase. You may sit. I'll return in a moment."

Violet hurried from the room, wondering if she would ever want to marry Robert. The flowers should have impressed her, since she did love flowers, but somehow she didn't feel anything romantic for him, only a bit of annoyance.

She found a pottery vase and put some water in it.

"Do you need help with something?" Ada asked, coming in the side door from the vegetable garden.

"No, I thank you, Ada. Robert Mercer brought these flowers and I'm putting them in water."

"Is he here?" Ada whispered.

"Yes, I'm afraid so." Violet gave Ada what she hoped was a bemused grimace and then walked back to the front room with the vase of flowers. She set them on the windowsill before turn-. ing to Robert.

"I hope all is well with your family."

"Yes, very well. My mother and father are hardy people. My sisters are all married and living elsewhere, but the last I heard, they were all well. And the planting has gone well this spring. We should have a great harvest this year."

She wasn't sure how he could state that so confidently when no one ever knew how the weather would be, if they would receive enough rain, enough sun and warmth, or if some pestilence would come and wipe out the crop. But she said nothing, determined to quietly observe his character and actions.

"Has Theo finished his planting?"

"Most of it. His helper was sick for a week, so that put them behind."

"A week? Perhaps he should find a new helper."

Lack of compassion, Violet listed mentally, adding, *Judges me by my physical size and appearance.*

"I have never been sick for more than a day. Perhaps his helper was only pretending. But even if he was sick, your brother needs a helper who is healthy."

"I suppose you can speak to Theo about that, if you wish." She resisted the urge to roll her eyes.

"I came here to speak to you, Violet." He stood up and took a few steps toward her.

He stared hard at her face. Was he about to ask her to marry him? And if so, shouldn't he look a bit nervous?

"I am sure your mother told you of my wish to marry you. You are of age now. What are you? Eighteen years old?"

Presumptuous. She would not answer his impertinent question this time. But she found he did not need an answer, as he continued talking.

"You will have a comfortable home with me, better than any you can hope for from anyone else. I shall have the priest cry the banns this Sunday."

"No, you shall not, for I have not given you my answer. And if you must have it today, then my answer is that I will not marry you."

His eyes opened a bit wider, then narrowed. "You know that I own more land than your family?"

"Yes, I believe I knew that." *He thinks I'm as impressed with the size of his land as he is.*

"And I have no brothers to lay claim to any part of it."

He's glad he doesn't have to share his wealth.

"Yes, and your sisters have all married and live with their husbands. I thank you for the flowers and for the visit." She stopped short of wishing him a good day and opening the door to usher him out. She even smiled to show that she felt no ill will toward him.

"I am not sure how long I will wait for you to change your mind. I do hope you will accept my offer, as I do think you are pretty."

She couldn't bring herself to thank him for the compliment. She was not going to change her mind and accept his offer. Her grandmother's words that love was everything echoed in her heart, and she was sure that she would never fall in love with Robert Mercer.

Finally, after staring at her for several long moments, he glanced at the vase of flowers behind her and said, "Good day, Violet."

"Good day, Robert. Please give my good wishes to your mother."

He nodded before continuing down the lane that led from her door to the road that ran to the village half a mile away.

"Was that Robert Mercer?" her mother called to her, coming into the room.

"It was. I would say he came to ask me to marry him, but indeed, I don't believe he ever asked me, exactly. He did say he would have the priest cry the banns this Sunday."

"And what did you say?"

"I said no, if he needed an answer today."

"Oh, Violet, you didn't!"

"Mother, I don't love the man." She didn't even like him.

"You won't know him until you marry him. And think of your future, Violet. Your father is already gone. When Theo marries and I am gone, you may not wish to stay here, living on the charity of your brother."

Violet blinked. Her mother didn't mean to hurt her, but she felt a cruel stab in her chest.

You are a burden to your family was the message she imagined behind her mother's words. *Haven't you lived off our charity long enough?*

"You should marry Robert Mercer. You will be safe and well-fed with him."

Part of Violet wanted to lash out at her mother, who seemed to think being safe and having enough food were the only important things in life.

"Love is everything," Violet said softly.

Was Grandmother right? Or was being safe and well-fed the best she could hope for?

FIVE

THE SUN WAS SINKING LOW AS VIOLET WALKED HOME WITH an empty basket on her arm, having taken the cakes she had made to a poor widow whose children were not yet old enough to help her very much and to an older husband and wife. The man had broken his hip and his wife was sickly, with a persistent fever and cough.

When she was walking up the lane to her home, she saw three horses in front of the door and heard strange male voices through the open windows.

Violet hurried forward, having to push one horse out of the way to reach the door.

A man was standing over her brother and mother, who were sitting on stools in the front room.

Violet's heart leapt into her throat. Mother and Theo were in danger!

Her blood boiled at the way the guard—for she could see he

was wearing Baron Dunham's colors—shook a bag of coins and said, "Is this all the money you have? If you are lying to me—"

"Who is this?" another man said, staring at her.

Mother's face was pale, and her bottom lip trembled.

Violet's heart constricted painfully to see her mother so frightened. Her brother's face was expressionless except for a hardness around his eyes and his jaw.

Violet wanted to demand that they get out of her house, but to do so might put Theo and her mother in even more danger. These men could obviously do as they liked, and Violet could not stop them.

The two men stared at her a moment, then one of them stepped toward her and grabbed her arm. Mother put her hand over her mouth, stifling a strangled cry.

"Take the money," Theo said.

"Let go of me," Violet demanded, wrenching her arm free from the man's grasp.

"A feisty one," the man said.

"We don't want any trouble," her mother said in a trembling voice. "Please, don't hurt us. Just take the money."

What did the men want? Were they only there for money? Or had Sir Merek told the baron about her defiance and accusations?

"What do you want?" Violet asked, trying to pretend she didn't think the men meant them any harm.

"We are collecting the tax required by Baron Dunham," the man holding her mother's coin purse said.

"What tax?"

"For the protection the baron provides you ungrateful people."

"Is this a lawful tax approved by King Richard?"

"Shut your mouth, girl," the man said.

Just then, a third man came from the back of the house holding another coin purse. He shook it, making it rattle.

"There was more. I thought so." The man who appeared to be in charge grinned. "That will cost you extra."

"We also found this letter." He held up the familiar piece of parchment. "It looks like it's addressed to the king."

Violet's face went hot, then cold. *Please forgive me, God.* How afraid her mother must be now. She felt sick thinking the letter she had written would bring fear and panic to her gentle mother.

The leader, whose face bore a scar from his nose to his mouth, just as Grandmother had described, snatched her unfinished letter from him and stared hard at it, holding it close to his face. Then he held it up and looked at Violet's mother and brother.

"Who wrote this? Do you know the king? Answer me."

"No! No!" Mother cried out.

Theo shook his head. "We don't know the king. We are simple farmers."

"I wrote it," Violet said. "I don't know the king, but I wrote the letter. They had nothing to do with it."

The man sneered at her, then looked around at his companions. "Writing a letter to the king? This girl thinks the king wants to read her letters."

The men laughed, then ignored her as they poured the coins

out on the table. They took about half, stuffing them in a pouch, and the leader returned the pouch to his pocket.

One of the guards started toward the door and then stopped. "What about the girl? I think we should take her with us." He leered at Violet, revealing a missing tooth in front.

Violet's stomach turned inside out. She frantically tried to plan how she would defend herself from these men.

"No," the leader with the scar said. "We were sent only to take the tax."

Violet stared hard at each of the three faces so that she could identify them later, taking notice of any defining features. Another one of the men had a scar on his chin, but the third man was rather ordinary looking besides his missing tooth.

As they passed by her, the one who had leered at her deliberately brushed against her.

Her blood was boiling, but what could she do? Anything she said or did would be fruitless at best, dangerous to herself and her mother and brother at worst.

She noticed her letter lying on the floor and snatched it up. Thanks be to God, they had not taken it with them to show to the baron.

Sir Merek said Baron Dunham's men did not take money from people in the name of protection. What would he say if he were here now?

She heard the guards' horses' hooves tearing up the dirt lane as they galloped away.

Her knees shook as she thought of those men coming into

their home, frightening her mother, intimidating her brother, and stealing from them.

"Violet, now do you see how dangerous it was to write that letter?" Mother's bottom lip trembled, a tear running down her cheek. She wiped it away with her hand. "Did you not see their swords strapped to their backs? They could have killed you, or worse." A small sob escaped her, and she pressed her hand to her lips.

Violet's heart sank to the pit of her stomach. She opened her mouth to apologize, but Theo rose to his feet and cut her off.

"Did you really think you could stand up to them? Ridiculous." Theo's face was scrunched into a look of disgust. "Do you think you can say anything you want and they won't harm you because you're a woman? You're foolish, that's what you are. Those men could have done anything they wanted to you. And I could not have protected you." He snorted, shaking his head. He strode to the side door and left, slamming the door behind him.

"He's right, Violet. Those men could have taken you away and hurt you, killed you." Mother's voice was low, tears streaming down her face.

"But why is Theo angry with me?" Conflicting thoughts crowded her mind.

"I suppose because you spoke boldly to them and you told them you wrote the letter. He's probably embarrassed because he didn't stand up to them. But it was very foolish of you to talk to them that way, and even more foolish to have written that letter."

Violet's breaths came faster. "I would never want any harm

to come to you and Theo, Mother, but if we cower before them now, we'll always be cowering."

"We have no choice, Violet." Mother's voice turned hard, as did her expression. "We cannot defy the baron and his men. They have all the power and we have none. You have to accept it and stop trying to think you can fight this."

Violet's stomach churned at the warring emotions inside her. Finally, she went to her bedroom and shut the door.

Hot, angry tears dripped from her eyes. She hated feeling helpless. She'd been helpless to save her birth mother as a child, but she did not, could not believe she was that helpless now.

She looked down at her unfinished letter still clutched in her hand. She went to her little writing table and placed the letter on it.

She would finish writing the letter and she would find a courier to take it to the king. Most likely nothing would come of it, but she had to try. The pain of doing nothing, of watching helplessly as the baron perpetrated his injustice on everyone around her, was greater than her fear.

Perhaps the king would never learn the truth of what a terrible man the baron was. But she would do what she could, and she would pray that God would make a way for them to stop the baron from taking advantage of them all.

Merek was sitting near Baron Dunham in the Great Hall, a place of honor. It was late, the evening meal had been eaten, and he was about to go to the barracks.

How had Merek not realized what a greedy man the baron was? How had he not known what the baron had been sending the guards out to do?

In the two weeks since Merek had come to serve under the baron, he'd been kept near the castle other than to do small errands for the baron, such as delivering a missive to a neighboring region, or accompanying the baron on a hunt.

Now Merek listened to the other guards and knights. Most of them spoke profanely, especially about women. It was clear that they did not take seriously their oath to uphold righteousness and to conduct themselves with honor. A knight without chivalry was no knight at all. And Baron Dunham obviously was the worst of them all, without a conscience, greedy and devious.

But the baron couldn't hope to fool Merek forever into thinking he was a good and benevolent leader. Surely he must know the truth would come out eventually. Did he think Merek could be bribed? Threatened into submission? How long before he openly showed his true nature to Merek?

It was against Merek's temperament to sit and wait for something to happen. He wanted to confront the baron, to accuse him to his face, to demand compensation for those he had wronged. But he also needed proof of his wrongdoing to present to the king.

Two of the baron's men came into the Great Hall, probably from raiding the villeins and landowners since sunup.

"Pardon us, Lord Dunham," one of them said as they bowed before the baron.

"What is it?" the baron asked.

"Sir, we don't wish to disturb you, but we felt it necessary to speak to you. However, if you are about to retire, it can wait until the morrow."

"Speak now. I'm listening."

"We have come from the village of Burwelle, where we were extracting taxes from your subjects, and we discovered a woman who had been writing a letter to the king."

"What woman? What did the letter say? Speak up!"

"I don't remember the exact words, but—"

"Where is the letter?"

"We didn't bring it, but she was telling the king that you are taxing the people unlawfully."

"Who was the woman?"

"Her family's name was Lambton. She was young and had violet-colored eyes."

Merek's breath caught in his throat. They must be speaking of Violet.

The baron's expression changed. He had a strange look in his eye as he seemed to stare past the guards. Then he said, "How old was this woman?"

"Probably eighteen or nineteen," the man said.

The baron said nothing.

"She was nobody. She obviously doesn't know the king, but we thought you would want to be made aware of what she was doing."

The baron sat motionless in his thronelike chair, staring at the opposite wall. Finally, he shifted in his seat and waved his hand slightly. "That is all. You may go."

When the men were gone, Merek started to rise from his bench.

"Sir Merek, I have a mission for you." The baron waved to him to come closer as he continued to stare at the wall.

Merek approached the baron, who motioned him even closer. Merek leaned down and the baron spoke quietly next to his ear. "I want you to go to the village of Burwelle, find this girl with violet eyes whose family name is Lambton, and bring her to me. Do you understand?"

Merek tried to pretend his mind wasn't racing. "Yes, sir."

"And take Sir Willmer with you."

"Yes, sir. Should we go tonight?"

"No, but go at dawn."

When Baron Dunham said nothing more, Merek bowed and left. As he went toward the soldiers' barracks, he wondered what the baron would do to Violet. But Merek was not about to let him punish her. Whatever was in the letter, he was sure now that it was all true.

So Violet had written a letter to King Richard. She had courage, more than most men.

He didn't want to pretend to still be loyal to Baron Dunham. But if he didn't go and fetch Violet, the baron would send someone else to get her, someone who might not treat her as respectfully as he would.

Merek was glad that the baron was sending Sir Willmer with him. He had noticed that Sir Willmer didn't drink strong spirits with the other guards and knights, and he did not join in with the vulgar talk. He would get to know Sir Willmer better, however, before he decided to trust him.

Merek entered the barracks and found Sir Willmer lying on his narrow bed, his arms crossed, staring up at the ceiling.

"New orders from Baron Dunham," Merek said.

Sir Willmer sat up.

"He wants us to go to Burwelle."

"Burwelle?" Sir Willmer squinted.

"The village to the south and west where we encountered that girl with the violet eyes."

"Ah, yes. The one you kept arguing with." The corners of his mouth twitched, but that was the only indication that he may have been amused.

"The baron wants us to bring her here."

Sir Willmer stared hard at him. "Why?"

"Apparently the baron's men found a letter she had been writing to the king." Merek watched for the reaction of his fellow knight.

Sir Willmer looked away, then said, "What else did the baron say?"

"Only that we are to leave at dawn."

Sir Willmer looked Merek in the eye. "I do not harm women," he said. "And neither will you."

Heat rose into Merek's face at the clear warning in Sir Willmer's words. Merek glared at the man. "I took an oath of chivalry. I do not harm women either."

"I am glad to hear it," Sir Willmer said placidly. "If we are to leave at dawn, we had better get some sleep." He began taking off his outer clothing.

Sir Willmer's calm reaction took the steam out of Merek, and he realized he was right. It was already well past dark, and Merek needed to have his wits about him tomorrow. But he had been worrying about the seven-year-old twins, Conner and Sigrid, as he went about his duties around the castle, and now that his time was his own, he put on his liripipe with the hood that would cover most of his face and walked to the town.

A small group of men were outside the alehouse, squatting or sitting on stools. They stared at him suspiciously, so he walked past them and to the butcher's shop, which was closed and the windows dark.

He wanted to peer inside to see if the children were home, but he couldn't do that without being seen, so he walked toward the field where the children had found him, thinking perhaps they might be playing there.

He thought about the alewife and her son and how rudely they had treated him. He was only trying to help. He winced and his blood grew warm. But now he knew the extent of the baron's greed and misdeeds. He only wished they had trusted him enough to tell him about it. In his anger, he imagined challenging the son to a fight and beating him soundly.

That was unchivalrous. Merek was a trained fighter, and the young man was not, and he was only protecting himself and his mother. Merek's thoughts showed that he had not overcome his wrathful temperament.

Since he was a child, if someone hit Merek, he would hit

them back twice as hard. If someone hurt his family, he wanted to avenge them. In fact, after he and his brothers had been wrongly convicted of murder and treason, he'd imagined, many times over, getting his revenge on the people who were responsible. He saw himself traveling to the Continent, tracking them down, and killing them the way they'd killed his father, the way they'd tried to kill his whole family.

His priest had told him that such imaginings were the same as murder, for Jesus had said that whatever you imagine in your heart was the same as actually doing it.

Merek told him, "But I would get more satisfaction from doing it. Thinking about it isn't satisfying."

"'Vengeance is mine,' says the Lord." The priest gave him a grave look.

"Wouldn't you want to kill the people who killed your father and tried to have you and all your brothers killed?"

"No. I would pity them, for murderers spend their eternity in the lake of burning fire. And I would forgive them, for God will not forgive my sin if I refuse to forgive my enemies."

The priest's words had done little to extinguish the fire in Merek's gut, but he'd said nothing. When he left the church, he took his small axe, went into the forest, and chopped down several trees, trying not to imagine that the trees were his family's betrayers, Baldric and Merek's stepmother, Parnella.

He'd made some progress toward controlling his anger and thirst for vengeance since then, finally accepting that avenging himself on his enemies would not change the past. Certainly he didn't think as much about vengeance as he once did, and he had been able to speak the words "I forgive them" several times while in prayer to God.

He took a deep breath as he stood in the field and murmured, "I am sorry I was angry with the townspeople for not answering my questions. I forgive them, for they were only afraid. Forgive me, Father God, for my sin of vengeful thinking."

He didn't feel as though his words were completely sincere, but perhaps when he said the words again the next time he prayed, he would sincerely mean them.

His glance took in the expanse of the field, but he didn't see any sign of Conner and Sigrid. He started back toward the town, and as he passed the butcher's shop, he saw two children run from the back of the shop and go in through the front door.

Good. At least they were at home and safe.

He made his way back toward the castle and to his bed. He needed all the sleep he could get in order to deal with both the young maiden, Violet, and whatever the baron had planned for her.

Six

In her bedroom, Violet tucked the rolled-up and sealed letter to the king, which she had finished early that morning, in the little purse hanging from the belt around her waist. She also dropped a few coins in, payment to the courier.

She emerged from her room and heard the snuffling of horses as a knock came at the front door. Through the open window Violet saw Sir Merek and the man who had been with him before.

Violet froze. Her heart pounded and her hand went to her purse. Would they find her letter describing the evil actions of Baron Dunham and his men?

She turned and went to the back door. As she slipped out, her mind was focused on the barn where her mule was already saddled and ready. If she could get to her, she could ride across the fields, and they'd never see her.

She closed the door as gently as possible, held up her skirts, and ran toward the barn.

Inside there was a lantern burning, along with the light from the open windows. Her mule was standing at the ready, as the field helper had saddled her for Violet. Mistress Sally greeted her with a soft snort.

"We can do this," she said in a low voice, leading the mule by her bridle. "We just have to move quickly."

As she emerged from the barn, Sir Merek was striding toward her. He must have seen her leaving.

She led the mule to the mounting block and stepped up onto it. The knight was coming faster now, so she threw her leg over the saddle and boosted herself up. But before she could raise herself upright, he grabbed her arm in one hand and her mule's bridle in the other.

"Forgive me, but you must come with me."

"Get off! Let go of me!" Violet tried to urge her mule forward, but Sir Merek was holding her fast while the other fellow came running up.

"You must get down," the knight said.

Violet did her best to snatch her arm away from Sir Merek, but he held her firmly.

"How dare you hold me against my will!" Violet let go of the reins and lashed out with her free hand, hitting Sir Merek on the chin.

Sir Merek flinched and leaned away from her, but he kept hold of her arm, tightening his grip, as the knight with him grabbed her other arm.

"Let me go!" Violet screamed, raising the hue and cry. She could not let them take her. She had to send her letter to the king. She screamed until she lost her breath, then took another breath and screamed some more, but neither Sir Merek nor the other knight loosened their grip.

Mother and Ada came running. A few moments later, Theo and his two field workers arrived from the fields. Theo, Mother, and the servants simply stared, stopping several feet away.

"I have orders to take her to Baron Dunham," Sir Merek said in a strident voice. "She will not be harmed. The baron only wishes to speak to her."

"Why?" Mother wailed. "What has she done? Please don't take her." She wrung her hands together.

"Don't worry," Sir Merek said. "I will not allow any harm to come to her."

"Liar," Violet said. "You cannot make such a claim. The baron can do anything he wants and you cannot stop him."

The knight frowned, a tiny downturn of one side of his mouth, but then it disappeared. "I am a knight in King Richard's service. I have taken an oath never to harm an innocent woman, and I consider my oath to be a sacred one to God."

Violet snorted. "You are harming me now by holding me against my will and taking me on a journey with only you and this other soldier."

He seemed to think this over. "It cannot be helped. And if you come with us, you will have an opportunity to tell the baron what you think of what he is doing, to say whatever you like."

"And have the baron throw me in his dungeon to rot, I

suppose." Truly, her insides quaked at the thought, but she would not give him the satisfaction of seeing her fear.

"You have my word that I will not allow that to happen." He spoke in a low voice, looking her straight in the eye.

"You told me you wanted to help," Violet said, tears stinging her eyes. She'd wanted to believe him. She hadn't realized how much she wanted to believe in his sincerity until this moment. But she would not let him see her cry. "You lied to me."

"I did not lie to you," he said. "I will help you, but you need to trust me."

"Trust you? You are taking me to Baron Dunham."

"Let us go," the other man said to Sir Merek. Then he slipped a rope around Violet's wrists.

"How dare you," Violet said, gritting her teeth. "The king will hear of this and then he will strip you of your knighthood, if indeed you are a knight. Which I doubt." She wanted to claw their eyes out. *O God, help me, please!* What would happen to her? Would she be locked in the baron's dungeon, or worse?

The weight in her chest grew heavier.

The second knight led another horse up to the mounting block and said, "We need you to dismount your mule and get on the horse we brought."

Sir Merek took hold of her wrists, which were tied together now, and she let him help her down. The other knight moved her mule out of the way while Sir Merek helped her mount the horse.

Her mother and brother, the servants, and even a few neighbors who had heard her screaming stood watching as Sir Merek held on to her elbow while his fellow guard tied the other end of the rope that was around her wrists to the pommel on the horse's saddle.

She felt her cheeks start to burn, and her heart ached when she saw her mother quietly sobbing into her hands.

Poor Mother. She didn't deserve to have this terrible worry. And though Violet felt guilty for causing her mother pain and anxiety, she also felt humiliated by the way she was being treated. But this was not her fault; it was Baron Dunham's fault. She had tried to stand up against his tyranny and injustice, and that was why she was being taken away from her home.

"Don't worry, Mother. I'll be all right, and I shall come back to you soon." *I'm so sorry*, she wanted to say, but she didn't want to give these men the satisfaction of seeing her express sorrow or wrongdoing. *God, rain down Your fire and brimstone on their heads for this.*

She silently accused Sir Merek of being a liar, but she couldn't even look at him, too afraid her emotion would get the better of her and she would start crying.

Sir Merek took charge of her horse's reins and tied them to his own saddle, and he and his fellow guard mounted up and started toward the road, bringing her along between them. She gripped the pommel, as the horse was quite a bit taller than Mistress Sally.

She was frightened, but she encouraged herself with the thought that if she suffered, at least she suffered for trying to right a wrong.

Merek listened to the quiet, which seemed to be a tangible thing hanging between them. He'd rather have Violet berate him than endure her silence as she hung her head and held on to the saddle as if she was afraid she might fall off.

He felt like the worst kind of man, oppressing an innocent—and courageous and unselfish—woman. And he realized he would prefer for her to be railing at him rather than to be silent and despondent.

They had been traveling for an hour when they stopped to let the horses get a drink. Merek could stand it no longer and broke the silence. "I am sorry for taking you from your family," he began, "but—"

"How is your conscience allowing you to take a young woman against her will? How do you live with yourself, knowing you are breaking your oath as a knight by stealing money from the poor and giving it to Baron Dunham?" She no longer hung her head but glared straight into Merek's eyes when he looked her way.

Sir Willmer groaned.

"These are sincere and reasonable questions," Violet said. "A knight should be ashamed to take orders from a man like the baron."

Everything she said was true, even though her accusations made the hair on the back of his neck rise. Merek was trying to think of how to answer her, to think before he spoke, as his priest had counseled him, when Sir Willmer spoke up.

He and Sir Willmer had dismounted to lead the horses to the stream when Sir Willmer, looking more flustered than Merek had ever seen him, went toward the maiden. Merek made ready to step in between them.

"Listen to me," Sir Willmer said, pointing at Violet. "I know what Baron Dunham does is wrong, and I don't like it, but I was sent to serve under him. Do you understand? Sir Merek and I have no choice but to do what he says. And if the king didn't like what the baron was doing, do you not think he would do something about it?"

Merek listened closely to Sir Willmer's words. Perhaps he could trust the man, since he at least admitted that what the baron was doing was wrong. If Merek could convince him that the king was ignorant of the baron's wrongdoing, he might be willing to help Merek bring the baron to justice.

"Perhaps the king does not know." Violet echoed his own thoughts, her colorful eyes sparking in the sunlight. "You should tell him, or let me tell him. Let me send him my letter." Her hands moved subtly to the little purse at her waist.

Did she, at this very moment, have the letter to the king in her purse? He would have to get it from her, and before they reached the baron's castle.

"If you are not willing to tell him, let me go," Violet said, "and I will get word to the king about the injustices happening here."

Sir Willmer's expression was sullen, his brows lowered. "We cannot. But as Sir Merek has said, we will try to keep the baron from harming you. It's the best offer you'll get, as the other knights and guards are very loyal to him, and they like that the baron shares his ill-gotten coins with them."

"He's right," Merek said. Truthfully, Merek wasn't sure why the baron wanted to keep him in his service. He must know that Merek was not interested in stolen money. And he also must know that he couldn't keep Merek from finding out about his nefarious activities for long.

Violet was silent for a moment, but only a moment. "You are knights. Where is your courage? Stand up to the baron!"

"He has twenty greedy men to replace every honest one," Sir Willmer said. "Sir Merek has not been with the baron long enough yet to know, but the baron doesn't allow any man to stay in his service once he finds out he is honest. In fact, he usually has those who disagree with his tactics killed by his favorite guard."

"The one with the scar?" Merek asked, drawing his finger from the bridge of his nose to the corner of his mouth. His anger was rising.

"Yes."

"His name is Sir Goring," Sir Willmer said, turning back to Violet. "As for me, as soon as I can find another place, I will leave. But in the meantime, I need to stay in the good graces of Baron Dunham to stay alive, and so does Sir Merek."

"Why should I trust you?" Violet narrowed her eyes at Sir Willmer, then at Merek as he untied the rope around her wrists and helped her down from the horse. "Sir Merek assured me that the baron would never take money unlawfully, and he said he wanted to help the people whom the baron is oppressing, then you both come and take me forcibly from my home, tying my hands in front of my family and neighbors."

"You should be thankful he sent Sir Merek and me," Sir Willmer said. "His other guards would have treated you badly."

"I feel so fortunate." Violet rolled her eyes heavenward.

Merek could tell Sir Willmer was clenching his teeth by the way his jaw twitched. Sir Willmer was the kind of man who liked peace and quiet, who didn't say much and seemed to prefer other people who also didn't say much.

"I still don't trust you, either of you. You grabbed my arm." She pointed at Merek. Then pointed her finger at Sir Willmer. "And you bound my hands together and tied me to a strange horse. Knights who are pure of heart do not do such things."

Merek said, "We wouldn't have grabbed your arm or tied your hands if you hadn't tried to escape."

"I wouldn't have tried to escape if I weren't being taken by men who work for the baron."

"The baron must have sent Sir Merek and me because he didn't want you harmed," Sir Willmer said. "He knows we, of all his men, are honorable. And he has had many men killed—and women, too, if the rumors are true. So you should count yourself fortunate."

"Give me your purse," Merek said.

She clutched the purse to her stomach. "Why do you want my purse? I knew it. You are not to be trusted."

"If you have a letter to the king in there, a letter that speaks ill of Baron Dunham, then you had better turn it over to me rather than let the baron take it from you and read it."

"He needs to hear the truth about what kind of man he is."

"Do you think he cares what you have to say?" Merek said.

Sir Willmer shook his head, turning away from her with a snort as he walked to where the horses were placidly cropping the grass at their feet.

Merek said, "We are only trying to help you. Give me the letter and I will find a courier to take it to the king."

"How do I know you will?"

"I can take it from you by force." Merek took a step forward, reaching toward her.

She slapped at his hand.

Merek crossed his arms and stared at her. He was rarely good at reading other people's thoughts, but he was fairly certain that she was conflicted, wondering whether she should give him the letter or risk having it taken from her by the baron.

Suddenly, she huffed, unfastened her purse from her belt, and thrust it at him. "Here. Take it. I suppose you will want coins to pay the courier."

"I will not take your coins." He forced himself not to glare at her. But she sorely tried his patience when she continued to misjudge his motives and his character.

He took out the rolled-up missive and returned the purse. "I will do my best to get this to the king."

He could see the look of mistrust in her eyes and quickly turned away from her to keep from unleashing the sarcastic words that were rising inside him.

The rest of the way to the castle, Violet Lambton said very little. Sir Willmer seemed quite pleased that she had ceased arguing with them, but Merek couldn't help wondering what she was thinking. Her countenance was sad and somber. He could easily imagine how frightened she must be. After all, she was a young woman with no power, being taken before a wealthy baron, having threatened that baron with telling the king of his nefarious deeds.

Merek and Sir Willmer had assured her they wouldn't let any harm come to her, but she didn't trust them, and he could hardly blame her. He had his own issues with trust. After all, the world was full of evil people who would eagerly stab a person in the back for a piece of land or a bag of coins.

For that very reason, if for no other, he could not let her down or break his promise to protect her from Baron Dunham.

SEVEN

VIOLET'S ANGER LEFT HER—UNFORTUNATELY—BECAUSE fear quickly replaced it.

Her instincts told her that Sir Merek and Sir Willmer were telling the truth. After all, they didn't have to agree with her that it was wrong for the baron to use his guards to take people's money, or to tell her that the baron had murdered people. If they were loyal to the baron, they would have defended him.

But she had been tied up like a common criminal and taken from her home unjustly. If the two knights were so noble, why didn't they do something to stop the baron? She was afraid to hope that they would protect her from him.

When Baron Dunham's castle came into view, she stared at the formidable fortress. Her first thought was that the fortified stone castle would live on long after its evil owner was gone.

"Come. Don't be afraid," Sir Merek said softly.

She wanted to snap angrily at him, but instead, to hide her

fear, she sat up straighter and urged her horse forward, up the sloping path to the castle gatehouse. The two knights had to hurry to catch up with her.

When they reached the castle, some young grooms came out to take their horses. Sir Merek helped her dismount. Her chest tightened, but somehow the concerned look on his face, and his gentle hands helping her down, calmed her. Perhaps he really was trustworthy. Perhaps God had placed him in the baron's service just at this time to watch over her, but she would never admit that to him, not until she was certain.

Sir Merek's intense blue eyes stared down at her. She thought he was about to speak, but some guards were striding toward them. Sir Merek and Sir Willmer simply fell in beside her, one on either side, and escorted her as they walked to the entrance to the castle.

Violet held her head high. If she knew anything from watching animals fight with each other, it was that she could not appear weak, and she considered Baron Dunham to be no better than an animal. Perhaps she was being naïve to think so, but her only chance seemed to be to stand up to him and refuse to appear powerless.

But it would be difficult to appear defiant when she was so worried about her family. The baron could punish them for what she had done, and no one could stop him.

She couldn't think like that. Her panic might rise, and she needed to be brave. She clenched her fists and stared straight ahead, setting her mind on standing strong in the face of this robber baron.

Sir Merek and Sir Willmer looked their part, with their regal bearing and the fierce expression of knights bent on bringing a wrongdoer before their master. No one would ever guess that they had pledged to make sure she was not harmed.

The guards were all staring at her, but she did her best to ignore them. If one did catch her eye, she gave him her best glare, imagining what insults she would hurl at him. *Churlish lapdog for the robber baron* was her favorite.

As they entered the enormous front doors of the castle, she struggled to keep her defiant countenance, not wishing to look like a country maiden who had never been outside her own village—which was not far from the truth.

The two knights led her into the biggest room she had ever seen, bigger even than the nave at her village church, with shields and banners across one wall, but her gaze was arrested by the man at the other end of the room.

He sat in a large chair. No one else was in the room except for a few guards who stood at the door. He was quite motionless, and he seemed to be staring at Violet, although it was difficult to tell with the lack of light coming through the windows.

"Come closer," he said, motioning with his hand.

Violet did not immediately comply, and a few moments later, Sir Merek and Sir Willmer each took hold of an arm and gently pulled her forward.

"It's so dark in here," the baron said irritably. He snapped his fingers at the guards at the door. "Bring me some extra candles."

The men hurried out.

The baron had weather-browned skin and a dark beard and

mustache. He looked to be about forty-five. He said not a word as he stared at her.

The guards came back inside carrying a couple of lanterns and placed them on the table beside the baron.

"Your name is Violet Lambton, yes?" the baron said, stroking his beard.

"It is."

"What is your mother's name?"

Why would he ask her that? After a moment's hesitation, Violet replied, "Mary Lambton."

He never took his eyes off her face. "Mary? Does she have violet eyes like yours?"

Why was he asking her this? "No," she answered. "Her eyes are brown." She hated that her voice quaked slightly.

"Who else in your family has violet-colored eyes?"

"I . . . I don't understand."

The baron's cold expression became even harder, and his eyes narrowed. "Why were you writing a letter to the king?"

Should she pretend to be meek and sorry in order to protect her family? Another part of her wanted nothing more than to confront the baron with the evil of his own deeds, but she had to be careful not to antagonize him. So she said, carefully weighing each word, "I was concerned that you were taking money unlawfully."

"And why would you think the king would listen to you?"

"I don't have any reason to think he would listen to me, particularly. I only thought . . ." She let her voice trail off. What could she say that wouldn't enrage this man? His mention of her mother had frightened the defiance right out of her. How could she bear it if he harmed her mother because of her foolish actions?

"Speak up!" he demanded.

"Please don't harm my mother. She had nothing to do with me writing that letter." She felt a sense of shame, heat building in her face, to beg this man for anything. But she was willing to do it if it kept her mother safe.

"Put this maiden in the dungeon," the baron commanded, "and go and fetch her mother."

"No!" Violet's breath rushed out. She spoke quickly, her voice rasping. "My mother has done nothing wrong. She is not to blame. Put me in the dungeon, but my mother doesn't know anything and hasn't done anything." Her stomach twisted at the thought of her poor mother suffering because of Violet's protest against the baron.

"You said your mother's eyes are not the same color as yours?"

"Yes. I mean, my mother has brown eyes." If telling the man everything about herself would keep her family safe . . . "But my mother, the one who birthed me, died when I was very young."

"Tell me more about your birth mother." The baron's eyes narrowed, his gaze even more intensely fastened on her.

"I don't know anything about her except that she starved to death and the mother and father who raised me took me in because I was left with no family. My father died a few years ago. Please, put me in your dungeon, not my mother. She does as she is told and disapproved of me writing a letter to the king."

The baron said nothing. He sat against the back of his chair, still stroking his chin.

God, please don't let him bring Mother here.

She glanced at the knights on either side of her. They both looked very stoic, but Sir Merek stared hard at Baron Dunham and she saw his jaw twitch.

"Did the people who raised you know your mother? How did you come to be living with them?"

"I don't believe they did know my mother." Violet thought about what she had been told. It was her grandmother who had suggested Violet's mother and father take her in. But she was too afraid to mention her grandmother. He might want to send for her, too, although she couldn't imagine why he was asking her these questions.

He seemed to be waiting for her to finish answering him.

"I was very young. I don't know exactly how it came about."

"Perhaps your family knew your mother. Perhaps they were related to her."

"No, I don't think so."

He stared at her, crossing his arms in front of his chest. Then he said, "Take her to the dungeon."

Sir Willmer grabbed hold of her arm.

"What is her crime?" Sir Merek asked.

Sir Willmer froze.

Baron Dunham stared back at Sir Merek. "She spoke against me. If I allow her to spread such tales, chaos will break out. People will not respect my law and there will be disorder. You are clever enough to understand that, Sir Merek. Are you not?"

No one moved. Then Sir Merek said, "Of course. But she is a woman, and though obviously unhinged, are you sure you want to throw her in the dungeon? Her family will wonder what happened to her. It is possible she is pledged to marry a land-holder, someone who will ask questions."

"Sir Merek, this is inappropriate to speak of in front of the prisoner."

Violet had to do something, to redirect the baron's attention away from Sir Merek before he got himself thrown in the dungeon as well.

"There is a man. His name is Robert Mercer. He owns some land in my village and—"

"Silence. You will speak only when asked a question." He turned cold eyes on Sir Merek. "Take her to the dungeon. We can discuss this later."

Sir Merek nodded and took Violet's other arm, and the two knights led her out of the Great Hall.

Violet felt strangely calm. Was this the peace that passes understanding that she had read about in the priest's Bible? God must surely be with her, as He was with Daniel when he was thrown into the lions' den.

No one spoke as they went through a corridor and down a long stone staircase. Then, after walking through another corridor, they went down a shorter set of stone steps to what was obviously the dungeon.

She heard a few moans coming from deeper within the cavernous, underground floor of the castle. After proceeding through a winding passageway, they stopped in front of a crude-looking iron grate serving as a door for a cell carved in the stone. Sir Merek pulled on it and the iron gate opened.

"We'll come back for you," Sir Merek said in a low voice. Then he turned to Sir Willmer, and they spoke to each other.

"We'll have to wait until after dark," Sir Willmer whispered.

"I'll find her a horse and have it saddled and ready," Sir Merek said.

Sir Willmer nodded, then Sir Merek shut her inside the tiny cell, stuck a key in the lock, and turned it until it clicked.

Violet stared through the bars at them. Sir Willmer avoided looking at her, but Sir Merek stared back. "I promise we will come for you. Don't worry."

"Please don't let him send for my mother. She would be so frightened."

"I don't think he intends to summon your mother. Do you know why he seems so interested in your mother?"

"I have no idea. But I am worried that if he finds out I am gone, he will take out his wrath on her."

Sir Merek and Sir Willmer looked at each other.

"She's right," Sir Willmer said.

"I will come to you after it is dark," Sir Merek said. "If you wish to be set free, I will help you escape."

"But I must not go if there is a possibility he will demand to speak to my mother."

"Maybe the baron will summon you again. Perhaps if you tell him what he wants to hear, he will set you free."

"I don't even know what he wants to hear." She shook her head and sighed. "He seems fixated on my mother's eye color and asks questions I cannot answer. Is the baron mad?"

Sir Willmer said, "He is not mad. I don't know what his interest is in your mother. Perhaps he knew her."

"If you can think of some way to satisfy his curiosity about your mother," Sir Merek said, "perhaps he will set you free."

"He doesn't even seem to be concerned about the letter I wrote to the king," Violet said, lowering her voice to a whisper.

"It is strange," Sir Merek said.

From deeper in the dark, windowless dungeon, one of her fellow prisoners started yelling and demanding water.

"I am sorry to leave you in here, even for a few hours," Sir Merek said.

"We should go," Sir Willmer said.

"We will return." Sir Merek touched the bars between them. "And I shall take care of the missive."

"Thank you. And please, if he mentions sending for my mother again, please try to persuade him not to."

"We shall do our best."

And then they were striding away, leaving her alone, the only light coming from a torch that hung on the corridor wall.

The air was damp and foul, smelling of human excrement. The man who had been begging for water let loose a string of curse words, then fell silent.

She could hear water dripping nearby and the occasional faint coughing. Glancing around, she noticed a bucket, probably for her use in relieving herself, and a narrow bench with a single blanket. Would she be here overnight and have to sleep on the wooden bench? She might stretch out on the stone floor instead.

The air was cool enough that she reached for the blanket,

sniffing it. It didn't smell terribly offensive. The gray wool material looked clean, so she wrapped it around her shoulders and sat down on the bench.

She closed her eyes and tried to arrange her thoughts into some semblance of a prayer. And there were many things to pray about, not the least of which was that her own fears did not overcome her courage.

Eventually she grew so weary that she lay down. She continued to pray, whispering, "God, please don't let the baron send for my mother. Give her—and me—peace, as You did for Shadrach, Meshach, and Abednego. Give me the courage You gave them to stand up to the king and to walk around in the fiery furnace. Even when faced with the king's wrath, they told him they would not serve his god or worship his golden image. Since You are the same God, I know You will give me the same courage You gave to them."

Feeling at peace, she fell asleep.

EIGHT

MEREK FOUND SIR WILLMER IN THE SOLDIERS' BARRACKS. He caught his eye and Sir Willmer nodded, got up, and followed him out. They didn't stop walking until they were in the woods behind the barracks.

"I talked to the baron," Merek said in a low voice, keeping an eye out for anyone who might be listening. "He was very arrogant about his position with the king. He isn't worried about her sending a letter complaining about how he taxes his people. But he also wouldn't tell me why he's so interested in Violet and her mother. He seems to think if he lets her sit in the dungeon long enough, she will tell him more about her birth mother."

"I'm surprised you got away with questioning him."

"I'm a little surprised myself." Merek's quick temper and tongue had gotten him in more trouble—and caused more regrets—than he cared to remember. But his only regret about standing up for Violet was that it may have stirred up suspicion in the baron about Merek's intentions, which would make it harder for him to rescue her.

"What is our plan?" Sir Willmer asked. "I take it you don't wish to allow the girl to rot in the dungeon any more than I do."

"If it were not for her concern for her family, which is understandable, I would say we should let her out of the dungeon now and make sure she gets far away from the baron. I could take her to my sister's or my brother's castle—they are both well outside this region."

"But then what? If we risk our lives for her, we may as well risk our lives to stop him once and for the good of all."

"I agree. How many more of the baron's guards might wish to help us? How many think the way we do?"

"None that I know of." Sir Willmer raised his brows and frowned. "I've been here three months and I've kept my mouth shut. As I said before, from what I've heard, anyone who crosses the baron ends up dead. But he probably thinks he can't get away with killing you without a lot of attention, since your family is so well-connected to the king and he trusts you. But eventually . . ."

"The baron will decide it's worth the risk to get rid of me too," Merek said.

"I've thought about it, and I think the best thing is for us to find some evidence against the baron. I had forgotten about it, but when I first came here, I heard the guards talking about a secret record book the baron keeps hidden. He has a record book he shows to the king's officials and a separate one that is an accounting of what he's actually taking in, so he can make sure no one is skimming off his profits. If we could find it, we could take it to the king."

"That is exactly what we need. But I'm not leaving here until the girl is free and safe."

Sir Willmer raised his brows again. "If you set her free tonight, the baron will just send more men after her, and after her family too."

"I at least want to talk to her."

"If you end up taking the girl somewhere safe, I'll try to secure the baron's secret record book." Sir Willmer crossed his arms, then uncrossed them, the only thing that belied his calm.

Merek sighed, wondering whether Violet would choose to go or stay. Finally, he said, "If you don't see me in the next hour or two, I am on my way to Strachleigh Castle, my sister's home, with the girl."

Sir Willmer nodded and Merek hurried to the dungeon to see Violet. He prayed again, *God, help me keep my promise to keep her safe and set her free.*

As he approached her cell, he could see she was lying down, motionless. She'd been in the dungeon for no more than two hours. Was she so unworried that she could fall asleep on that hard wooden bench? He knew women could be very brave, as his sister, Delia, had placidly knitted while all her brothers plotted to attack their guards and escape the Tower of London. Or perhaps Violet was paralyzed with fear.

When he turned the key in the lock, Violet roused herself and sat up, rubbing her cheek.

His heart contracted strangely. He wanted so much to save her, to spare her the cruelty of this dungeon and Baron Dunham.

"Sir Merek," was all she said.

"I spoke to the baron. He told me he was not concerned about you writing letters to the king. He has allied himself with one or two of the king's closest advisors and so believes he is impervious to the king's wrath. However, I will send the letter, if you wish, for I believe he is overconfident in that."

"Yes, of course," she said, clearing her throat. She had sleep lines on her cheek from where she'd been using her hands as a pillow.

"He says he knew a young woman who may have been your mother. He wants to know what happened to this woman. If you can give him any information that will help him determine if your mother was the woman he knew, then I believe he might let you go. But if you do not wish to speak to him again, I can help you escape."

"I am worried he will harm my mother. Besides, where would I go that he wouldn't be able to find me again?"

"I can take you somewhere you'll be safe, to my family who lives far away from here."

"But my mother would not be safe. No, I will try to answer his questions. But truthfully, I know so little about my birth mother."

"Do you not know her name?"

"I don't, but I think my grandmother might. But you are not to tell the baron that." She pointed her finger at Merek's chest.

"Of course not."

She let out a slow breath. "Can you take me to the baron?"

He couldn't help admiring her courage as well as her love for her family. "Of course."

He led her out of the dungeon and up to the Great Hall.

The baron was speaking to the knight who seemed to be his right hand, Sir Goring, the one with the scar. When Baron Dunham saw Merek and Violet enter the room, he said something to Sir Goring and that man left the room, staring hard at Merek as he went.

As soon as Merek brought Violet near, the baron said, "Tell me everything you know about your mother. If you tell me anything useful, I shall let you go home."

"As I said, I don't remember much about my mother. I was only about five years old when she died. I remember her being young and beautiful. I was told she starved herself to feed me, for she had no family and was very poor."

"Do you remember the color of her eyes?"

Violet shook her head. "I do not. Only that she had long brown hair, similar to mine."

"Her name? Surely you know your own mother's name."

"I can ask my family if you let me go home. Perhaps someone knows."

His cold eyes seemed to stare past her. "Very well, you may go. But you must return in two days' time to tell me what you discover about your mother. If you do not, I shall send for your entire family. And if I cannot find out what I wish to know, you will all be thrown in the dungeon."

He leaned forward, menace in his expression. "You have had a taste of it and would not like staying there indefinitely, would you? Or be responsible for your family members living in my dungeon?"

It was on the tip of Merek's tongue to say, "She seemed to be napping peacefully in your dungeon, as an innocent mind is a peaceful one," but he refrained.

Would Violet shoot back a defiant reply, as he had known her to do? Or would she feign compliance? He held his breath, waiting for her to speak.

"As I do not wish my family to suffer from your cruelties any more than they already have, I shall do my best to discover my birth mother's name, though I cannot imagine what your interest in my mother could be."

If Merek had thought the baron's face cold and menacing before, it was nothing compared to the way his jaw visibly hardened and his face turned red.

Merek's mind went to his sword strapped across his back, and he calculated how many of the guards he might need to take out if the baron attacked Violet.

The baron finally unclenched his jaw and said, "If you are not here in two days, I will send for your family. Do not test me." His eyes shifted to Merek, and he flicked his hand, as if to tell him to take her away.

Merek gave a quick nod and took Violet by the arm, leading her out of the Great Hall.

Neither of them spoke as they passed through the corridor and out the door closest to the stables. As they walked across the open yard, Merek said, "I hope you can discover your mother's name and—"

"Why are you trying to help me?"

"I wish to help you because your cause is just. And I am a knight." The hair on the back of his neck bristled at the way she continued to question his motives, but he couldn't get too offended; he was just as mistrustful as she was.

"Forgive me." She sighed, her expression crumpling. "You have been very kind. I am just worried about my mother."

She turned and continued walking toward the stable, her hand clenched in a fist by her side as she strode away from him.

He understood her anger more than she could imagine as he thought back on his own rage at those who had hurt his family only a few years before.

He did think she could be a bit more grateful. Didn't she realize that he was risking everything by helping her? He'd been willing to take her out of the dungeon and give her a horse and let her escape, and he still would, if the situation warranted it.

Nevertheless, there was nowhere he'd rather be than here, helping the courageous girl with the violet eyes and the scarlet cloak.

Violet was finally starting to breathe normally as she rode toward home. She had to figure out what to do, what to say, and what not to say.

Mother was probably crying and worrying herself nearly to

death. And Violet had the baron's threat hanging over her that he would imprison her mother. Would he find her grandmother and put her in his dungeon as well? Of course he would. The man was obviously heartless.

But now that her head was cooler and her thoughts calmer, she realized she should have thanked Sir Merek instead of questioning why he was helping her. He and Sir Willmer had not harmed her in any way, and they had even pledged to set her free and protect her. They had behaved honorably toward her and seemed to be decent men. In fact, it was because of Sir Merek taking her to the baron that she was on her way home.

Sir Merek was risking a great deal to help her.

She was leaving the town of Bilborough, so she slowed the horse the baron had allowed her to borrow and patted her neck.

If Violet was honest, she had been afraid. Anything could have happened to her. And she worried about her mother, whose fears about far lesser things had caused her to break down in tears many times.

"O God, forgive me for my selfishness. Please spare my mother this anguish. How much worse will that be if real harm comes to her because of me?" Tears sprang to her eyes and slid down her cheeks.

She thought of the distress on her mother's face when Sir Merek and Sir Willmer came and took her. Did her mother and brother blame Violet for this trouble that had come to their family? After all, Violet had written a letter to the king with accusations against the powerful Baron Dunham even though her mother had told her not to.

"I'm sorry, Mother." Tears continued to flow down her face now that the sun was going down and it was growing dark.

It was not safe to be on the road at night. She'd been told that by her mother many times, and she was still at least two hours from home. But she couldn't push her horse to go faster or she would run the risk of exhausting her.

She rubbed the tears from her cheeks, taking deep breaths to make them stop coming. Crying did no good at all and would only make her more tired.

Suddenly she was aware of the sounds of a horse behind her.

Violet glanced over her shoulder. A man was riding toward her, gaining ground.

Her heart lurched inside her chest. Was this man a brigand bent on robbing her? What would he do when he found that she was alone?

She clutched the reins tightly in her hands, ready to urge her horse into a gallop.

"Violet, wait."

The man knew her name.

When she turned her head, she saw it was Sir Merek. Her heart immediately slowed its frantic pace.

He pulled up his horse alongside her. "I want to make sure you get home safely."

"Thank you." She nodded at him. "And thank you for looking out for me and for helping me."

She had to swallow her pride to say those words, but he deserved her gratitude. He had been very kind to her.

"I am honored to help." His words were simple, his manner surprisingly humble.

They rode along in silence for a while, her mind churning with questions.

"Why do you think Baron Dunham is so interested in my birth mother?"

Sir Merek gazed at her from atop his horse. "I don't know, but it seems as if the baron may have known a woman who had the same color eyes, someone who was of an age that she could have been your mother."

"But my mother was poor. Surely the baron will realize he could not have known my mother. There must be other women in the world with violet eyes."

"I would imagine that is so."

She must speak with her grandmother. She was the only person who might know something.

Sir Merek was staring at her.

"I've heard the baron had a sister who disappeared, but that was only from someone who likes to gossip. We can ask Sir Willmer, since he's been here longer than I have." Sir Merek raised his brows. "If you are the baron's sister's child, the baron will want to marry you off to someone powerful and wealthy, which could be a good thing. You would have far more if you wed one of the baron's friends than if you married the man you are pledged to now. Did you not say he was a landowner?"

"The truth is, I am not pledged to be married to him. He asked me to marry him, but I refused him."

Sir Merek's expression changed slightly. Was he relieved that she wasn't pledged to marry? No, she was surely imagining that.

"If you are not pledged to marry him, why did you bring up his name?"

"You suggested to the baron that I might be pledged to marry someone, someone who would ask questions. I only mentioned Robert Mercer in the hope that it might deter the baron from harming me—and to distract him from becoming angry with you. But I would never ask Robert Mercer to help me."

As they rode, Violet thought about the rumors Sir Merek had heard. What if her birth mother was somehow related to the baron? Violet had always imagined that her mother was noble and good, perishing in order to save her daughter, and that her birth father was good but had died before he could provide a future for his family. How awful if the truth was nothing like her imaginings. Indeed, she knew almost nothing of her origins. Could it be that what she had been told—that her mother was destitute and alone—was not even true, that she was actually related to the baron and had not been poor at all?

Her stomach felt sick at the thought that her family may have lied to her.

They rode along in silence for a few more minutes before Violet wondered aloud, "Did the baron send you to accompany me home?"

"He did not."

If he was telling the truth and he truly was concerned only for her welfare, then it was a bit disconcerting. He was a knight, the son of an earl. He was risking so much, his position and possibly even his life, to help a young woman of lowly birth. She was causing so much trouble for her mother as well. Was she now to feel the same obligation to him, the same guilt?

When they reached the lane leading to her home without incident, Violet said, "That is my house, down this lane."

Sir Merek stopped his horse. "I will watch you go the rest of the way."

Violet started to dismount from the borrowed horse.

"Keep the horse and bring her back in two days—unless you change your mind about going back to the castle. If you discover something that makes you want to flee, send me word and I shall take you to my sister's home at Strachleigh—and your mother and siblings too."

Her only sibling was Theo, and he would never leave their farm, but there was no need to mention that. "I thank you. You have been so kind."

"It is my privilege as a knight to serve those in need."

She stared at his profile. He was very serious and rather gruff, but she felt safe with him. And he was quite handsome and well-favored, though his expression was often so unreadable.

"Good night, Sir Merek."

"Good night, Violet."

When Violet knocked on the door, her brother opened it. Mother was right behind him, and she cried out, "Violet!" and threw her arms around her.

"I'm safe, Mother. Don't cry. All is well."

Violet told her mother all that had happened and how she had left the castle accompanied by one of the knights.

"But I don't know your mother's name," Mother wailed. "I never even saw her. Your grandmother found you and brought you to us."

"Then I must go see Grandmother in the morning."

Mother started to cry, wiping the tears as fast as they puddled under her eyes. "I don't understand why this trouble has befallen us. It is too hard, too unjust."

"Don't worry, Mother. All will be well. We must trust that God will take care of us."

Mother continued weeping and speaking her fears, all the things she imagined the baron might do to them. Violet didn't mention that she and Sir Merek thought it possible that the baron was her uncle, since it seemed so unlikely.

Theo stared hard at her, though he said very little. But she could imagine what he was thinking—that she, the adopted daughter, had brought trouble on their family.

NINE

THE NEXT MORNING MEREK RODE TO A VILLAGE ABOUT AN hour away. He had read Violet's letter to the king. It was a good letter; he could not have written a better one. So he resealed it, wrote a short letter of his own, and took them to a courier he knew who had once been a guard.

"Where are you now?" the man asked.

"At the castle of the Baron Dunham."

The man's brows shot up. "That sly thief?" he said in a low voice. "He's a whitewashed tomb if there ever was one."

"So I'm discovering." After thinking a moment, Merek said, "Would you be willing to band together with me and some other honest men to try to stop Baron Dunham?"

The man took a step back. "A few honest men against the wiliest and richest man in the region? I am not so eager to meet the Almighty. I have a wife and children to provide for."

"I understand."

"I will take your letters to the king, though, and I won't tell a soul. But I'm sorry to say that I can do no more than that."

Merek was disappointed, but his spirits rose nevertheless. He never shrank from a challenge, and in fact, he rather relished tasks that other people felt were too difficult. He had learned that others were not so attracted to a nearly hopeless cause.

Merek rode back to Dunham Castle to make sure he was there for Violet should she need him. When he returned, he went in search of Sir Willmer, whom he found sitting on a stool in a shady, out-of-the-way spot, sharpening his knives with a whetstone.

Merek told Sir Willmer about the baron giving Violet two days to find out more information about her mother, then asked, "What about the record book you mentioned, the one he keeps to account for the monies his men collect? Are you any closer to finding it?"

"I found out that the baron's men hand whatever monies they collect on their raiding parties and tax collections to Sir Goring, and he puts the coins in a cell full of strongboxes in the dungeon. It made me wonder if the record book might be with the coins in the dungeon."

Merek nodded. "Sounds like a good place to start looking."

Together, they formulated a plan, including what they would say to the other knights and guards to try to discover how loyal they were to the baron and whether they might be trusted to join with them.

"But we must wait and see what happens with Violet first."

Sir Willmer said, "I was thinking he might be trying to make her his new mistress, since his old one disappeared some months ago."

"I don't think that's his motive." Merek explained what he had overheard about the baron's sister.

"I've never heard anything about a sister, but that would make sense, I suppose. But even if the maiden's mother was the baron's sister, why would he care to know, beyond mild curiosity? It seems unlikely he could have cared so much about her, even if she was his sister."

"You have a point. But if she is his niece, the baron could want to make an alliance by marrying her off to someone powerful."

Merek hoped Violet would uncover something that would satisfy the baron's curiosity. But if he tried to harm Violet, all the more reason to defeat him and save the people of this region from the despotic robber baron.

Violet slept fitfully and awoke at dawn with a nervous feeling.

"Don't worry," she insisted to her hovering mother. "I will visit Grandmother and find out what she knows about my birth mother. All will be well."

"I'm just so afraid," Mother said, starting to cry as Violet quickly ate some buttered bread for her breakfast. "So afraid of what will happen to you when you go back to the baron. But what can we do? It will only make things worse if you try to run away."

"He's not going to hurt me, Mother." Violet tried to sound as if she wasn't worried at all. "I'm just a woman, with no title or position, so he has no reason to fear me, and therefore no reason to harm me."

"Yes, you must emphasize that you don't know anything and you don't know anyone of any importance. You're a simple maiden of simple means and—"

"Yes, yes, Mother. I know nothing. I am no one and nothing and the baron need not bother with me at all."

"Well, it is true, and you must say whatever you need to say to keep yourself safe."

"Yes, Mother. Of course."

She hated the truth of her mother's words, and something inside her wanted to rebel against them, to prove her worth, to prove that she was not "no one and nothing." She was of great value—to God, at least.

All were equal in God's sight. She'd read that in the Holy Writ that the priest kept in his chambers in the village church. God was no respecter of persons. But how well she knew that most men and women *were* respecters of persons.

Violet had tried to please her mother and father, to earn her place in the family, always aware that she was adopted. She feared that if she wasn't a blessing to her family, they would cease to love her and care for her. She wasn't sure where this idea came from. It had just always lurked in the back of her mind.

Theo often pointed out Violet's many strange characteristics, as if trying to prove that Violet was not like the rest of the Lambtons. But if Violet had many quirks, her mother's one characteristic that stood out was being fearful of absolutely everything.

She loved her mother. Her mother had taken her in, cared for her, never mentioning that she was not her natural-born daughter. She took good care of her when she was sick and made sure she stayed clean and fed and well-clothed. If not for her, Violet very well might have perished or become the victim to some malicious person.

It was true that Violet had often wished her mother was more affectionate. She longed for her to hug her for no particular reason, to smile at her and touch her cheek in passing, to call her loving pet names. But surely it was wrong of Violet to find fault with her mother. Effusive affection just wasn't her mother's way. Besides, those were the kinds of things her grandmother did— kissing her cheek and calling her "loveliest girl," "sweeting," and "sweet child"—so Violet could only be grateful and count herself fortunate indeed.

And if she could save her generous mother the torture of being fearful for her safety, she would.

"Mother, I am sure I will be all right. Please don't worry."

She hurried out of the house, saying a silent prayer for her mother's peace of mind. As she neared the stable, Theo stood outside with the baron's horse.

"Keep this in your pocket," he said. It was one of his knives, along with its sheath. "Men respect a woman who is willing to defend herself."

"Thank you, Theo." She took the knife and put it inside her red cloak.

"I hope you find out something from Grandmother," he said.

"Thank you. And thank you for saddling my horse."

He nodded.

Violet mounted and set out, and when she came to the crossroads, she happened to glance over her shoulder. A man on horseback was behind her. He ignored her glance, almost too purposefully. Was he following her?

She urged her horse to go faster, and as soon as she had gone around a bend in the road, she dismounted and led her mare into a stand of trees.

She waited, holding the horse's harness and rubbing her neck. Soon the man came into view. He slowed his horse and looked back at the crossroads, then turned his horse around and went the opposite way, going down the east road.

Violet led the horse out of the trees, mounted, and urged her into a fast trot toward her grandmother's.

Violet hid her borrowed horse in her grandmother's small barn and went inside the house.

"Grandmother? Are you here?" Violet's heart beat hard and fast as she searched through the house and out the back door. She found Grandmother in her garden.

"What is it, child? You look frightened." Grandmother came toward her with a basket of peas on her arm.

They went inside the house and Violet explained all that had happened since the last time she'd seen her. Grandmother's eyes grew cloudy and her slightly wrinkled face tensed more the longer she spoke.

"Do you know my mother's name?" Violet ended.

"My darling girl, I am very sorry you have come to the attention of the baron. I had hoped this would never happen."

"What do you mean?" Her stomach sank. Grandmother was about to tell her something, and it wasn't good news.

"I mean that your mother was known to the baron. In fact . . . did you know that after your grandfather died and my daughter Mary was married, I worked for a short time in the baron's castle?"

"No." Violet sank down on the bench at her grandmother's table, her knees suddenly weak.

Grandmother took her hand in hers, holding it gently but firmly. "I was a cook and worked in the kitchens. And that is where your mother worked. She was an orphan and had been a servant in the castle since she was a little girl. She grew up to be quite beautiful, with eyes the exact same color as yours. Unfortunately, she caught the baron's eye, and he took advantage of her powerlessness, and she became pregnant."

Violet felt sick and her mind was whirling. She held her breath, trying to brace herself for what her grandmother would say next.

"I wish I could protect you from the truth, but perhaps I should have told you sooner. I am sorry, my dear, but you are the natural daughter of Baron Dunham."

"Have you known all this time?" Tears flooded Violet's eyes. She felt betrayed by her grandmother. How could she keep such a secret from her?

Her grandmother had a pained look on her face. Violet said in a breathless voice, "What happened to my mother?"

"The baron mistreated her, and she ran away before he could learn she was pregnant. She hoped he wouldn't come looking for her. I did not hear from her for a few years, but she showed up at my door when you were five years old. She was sick and starving, and I did my best to help her, but she was too far gone and I couldn't save her. But I promised her I would ensure that you would be well taken care of.

"I asked Mary and her husband, John, if they would like to adopt you as their own. Mary's pregnancy with Theo was difficult and she almost died, as you know, but you probably didn't know that Theo had a twin who was stillborn."

"I didn't know that." Violet felt numb at so much new information.

"I never told Mary or John that you were the child of the baron and his servant girl. Mary is such a fearful person, and I didn't want . . . It seemed best not to tell her."

"Why did you never tell me this before now?" Tears sprang to Violet's eyes, her thoughts jumbled and confused.

A boulder was inside her chest, crushing her heart. *O God, why was I born? How could I be the child of so much evil?* And how could her grandmother keep such a secret from her all these years?

"Forgive me, my dear. I felt you were better off not knowing. After all, if the baron never knew you existed, how could he harm you? I hoped you would never know of your connection to him."

"But it hurts that you kept a secret from me." Violet couldn't stop the tears from spilling over onto her cheeks.

"Oh, my precious girl, I'm so sorry." Grandmother's voice was soothing and contrite. "I never meant to hurt you. I see now that I should have told you. You deserved to know the truth.

When you asked me about your mother, I should have told you everything. Will you forgive me?"

"Of course I forgive you. You were only doing what you thought was best for me." She still felt an actual physical pain deep in her chest, but she knew her grandmother would never purposely hurt her. And just as her tears finally seemed to be dissipating, they started afresh as a new thought forced itself on her.

"I don't want the baron to be my father." A sob escaped her as she buried her face in her hands. Instead of being the good man she'd imagined, her father was a monster.

"Oh, my dear. I hope you know that you are not responsible for anything that befell your poor mother. You are not responsible for anything the baron has done, and it is no reflection on you. Indeed, I have heard the priest say that when the father eats sour grapes, God does not set the children's teeth on edge. You will not suffer the consequences that rightfully belong only to the man who committed the wrongs. He and only he shall answer for his evil actions. What we do need to think on is how to set you free from him."

Violet quickly wiped the tears and took a deep breath to calm herself. "I must decide what to tell the baron about my mother." There was a note of bitterness in her voice. She took another deep breath and let it out. "Sir Merek said he will protect me from the baron, but . . ."

"Yes, I remember this Sir Merek. He said he would help you?"

Violet explained how Sir Merek and Sir Willmer had been sent to bring her to the castle, had pledged to protect her from the baron, and how Sir Merek had made sure she made it home safely.

"He seems like a very good sort of man, and he's handsome too. Perhaps God has provided him to protect you."

Violet wanted to ask why God had not provided anyone to protect her poor mother, but the thought seemed resentful and bitter.

Forgive me, God. The last thing she wanted was to allow bitterness to fill her heart.

"So what should I do?" Violet asked. "Should I tell him the name of my mother?" Could Violet be in danger if the baron discovered she was his child? He might wish her dead if he did not want to acknowledge her as his own, and if he knew that she knew that she was his daughter.

"I have not told you her name yet," Grandmother said, staring thoughtfully past Violet. "And I don't think I will. That way you aren't lying if you say you don't know."

Violet closed her eyes and prayed silently, *God, help me. What should I do?*

"I don't want to cause harm to Mother and Theo, and the baron has already threatened to put Mother in the dungeon. Do I tell the baron that I know what he did to my mother? Or should I pretend not to know anything and hope that he believes me?"

"I don't know what will happen, but I believe you will do what is best."

"But what is best?"

Grandmother seemed thoughtful, but her expression was as calm as if they were discussing the ingredients for a cake.

"Why are you not afraid?" Violet asked. "If the baron finds out that you knew my mother, he may come after you as well."

Grandmother sighed and squeezed Violet's hand. "When I promised your mother I'd make sure you were cared for, I held you in my arms and I heard God speak to me."

"God spoke to you?"

"It was only one of a very few times I heard God's voice. He said, 'This child will bless you and everyone around her.' God knew your future, and He knew you would do good and not evil."

Violet wanted to argue with her that it had been many years after God had made that promise to her, and what had Violet done in her life to bless her family? But surely God wouldn't have said that she would bless them if she was destined to cause her family to be sent to the dungeon.

"But what should I do? Tell the truth? Or pretend I don't know anything?"

Grandmother still did not look worried. "I cannot tell you. You will have to decide that for yourself. But I believe God will lead you to do what is best."

Violet didn't want to say so out loud, but Grandmother's words frustrated her.

"Don't be afraid to ask God for direction. He has promised to give wisdom to those who ask."

"But what if I hear Him wrong?" Or what if He told her to do something she was too afraid to do? Wasn't it better not to know His will than to know it and be too afraid to carry it out?

"Just ask Him. His children know His voice."

"Thank you, Grandmother. All will be well, I'm sure." But

she said the words not out of surety but in the hope that she would actually believe them. At least her grandmother believed them. That was some comfort.

After embracing her grandmother and kissing her wrinkled cheek, Violet left.

As she turned her horse onto the road, she caught a glimpse of the same man on horseback who had been following her earlier. Had he seen where she had gone? Had he overheard her conversation with her grandmother?

The man took off before she could get a good look at him, his horse breaking into a gallop, disappearing around a bend in the road.

Violet's stomach took another dive. *God, please don't let the baron do anything terrible to Grandmother.*

T E N

AFTER PUTTING THE BORROWED HORSE IN THE STABLE, Violet walked to the village church, the door of which was always open to anyone who wished to go inside and pray.

Violet walked through the nave, genuflected before the crucifix, and lit a candle, saying a short prayer as she did so. Then she knelt in front of the chancel.

Her mind was racing to and fro so much she could hardly form a sentence. "God of heaven," she whispered, "what should I do?" Images filled her mind of her mother lying on the cold stone floor in the baron's dungeon, crying in fear and despair. "God, please help me do the right thing. Please protect my mother and my grandmother. Give me the words to say to the baron."

As she prayed, she did her best to fight off the fears that kept attacking her. When she was only able to whisper over and over, "Help me, God. Please help me," she lifted her head and gazed up at the crucifix.

Jesus had suffered, hanging from the nails in His hands and feet. Why should she think her life would be free of suffering? Jesus said that in this world His followers would experience trouble. But He said that they should not despair, as He had overcome sin and death.

"God, I can bear suffering at the baron's hand, but please don't let me be the cause of my mother's and grandmother's suffering."

I hold you, your mother, and your grandmother in the palm of My hand.

The words came into her mind so suddenly, her heart quickened and she sucked in a breath. In that moment she was certain God had spoken to her.

"God," she whispered, "You hold us in the palm of Your hand, but what does that mean? That we will not suffer?"

She waited, but no other words came to her.

"Since You hold us in the palm of Your hand, I will trust You." She would hold on to those words no matter what happened. They were in the palm of God's hand, and that must be enough for her. "Thank You, God."

She stayed on her knees for several more minutes, whispering prayers of thanks and praise to God. Then she stood, crossed herself, and went home.

Not wanting to delay any longer, Violet told her mother she was leaving for the baron's castle and packed a small bag with a few items, including her Psalter.

Mother was wringing her hands as she watched Violet gather some bread and cheese. The day was warm enough that she didn't need her red cloak, but she folded it and tucked it under her arm.

"You are taking those things because you think the baron will put you in the dungeon." Mother's chin quivered.

"I may spend some time in the dungeon." Violet's heart squeezed painfully as a tear rolled down her mother's cheek. "But please don't worry, Mother. God is holding me—and you—in the palm of His hand."

Mother looked slightly bewildered as she wiped her cheek, her eyes widening. She shook her head. "You talk in riddles."

"No. I was praying, and God spoke to me. He said He holds us in the palm of His hand."

"God didn't speak to you. God only speaks to priests and prophets and . . . You talk nonsense. You should go to the priest and ask him to give you last rites." She let out a small sob.

"Mother, no. I shall be well. You will see. Don't worry, for I believe—"

"Theo, say your fare wells to your sister." Mother was crying in earnest now, tears streaming down her face as Theo walked into the room. "She's going to the castle and—" Her sobs cut her words short.

"Do not let yourself be so troubled, Mother." Violet's own heart was strangely calm. "I believe all will be well."

Mother only turned away from them and found a clean apron to wipe her face on.

"Fare well, Violet. I hope you don't get yourself killed." Theo frowned slightly and left the room.

Mother seemed to get control of herself after Theo left. She wiped her face and nose and said, "He will be devastated if something happens to you."

Violet wanted to shrug but nodded instead.

She drew the drawstring closed on her small bag, which she hoped she'd be allowed to take with her if she was locked in the dungeon again, then tied it to the tapestry belt around her waist and hugged her mother.

"I'm sorry for the trouble I've brought on you," Violet said, tears clogging her throat. While her mother clung to her, she said, "Thank you for being my mother, for taking care of me and teaching me to be good. I love you very much."

When she pulled away, her mother's face was scrunched, as if she was trying to hold back her tears.

Violet hurried away, saying a prayer that her mother would be well while she was gone and that God would comfort her.

Merek saw Violet making her way from the gatehouse between two guards. She was a day early, but he wasn't surprised. It was the kind of brave thing she would do.

He walked toward the maiden, who carried her now-familiar red cloak in her arms. Their eyes met in a long gaze before she redirected her eyes forward. Merek followed her and the other guards into the castle.

Once inside, one of the guards took hold of her arm. She immediately jerked her arm out of his grasp. "Do not touch me," she demanded.

To Merek's surprise, the guard did not take her arm again, and together they walked to the Great Hall.

Merek followed close behind them, as if he was meant to be of their party. When the men saw that Baron Dunham was not in the room, one of them glanced around and saw Merek.

"Can you wait here with this woman while I go find the baron?"

"Of course," Merek said, stepping up to take his place beside Violet.

Violet looked at him. He wanted to reassure her that he and Sir Willmer had a plan—of sorts. It was a simple plan, but it was a plan nonetheless. They would find the baron's secret record book, steal it, and take it to the king. They would also make sure the baron did not harm Violet or her family by taking them to Strachleigh, if necessary, where his brother-in-law, the duke, would protect them. But of course, he couldn't tell Violet all of that in front of the other guard, whom Merek already knew to be an often-drunk, harsh-talking, unscrupulous sort of man.

So they stood silently waiting until the guard returned with the baron.

When the baron entered the room, Merek noticed that he was rather short in stature. It occurred to Merek that he had rarely if ever seen him standing or walking. He was also mostly bald. Merek wondered if he was trying to make up for his lack of hair with a long black beard and mustache. His beard was so black, in fact, that Merek had heard rumors that he colored it with some sort of dye.

The baron stopped a few feet in front of Violet and stared at her. He crossed his arms over his chest and said, "You are here early. You must have discovered some information about your mother."

"I did. But if I may ask, why you are so interested in my mother, and what will be the consequences for me?"

The baron narrowed his eyes at her, but then his face broke into a smile. Finally, he shook his head and looked at Merek. "Have you ever seen a maiden with more fire and vinegar?"

"She is rather clever too," Merek said with what he hoped was a look of begrudging admiration.

The baron turned his attention back to Violet. "You do not have the luxury of making demands. But I shall not punish you for your boldness, as long as you tell me forthwith what you know." His voice and his demeanor changed as he spoke, becoming hard, cold, and unflinching again.

Violet's delicate throat bobbed ever so slightly as she swallowed. Then, a look of defiance flashing in her eyes, she said, "I know that my mother was an orphan who worked here at the castle and that she fled this place when she learned she was with child."

Merek focused on the baron's reaction even as the blood flowed through his limbs in heightened alert.

"And I discovered that my mother did have eyes the color of mine."

The baron's expression hardened. "And what was her name?"

"I don't know. I did not learn her name."

"But she was quite young?"

"Yes, I believe so."

"And her eyes were violet, like yours?"

"Yes."

The baron turned and ascended the dais at one end of the room, then sat down in his chair. "And who gave you all this information? I suppose they also told you who your father is."

"I was told that you are my father."

Merek felt heat rise to his forehead. This was worse than he'd imagined. And it remained to be seen if the baron would take this news well, treating the girl as his long-lost daughter, or if he would want her dead.

The baron's expression did not change, except perhaps to grow colder and darker. "Who told you this?" he demanded in a low voice.

"It was not my mother, the woman who was kind enough to take me in and raise me as her own, nor my father, who made sure I was clothed and fed and taught me how a man should treat his wife and children."

The woman had spirit, and Merek's admiration rose. But he also wondered if her boldness would force him to have to defend her sooner rather than later with his sword.

"What if I don't believe you? What if I send someone to fetch the woman you call Mother and throw her in the dungeon?"

"Why would you do that? My mother has done nothing wrong, and she cannot tell you anything because she doesn't know anything."

"I can do as I please and I don't need to explain to anyone. I am the Baron Dunham."

Violet remained silent, thankfully. How must she be feeling, knowing the baron was her father and the circumstances of her birth? The baron must have cruelly mistreated her poor mother for her to flee from him when she found she was with child.

"It matters not whether you choose to tell me who gave you this information. My men will be here any minute with your grandmother. Perhaps she will be more forthcoming."

Violet's expression fell at these words.

No doubt he was bringing her grandmother so he could threaten her safety in order to manipulate Violet, to force her to do what he wanted. But Merek would do whatever he had to do to protect her grandmother, just as he had pledged to protect Violet.

Violet felt the blood leave her face.

The man who had followed her to her grandmother's house. He must have reported back to the baron. *O God, please don't let him hurt Grandmother.*

"Your grandmother worked at the castle. She knew your mother, did she not?"

Violet did not answer.

"I suppose she told you I was a terrible person who sent your mother away when she was carrying my child. But I knew nothing of the child. She did not tell me. Did she give the child to the woman you call Grandmother before she died? Is that what happened?"

A sound came to them of footsteps approaching.

"Never mind. I shall ask her."

Violet's heart was in her throat. She had to try to force her breaths to slow down so she wouldn't faint as two guards entered the room with Grandmother walking between them.

The strong, unworried look on her grandmother's face reminded Violet to stand up straight and keep her head high. Grandmother's eyes fell on Violet, and she actually smiled and winked.

"Alina Markeley. Is that your name?"

Grandmother said in a strong voice, "It is."

"Do you know why you were brought here?"

"They told me you sent for me."

The baron frowned slightly on one side of his mouth. "You knew this woman's birth mother, did you not?"

"I did."

"And what was her name?"

Grandmother was standing only a few feet away, and she looked at Violet.

"It's all right," she said quietly. "I told him the truth, all of it."

Grandmother nodded and turned her gaze on the baron. "She was a precious, dear girl, and her name was Annora."

The knot in Violet's chest tightened. Annora. She finally knew her mother's name.

The baron was very still. His eyelids were so low on his eyes, she could not really tell whether his eyes were open or closed. Finally, he said, "Did you not know that I was looking for her? Why did you not send word to me that you had seen her, that you knew where she was? I could have taken care of her and made sure she had anything she needed. Her death is on your head."

The baron sat up and leaned forward, his hands gripping the arms of his thronelike chair.

Grandmother looked and sounded unperturbed. "I did not see her after she left the castle. When she came to me, she was already very sick and near death. She asked me to care for the child, who was five years old at the time, and I assured her the child would be well cared for by my daughter and her husband. She died the next day."

The baron glared at Grandmother for a few more moments, then sat back in his chair. He laced his fingers together in front of him, so still that Violet began to wonder if he had fallen asleep. The guards began to shift their feet.

The baron said, very quietly, "Throw them both in the dungeon."

The guards took hold of Grandmother's arms even as the guard on Violet's left took hold of hers.

"But put them in the same cell," he said. "See how forbearing and merciful I am?" An ironic smile pulled his lips back to show his crooked teeth.

A pain shot through Violet's chest. This man was her father. What a horrible thought. Nevertheless, she was thankful that she would not be separated from her grandmother. But oh, the guilt at being the cause of her grandmother's imprisonment in the baron's dungeon. The weight of it settled on her shoulders as she walked behind her grandmother.

I am holding you, your mother, and your grandmother in the palm of My hand.

Surely God had given her those words so that she would not despair now.

God, I trust You. Help me not to be afraid.

She watched her grandmother walk calmly in front of her. Her heart was in her throat, fearing the guards would push Grandmother or otherwise intimidate or harm her, but as they made the long walk, Violet realized her grandmother was actually chatting with the guards, asking them about themselves. Violet would not be surprised if she was even smiling placidly.

Violet reminded herself how she had defiantly told the baron the truth. He was undoubtedly unaccustomed to people being so bold. At least she could be proud of herself for not cowering before that tyrant.

ELEVEN

VIOLET'S GRANDMOTHER WOULD FORGIVE HER FOR LEADING the baron's guard to her house, and would probably even say there was nothing to forgive, but Violet wasn't sure how she would forgive herself.

But all of this was Baron Dunham's fault. How she hated him!

God, I know I must love my enemies and must forgive them. Please help me.

She suddenly realized Sir Merek was beside her. As they paused at the top of the steps that led down to the dungeon, he turned to the guard on Violet's other side and said, "I will take her the rest of the way."

The guard left her with Sir Merek, but in front of them were still the two guards who had accompanied her grandmother. They were a few steps down into the dark, dank dungeon when

Sir Merek turned to her and whispered, "Sir Willmer and I will get you out as soon as we can."

"But he will just send for us again," Violet whispered back.

"We have a plan. Trust me. It may take a few days, but—"

"You." One of the guards with her grandmother was calling up to them from several steps below them. "What are you— Oh, it's you, Sir Merek."

Sir Merek merely nodded to him.

Violet watched the guard below them, wondering if he had overheard the comment, but he didn't react. He kept going down, and she let Sir Merek take her arm and lead her the rest of the way down the narrow steps.

Thank You, God, for Sir Merek.

His presence beside her made her feel safe. Just knowing that he cared enough to try to help her gave her hope.

When they reached the bottom of the steps, they walked around a bend and saw the two guards motioning her grandmother into a stone cell with two benches. Violet followed her inside, still clutching her red cloak, which hid the cloth bag underneath it.

The guards closed the door, which looked like an iron gate, and one of them locked it.

Violet held on to her grandmother's arm. "Are you all right? They didn't hurt you, did they?"

"I am very well. And you?" Grandmother was smiling as if they were sitting in her kitchen, talking about how their day had been.

Violet nodded, then noticed Sir Merek was the only guard still standing at the cell door.

"I will come back later and make sure you are well," he said quietly. "And don't worry. Sir Willmer and I have a plan."

"Thank you," Grandmother said, her eyes twinkling.

Sir Merek nodded and moved away from the door, and Violet heard his footsteps on the stone stairs, then silence.

"My eyes don't see as well as they used to, but even I can see that Sir Merek is quite handsome," Grandmother said in a whisper.

"He is."

Grandmother's smile was even bigger now.

"I'm so sorry the baron put you in the dungeon because of me." Violet squeezed her grandmother's hands.

"It is not so bad, especially since we are together. I have never seen a dungeon before." She looked around at their cell. "We have two benches, so we don't have to sleep on the cold floor."

"How can you be so happy about being here?"

"Why, child, don't you know that God can give us blessings even through terrible things? Perhaps He wants you to be helped by this knight, Sir Merek, so that the two of you can fall in love."

"Ugh! Grandmother!" Violet said in a loud whisper. "So that is why you are so happy?"

"Sir Merek wants to help you and says he has a plan. Did you not hear him?"

"I heard him." She didn't want to assume that Sir Merek would save them, but in her heart she already trusted him. And she also feared that her grandmother's hopes about Sir Merek might become her own and she would be heartbroken when this was over.

Sir Merek was brave and noble, putting the safety and well-being of two lowly women above his own. And that was exactly what she and her grandmother were, two women who were neither wealthy nor highborn. Sir Merek, on the other hand, was from a wealthy noble family. He could expect to marry well. But if he were lowborn and poor, she was sure she would fall in love with him. He was good and kind and handsome. He was passionate about doing what was right, and he seemed to feel things very strongly. And yet, before she knew the sincerity of his intentions, he had borne her accusations and anger with great patience.

"Child." Grandmother looked her in the eye. "Don't let your mind be tormented with fear."

"How can I not? We are in a dungeon, and the worst man in the region is my father."

"He may be evil, but he is not more powerful than God. Just remember that." Grandmother gave her a perfunctory nod and sat down on a bench.

Violet remembered the words God had given her when she was praying, and her conscience smote her. Was she still afraid despite God's direct reassurance? Truly, her grandmother's faith was so much bigger than her own.

Forgive me, God.

Violet sat down beside her grandmother, unfolded her red cloak, and draped it over her grandmother's shoulders. "You are right. I need to choose to trust God instead of believing in my fears."

Grandmother patted Violet's hand. "It's all right, child. Old age has taught me that most everything works out in the end even better than I imagined, and when things don't work out, all I need to do is wait, because I just haven't given it enough time. God always has a plan."

Was Grandmother right? Mother's way of thinking was completely opposite. How were those two people mother and daughter?

Violet had heard her mother fretting so many times, wailing even, over the smallest fears of what might happen. Usually her fears never came true, and when Violet had pointed that out to her once, she gave her a sullen look, tossed her head, and said, "If I could stop worrying, I would. Now go milk the cow so I won't have to worry about that."

Violet felt sorry for her mother. Truly, it must be a hard life to fret as much as she did.

"How do you not worry, Grandmother?"

"I still worry a bit, but not as much as I used to. I suppose I've learned that being anxious does no good and only torments the worrier. Things may not work out the way I want them to, so I have to be humble and look to God and trust that His plan is better than mine."

Now that they were sitting here with nothing to occupy them, Violet's mind went to the uncomfortable feelings that had been building inside her about the huge secret her grandmother had kept from her.

There was an actual pain in her chest, knowing that Grandmother knew all this time that Violet was the daughter of the baron and his servant and didn't tell her. Violet had said she forgave her, and she did forgive her, but she was still struggling with the fact that her grandmother could have told her but didn't. She could have been spared the pain of finding out that all her imaginings of what a good man her birth father might have been were the furthest thing from the truth.

Her heart ached to think her grandmother had been less than honest with her, and it hurt to accuse her grandmother of anything, as she had always been Violet's ideal of a perfectly good, kind, and wise woman. But Violet couldn't shake the feeling that her grandmother had lied to her, even though she hadn't, not really. She had only omitted a lot of important information.

"My darling girl, you look so sad. Is it because I kept your father's identity a secret from you?"

"I was thinking about that, but I know you did it to keep me safe."

Grandmother's eyes were full of compassion. "Perhaps it was wrong of me."

Tears dripped from Violet's eyes. She shook her head. When she was able to talk, she said, "No. If my birth mother asked you not to tell me, and you were doing it to protect me, then it wasn't wrong. It is just such a shock, that is all." Violet let the tears come while her grandmother held her. She cried from disappointment and even shame at having such a father. She cried from sadness for what her poor mother had suffered. But somehow when the tears stopped, they seemed to have washed away the ache in her chest.

They huddled together, but even with Violet's red cloak, her grandmother was cold. So Violet stayed by her side with her arm around her to keep her warm with her body heat, and they talked of many things until they guessed it was probably close to nighttime. Just as they were considering how they would sleep, they heard footsteps, and presently Sir Merek was standing at their grated door with two wool blankets.

"I thought you might need these," he said, pushing them through the bars. "I shall return tomorrow or the next day to set you free, if all goes well."

Violet's heart squeezed at his kindness, at the look of sincerity and compassion on his face. The tears that had so recently vanished sprang up again, and she couldn't speak, even to thank him.

"Thank you," Grandmother said. "You are a noble knight. May God save and bless you for your kindness."

"Thank you, and you are welcome." He also handed them a cloth bag and then left without another word.

When they opened the bag, they found cold meat and cheese inside, along with bread and nuts and dried fruit.

Grandmother smiled. "Do you see how God is caring for us?"

Violet almost said, "And how Sir Merek is caring for us," but she stopped herself. This tender feeling toward the handsome young knight was too new, too fragile, to speak of aloud, even to her grandmother.

Merek and Sir Willmer stood at the edge of the forest behind the barracks and talked over their plan. They had discovered from a guard who had drunk too much wine that the secret record book they needed was indeed in a strongbox in the dungeon. They'd even managed to steal a key the guard had on him, which they hoped would open the cell door and the box.

"I still think you should let me get the record book by myself." Merek stared Sir Willmer in the eye. "Then if I get caught, you will still be able to set the women free."

Sir Willmer shook his head. "I say we do it together. I can keep watch for you at the top of the stairs."

Merek liked his chances better alone. He disliked the idea of depending on Sir Willmer, or anyone, for that matter. But it was probably wise to have a lookout. "Very well."

Sir Willmer said, "First let's make sure there are no guards in the dungeon."

Merek nodded.

They went to the top of the dungeon stairs and listened. Not hearing any sound except the occasional coughing of a prisoner and the slow dripping of water, they started down the steps. If there was a guard in the dungeon, they would say the baron had sent them to check on Violet and her grandmother.

At the fork in the dungeon, Sir Willmer went right and Merek went left so that he could check on the two women.

When he arrived at their cell, they both appeared to be asleep. The grandmother was snoring softly, covered with both of the woolen blankets he had brought them, while Violet was covered by her red cloak. Neither of them moved as he approached.

How wrong it was that these two women should be locked in

this damp, stinking dungeon when they had done nothing bad. *God, help me set them free once and for all.*

Merek went all the way to the very back of the dungeon, which was dug into the rock of a natural cave, and saw a shorter cell, roughly half the height of the other cells. Sir Willmer appeared behind him.

"No guards," Sir Willmer said. "Let's get the book and go." He went toward the cell door with the key.

"Only one of us needs to get it. Let me have the key and you be the lookout, as we planned."

Sir Willmer gave him a suspicious look. "If you decide to take some of the money, we will give it back to the people. Agreed?"

"I'm not taking any of the money." Merek glared at him. "I just don't want us both getting caught down here, and I don't know how long it will take to find the book."

"Very well." He handed Merek the key and disappeared around the bend in the dungeon corridor.

Merek pushed the key into the lock on the iron door. It turned with a squeak and a rattle, then the door opened.

It was too dark to see, so Merek took the nearest torch from its iron sconce off the wall, then bending down, he half squatted, half crawled into the dark cavern.

Inside there were strange circular pools of water about the size of his outstretched hand on either side of a path that led deeper into the darkness. He moved carefully and came to a portion of the cavern where he could stand upright. There he found rows and rows of metal strongboxes stacked on top of each other against the wet rock wall, all of them covered in various amounts of rust.

He looked around. They would have to keep the book in a metal box, because rats would eat the parchment pages, or else it would mold in this damp place.

All the strongboxes looked the same. The record book was supposed to be in one of those boxes, but which one?

He followed the line of strongboxes around the wall, walking deeper into the cave. He found a dead bat on the rock floor and stepped over it. Finally, he came to a strongbox that was lying open. The torchlight showed it was empty. It was the only thing he found that looked out of place.

He heard footsteps right before a loud whisper. "Merek! Get out! Someone's coming!"

Merek ran back toward the entrance.

Twelve

Merek closed the door and locked it, placed the torch back into its sconce, and he and Sir Willmer ducked into an empty cell, flattening themselves against the wall.

They both stood motionless, hardly breathing, as two men walked past. One was carrying what looked like a recordkeeping ledger.

He held his breath, trying to hear if the guards were speaking. Had he left anything behind that would indicate that someone had been there?

Their voices were too low for him to make out any words, especially after they unlocked the door, which must have had more than one key, and went inside the grotto. When they came out, they locked the door and left.

When Merek was sure they had gone, he held up the key he'd used to unlock the stronghold door and whispered, "You might as well come with me. I don't think they'll be back in the next few minutes."

"That's what I was thinking."

"Let's go get that book."

Merek and Sir Willmer again opened the little door to the stronghold. Merek was more careful this time not to make noise, but as he opened it, the door squeaked extra loudly. He cringed.

Sir Willmer whispered, "They're long gone by now."

"Hopefully."

Merek went inside, wishing he'd told Sir Willmer to go back up the stairs to make sure the guards were gone and to keep watch.

Suddenly Merek had a thought. "Are you sure they didn't see you come down here?"

"No, no, I don't think so."

He didn't think so. Merek's stomach sank. At least he had his sword strapped to his back in case he needed it.

Merek moved quicker this time, avoiding the pools of water and stepping over the dead bat. His hunch that the open box was where they kept the record book seemed to be correct, as the box was now closed and locked.

"How do we get into it?" Sir Willmer asked.

"Not sure." Merek suspected the key that had worked on the cell door probably wouldn't open the strongbox, but he tried it anyway. Unfortunately, it was much too big. Merek took out his knife and used the tip. He worked at it for a minute, then asked, "Do you have a knife with a narrower blade?"

"We could just pick up one of these other boxes and beat it."

"I don't think that will work, and it would make a lot of noise."

"You're right." He pulled out a knife from his belt and handed it to Merek.

Merek tried it. It wasn't any narrower than the blade of Merek's knife. "This isn't working. We may have to take the box."

"They will surely see us carrying around a big metal strongbox."

The box was about a foot wide, a foot and a half long, and half a foot deep. It was not too heavy for one man to carry, but it was bulky.

"Is there a blanket in here? We could cover it and walk out with it."

Sir Willmer seemed to consider this, finally saying, "All right. It seems like the only way, unless we want to wait and find a key that opens it."

"I don't want to wait." They needed to get this book and Violet and her grandmother out as quickly as possible and get them all to London and to the king. The women wouldn't be safe otherwise.

Sir Willmer nodded. "Let us do it, then."

Merek picked up the box. When they were both out of the stronghold, Sir Willmer said, "I saw a blanket in one of these cells." He ducked into an empty cell and came out with one of the nondescript gray woolen blankets they sometimes gave to the prisoners. He thrust it at Merek. It smelled of urine and underarm odor.

"That's disgusting." Merek recoiled from it.

"You got a better idea?"

He didn't, so he took the blanket, wrapped it around the box, and tucked it under his own arm.

When they reached the top of the stairs, Sir Willmer went first, to make sure no one was around. Then he came back, sticking his head through the door and motioning with his hand.

Merek climbed the rest of the steps and went through the door, the cumbersome box under his arm.

"Don't follow me," Merek whispered, in keeping with their plan, which was to stay separate so that the two of them would not be captured together.

Merek walked toward the door to the outside that was closest to the stables, while Sir Willmer went the opposite direction.

As soon as Merek exited the castle and started toward the woods behind the stable, he heard men behind him.

They tackled him before he could turn around. He fell on the box, which struck him in the ribs, knocking the breath from him. They slammed the back of his head with something hard and his vision went black.

Merek awoke with a headache. As soon as he drew in a breath, he felt a sharp pain in his side.

He opened his eyes. He was on the floor of a small room with a guard standing over him, sword drawn.

"The only way you were able to strike me down was because

you attacked me from behind. Hitting a man in the back—how cowardly." Merek's voice was strained, but he refused to allow himself to groan, though the pain took his breath away when he moved. They must have kicked him in the ribs after he lost consciousness.

The guard did not answer him but knocked on the door behind him, a signal to someone on the other side.

Merek reached up and touched his head. His hair was matted with sticky blood. While still lying on the floor, he tried to assess the rest of his body for injuries. His arms and legs seemed to be unhurt, thankfully. If his injuries were just broken ribs and the pain in his head, then he was confident he could escape.

His sword was nowhere to be seen, but he could get another one.

He calculated how long it would take him to get to either his brother Edwin's house or his sister Delia's. Either one of them could supply him with a fresh horse and a sword.

Violet. The poor girl and her grandmother were probably waiting for him to fulfill his promise to rescue them. He prayed, *God, I must help them. I cannot leave them in the dungeon.*

But first he had to rescue himself.

He let out a frustrated breath. Why had he been caught? He was doing a good deed, trying to expose an evil man and save two innocent women from his clutches. And now he'd been beaten and captured. Had Sir Willmer escaped?

The guards must have been waiting for him. They must have suspected he was stealing something from the strongbox hold. But how?

Sir Willmer had seemed so honest, so eager to help him. Had he only been pretending so he could betray him to the baron?

He didn't want to believe anything evil about Sir Willmer. But if he discovered Sir Willmer had betrayed him . . . Heat built up in his already-aching head as a wave of rage swept over him.

He tried to take a deep breath, as his priest had taught him, but it hurt too much and turned into a gasp. Instead, he reminded himself how Sir Willmer had never done or said anything to make him question his integrity. No, unless Sir Willmer had been caught, too, he would be trying to figure out a way to rescue them all. His idea to separate had worked—hopefully.

He heard footsteps approaching and pushed himself to a sitting position, then rose to his feet just as the door swung open. He gritted his teeth against the pain as two guards came inside the tiny room, followed by Baron Dunham.

"Sir Merek." The baron expelled a breath. "What were you thinking, stealing from me? I thought better of you."

Merek said, "And I thought better of you. You said you cared about the people of this region, that you felt responsible for their welfare. Why did you say that when you were stealing from them, the poorest of the poor, the widow and the orphan?" Merek spoke slowly and in a low voice, trying not to show how painful it was to talk.

"My men saw you coming out of the dungeon after a guard reported that his stronghold key was missing. They saw you had stolen something, thinking it was money, but instead they found you had taken something else. But you didn't know what was in the box, did you? You thought you were stealing money, did you not?"

What did the baron expect him to say? Merek just glared back at him.

"You have taken a liking to my daughter, I think. Is that why you were seen talking to her? I sent you to fetch her because I trusted you. You seemed to have such high morals. But now I don't know what to think." He crossed his arms, then uncrossed them, rubbing his beard. "You want me to think you care about the widow and orphan, but I rather think it is my daughter who interests you. Or is it my money?"

"Your daughter is in the dungeon." Merek made sure to infuse his voice with irony. "And I am a knight. I uphold the king's purposes, the goals and morality of the Church, and the king's laws. I do not help rich men get richer by taking money unlawfully from the people of their region."

"I always knew you fancied yourself righteous and noble, but I never thought you were daft. Who is to say that I take money unlawfully? Will the king believe you over me? I suppose that is why you were trying to take the record book. I cannot allow you to do that, can I?" The baron grinned. "But we can still be friends. If you will not report me to the king, then I will not report you. If you will not tell the king that you think I am taking taxes unlawfully, then I will not tell the king that you were a troublemaker here, picking fights with the other knights and trying to seduce my daughter for your own gain."

Merek glared back at the man. The urge to defy him and fight with every ounce of his strength was almost overwhelming.

But he could control himself, for Violet's sake. He couldn't protect her or help her if he was locked in the dungeon or dead. The best way to help her seemed to be to play along with the baron. He could pretend to agree. But he could not break his promise to help Violet and her grandmother and set them free.

"You are right. I cannot defeat you. Therefore, I will not tell the king any of this." He had to clench his jaw to get the words out of his mouth. The very thought of giving anyone, especially the baron, power over him made his blood boil and his hand itch to hold a sword.

The baron rubbed his cheek. "I need to consider this. After all, the king is not likely to believe you anyway since you don't have any proof. Guards," he said, turning his attention to the three guards crowding the room, "lock him in the dungeon."

The guards took hold of his arms and pulled him from the room.

Merek did not resist. With every breath he was stabbed with pain in his sides. His head did not hurt as much, but he was still a bit dizzy as he tried to walk but ended up being dragged down the corridor.

They forced him to go first down the dungeon steps, probably afraid he would fall and drag them down with him.

Merek took each step slowly, his mind churning with ideas of how to escape, keeping his eyes wide open to any opportunity.

When he was still a few steps from the bottom of the stairs, Merek pretended to get dizzy, putting a hand to his head and falling backward. He fell into the guard and grabbed the man's sword.

The other guards took hold of his arms before he could swing it. They slammed the hilt against his head, then dragged him past the cell containing Violet and her grandmother.

The two women roused from their slumber as he went by. Had they seen and recognized him? He wasn't sure.

His stomach churned. He had failed them.

They came to an empty cell near the women's and shoved him inside, so hard he fell to his knees. Before he could get up, they slammed the cell door and locked it.

Merek raised himself into a sitting position against the wall. Somehow he had to escape.

Violet awoke to see some guards dragging a man past the bars of her cell door. Was that Sir Merek? Her stomach sank. Had the baron discovered he was not loyal to him?

"Are you well?" Grandmother said from the bench two feet from her own.

"Yes. Just some guards with another prisoner. Go back to sleep," Violet whispered back.

There was a loud *slam* and then the guards walked past her cell again without the man.

"Poor soul. God, help him," Grandmother said softly, and soon she was snoring again.

Violet was silently praying for Sir Merek, or whoever the man was whom the guards had just brought in, when she heard a man's voice say gruffly, "Violet?"

"Sir Merek?"

"I still have the key to the stronghold door, so I—"

"Stronghold door? What is that?"

"It's a place where . . . Never mind. I am going to try the key in my cell door and hopefully set us both free."

His voice sounded labored and strained, and his speech was halting, as if he was having to pause every couple of words to catch his breath.

"Are you injured?" Her heart squeezed painfully inside her chest. "Were you captured trying to set us free?"

Grandmother was starting to awaken. She opened her eyes and sat up.

"No. I was stealing the record book that would prove that the baron was taking money unlawfully from the people."

"The record book? You found it? Where is it now?"

"The guards attacked me from behind and took it. I don't know where it is."

"Are you hurt?"

"I am well enough. Just a broken rib or two."

An imaginary knife stabbed her chest at the thought of his pain.

"Please, don't put yourself in harm's way for us. I think the baron only wishes to frighten me into submission. Besides, even if you help us escape, where can we go that the baron will not find us? You should escape without us as soon as you have the chance."

"First of all, you are making a lot of assumptions. You don't know that the baron intends to let you go. You should trust me. I'll take you with me, either to London to the king or to my sister's house if necessary, and then Sir Willmer and I will find proof to show the king of the baron's misdeeds."

"I am very sorry you were injured by the baron's men, but I—"

"I am not seriously injured, and I will find a way out. When I do, I will protect you."

"I don't want you to be more seriously injured, or even killed, trying to rescue me when there is no need."

"No need?"

He sounded exasperated. Indeed, it was difficult having this conversation while not being able to either see his face or show her concern. Did he not understand she was worried about him? Just thinking of his injuries made her breath catch, and yet he was still thinking of her, wanting to save her and her grandmother. She longed to be able to see him.

He huffed out a breath. "This key doesn't fit the cell door. It's useless."

Far off, at the top of the stairs, Violet heard what sounded like someone opening the dungeon door again, then soft footsteps on the stairs. Soon Sir Willmer appeared at her cell door. Violet nearly cheered aloud.

"Let's get you out of here," Sir Willmer said. "Do you know where they put Sir Merek?"

"Yes! He's there." Violet pointed.

"Sir Willmer," Sir Merek said. "Thank God you're here."

He moved away in the direction of Sir Merek's voice.

"How did you escape the baron's men?"

"When I heard them chase after you, I stayed hidden until I could get into the dungeon without being seen."

"I wondered if you had betrayed me."

"I didn't betray you, you doubter. Why would you think that?"

Violet couldn't hear Sir Merek's answer. They were keeping their voices low, no doubt so the other prisoners couldn't hear what they were saying. Her heart was beating fast, but Grandmother had a gentle smile on her lips as she took Violet's hand in hers.

God, please help me make wise decisions in the next few minutes. Wise and brave.

THIRTEEN

MEREK STUDIED WILLMER'S FACE. HE LOOKED SINCERE. Besides, what motive could he have for coming down to the dungeon and freeing him and Violet and her grandmother if he wanted to betray him? He couldn't think of one.

"They beat you up pretty badly, I see."

"I am well," Merek growled back. "Just a broken rib or two. I can still wield a sword better than any of the baron's half-trained guards."

"Forgive me for not being able to save you from the guards," Sir Willmer said.

His words sent heat into Merek's face. Did he think Merek needed saving? That he was weak? And he said these things in the hearing of Violet and her grandmother. Was he trying to embarrass him?

Merek did his best to slow his breathing. *You need to check your temper and your pride.* That was what his priest told him every week when he confessed his sins.

"Just get us out of here and I'll forgive you." Merek sounded angry, but he didn't care.

Sir Willmer took out a key and opened Merek's door.

"Where did you get that key?" That was suspicious, wasn't it?

"I've always had a key to the dungeon cells. I told you that, remember?"

Merek moaned as he emerged from his cell while Sir Willmer went back to the women's cell door. When he inserted the key in their lock, the door didn't immediately open. He jiggled the key around for a minute until it clicked.

"Come," Sir Willmer said. "We need to hurry, before the next set of guards start their watch."

"I am not sure that is the right thing to do." Violet and her grandmother stayed in their cell, not coming out even when the door swung wide open.

"What? Why?" Sir Willmer asked.

"Go on and escape without us," Violet said.

Merek groaned.

"We will only slow you down and will keep you from getting away," the grandmother said.

"We want you to come with us so we can protect you. Come." Sir Willmer motioned for them to come out.

"I don't think the baron means to harm me or my grand-mother, and I believe he will let me out of the dungeon soon."

"And what if he doesn't?" Merek asked. It hurt to talk, but he was too exasperated to stop. "He is not a good man. You should come with us. We will hide you someplace."

"I need to stay here," Violet argued, "to find the record book that you tried to steal. We need it to prove to the king— Oh my!" She leaned closer to Merek. "You are hurt! So much blood."

He touched his lip and realized it was oozing. She probably also saw the blood in his hair and running down his temple.

The look of horror and concern in her eyes made him feel vulnerable, and he did not like that feeling.

"I am well enough. I've had worse injuries." *Though not at one time.* "We don't want to leave here without you."

"Let me look at your head at least and see if the cut needs to be sewn closed."

"There's no time." Why was she so exasperating? "I could defeat three men by myself if I had a sword. Now come."

"Just go and save yourselves." Violet looked him in the eye. "Please. I couldn't bear it if I caused you further harm."

His heart did a strange flip inside his chest. He couldn't decide whether he felt insulted at her lack of faith in his abilities, but the way she was looking at him, with tenderness and concern and great intensity, scattered his thoughts so much that he could only stare back at her.

"We should go." Sir Willmer had turned to Merek and was whispering with his head turned away from the women. "They would slow us down, and I think the girl is right, that the baron will not harm her."

"Yes, do please go without us," Violet insisted. "When the baron releases me, I will find a way to search for the record book in secret. Then I can take it to the king."

Why wouldn't she let him help her? She was both stubborn and . . . admirable and lovely and mesmerizing.

Merek didn't want to take them against their will—although he considered it. But in his injured state, he wasn't sure he could accomplish it, though he didn't like to admit that, even to himself. He also didn't want his pride to be the cause of getting the women injured or killed.

"Very well," Merek said, looking into Violet's eyes. "But I will not leave you entirely alone. I shall return to watch over you the best I can. I will disguise myself to get back into the castle, whatever I have to do."

"And I shall do my best to find that record book." Her expression was so stoic, so determined, he suddenly longed to kiss her.

Strange thought.

Sir Willmer said, "We will come back for you."

Violet looked back at Merek, grimacing sympathetically. "Take care of your wounds."

He did his best to stand upright and tall before walking away with Sir Willmer.

God, I feel like a terrible knight. He was leaving the young woman and her elderly grandmother in the dungeon. But he and Willmer had both told her they would come back. It was the best he could do at the moment.

"Look sharp," Sir Willmer said as they ascended the stairs and drew near to the door leading out of the dungeon. "We still have to escape ourselves without being seen."

They stood there and made a quick plan. Merek had to stay alive and free of Baron Dunham's noose to have any hope of coming back to watch over the brave young maiden with the violet eyes.

Violet watched the two knights leave, then turned to her grand-mother. "Did I do the right thing?"

"Yes, child. I, too, felt as though it was the right thing to stay here and let them escape. I am very proud of you."

Violet thought about the blood on the handsome knight's face and in his hair, and her breath caught in her throat. Would he be all right? She'd known of a man once who fell and hit his head and appeared to be well, only to die a few days later. "God, please keep Sir Merek and Sir Willmer safe."

"Yes and amen," Grandmother said.

She trusted Sir Merek. He'd obviously put himself in harm's way to try to save her and to get the evidence needed to convince the king of the baron's wrongdoing.

Besides how kind he seemed, and despite the blood on his face, he was so handsome. She could now admit that he was quite possibly the handsomest man she had ever seen.

"He will be back," Grandmother said, squeezing her hand. "Sooner or later. But now you should go to sleep."

Violet nodded and they both lay back down on their benches. But after Grandmother's breathing told her she was asleep, Violet lay awake, praying for the young knight who had promised to come back to the castle and watch over her. Something about that promise touched her heart and made tears dribble from the corner of her eye.

Her mind flashed to her birth mother, and she realized she felt responsible for her mother's death. After all, she'd starved herself to feed Violet. It felt as if an old wound had been reopened. How could she bear it if she caused harm to come to the other people she loved? To her mother, her grandmother, or this brave knight.

"God, protect him," she whispered.

Violet awoke to her stomach growling. She gazed over at her grandmother, who was lying with her eyes closed, still looking as peaceful as ever.

"Are you awake?" Violet said softly.

Grandmother's eyes popped open. "Yes, child. What is it?"

"I was only wondering if you were hungry. We could share some of the bread and cheese Sir Merek brought us."

She opened the bag.

"I don't need very much food," Grandmother said, only allowing Violet to give her a tiny portion. "I'm old and I don't get very hungry. You eat it."

Violet insisted her grandmother have some of the food, and they both ate minimally so that she could make the food last as long as possible, not knowing how long they would be in the dungeon. After all her assurances to the knights that she didn't believe the baron would leave her there, she realized she wasn't as sure as she let on.

After their small repast, they talked about various favorite memories and listened to the chatter of the few prisoners in the dungeon, who talked among themselves, sometimes quite loudly, their voices echoing off the stone walls.

Eventually the prisoners began to converse with her, and she learned that one of them, Roger, had been there at least three years. Another named Simon had been there six months, and a third man, Martin, had been there for two months. There were no other female prisoners.

"What did you do?" Roger asked. "Why'd the baron put you in here?"

"I wrote a letter to the king to tell him about the baron taking money from the people." It was true, but she didn't want to tell them that he'd also put her in the dungeon because she was his daughter.

"I'm surprised he didn't kill you," said Martin.

"I'm surprised he didn't torture you first, as he did to me," said Simon. "You must be young and pretty."

"I saw her when she was brought in," said Roger. "She is very pretty." He said it sadly and with quite a bit of feeling, punctuated by a sigh.

Then they all told why they were there. Roger said, "I was thrown in here for shaking my fist at the baron when he rode through my village. It was foolish. My wife told me not to do it, but I did it anyway."

Martin said, "The baron put me in here for taking my money back. I offered the guards a meal, and while they were eating, I took my coins out of their bag. They caught me and accused me of stealing. The baron sentenced me to the dungeon until I confessed, but there's never been an opportunity to confess anything."

Simon said, "I was put in here for stealing a horse from the baron's stable."

"Tell her why you did it," Martin said.

"I wanted to ride to London and tell the king what the baron was doing. But I got caught. And the baron tortured me until I confessed. He said he would choke my parents with his bare hands until they were dead if I didn't tell him why I stole the horse."

"How old are you?" Violet asked.

"Seventeen." Simon sniffed. "I'm so afraid my parents will come here asking for me. I can only hope they think I'm dead." His voice cracked on the last two words.

Violet let out a deep sigh. So much pain caused by one greedy man. And he was her father.

She felt sick. Her actual father was the man who had accepted her as his own child, who had provided for her and made her feel loved. He wasn't a perfect man, but he was a good man, and he was a good neighbor to those around him. He was never cruel to other men, never took more than his share. He believed that men should work for themselves and their families, to provide whatever was needed, and he believed in sharing with the poor.

"I am so sorry the baron has been so cruel to you all," Violet said. "You did not deserve to be so treated."

God, when I get out of here, let me be able to free all these men from this terrible, sunless place.

A few minutes later, after the conversation had died down and Grandmother had fallen asleep again, she heard the now-familiar sound of the dungeon door opening and several sets of footsteps coming down the stairs, drawing closer.

A group of guards came to a halt in front of her cell door, waking her grandmother.

"Violet Lambton?" the lead soldier asked.

"Yes?"

"Baron Dunham has summoned you," he said, unlocking the door and swinging it open.

"What about my grandmother?"

"Your grandmother is to be taken to her home."

Violet exchanged a look with her grandmother and squeezed her hand. At least she would be safe. If he was telling the truth.

"I would like to stay with my granddaughter, if you please," Grandmother said, lifting her chin and staring up at the guard.

"That is not for me to decide," he told her.

"Then go and ask the baron," she ordered.

The guard cleared his throat and seemed at a loss for words. Finally, he turned to a soldier behind him and pulled him a few feet away, and they seemed to discuss it for a minute. Then he came back and said, "We must obey the baron. You will be taken to your home."

Grandmother shrugged and gazed up at Violet. "It was worth a try."

"Don't worry about me," Violet told her grandmother. "I will feel better knowing you are safe at home."

"And you have been promised help, should you need it. Don't forget that." Grandmother winked.

Grandmother was always the romantic. She had more faith than anyone Violet knew.

Violet expected the guards to take her by her arms and pull

her out of her cell and up the steps. But they only stepped back from the door, letting her and her grandmother proceed ahead of them.

Violet held on to her grandmother's arm as they went slowly up the steps. She was careful not to rush her grandmother or let her stumble and fall.

When they reached the top, one guard came up beside them and unlocked the door, again stepping back and waiting for them to go first.

Once outside the dungeon, two guards escorted Grandmother away.

The remaining guards walked with Violet up some stairs and into the baron's solar, a round tower room with several windows that let in more light than Violet would have expected in a castle. She was also surprised to see that the sun was already high in the sky.

Inside, Baron Dunham appeared to be waiting for her.

"Come in," he said. He nodded to the guards behind her. "You may go."

Fourteen

Violet was alone with the baron, and she felt a bit sick at the sight of his face. She was still holding on to the bundle she had taken from home, plus the bag of food Sir Merek had given them. Her red cloak was wrapped around it.

"You are my daughter, and as such, you will be expected to do as I say. Do you understand?"

His face was cold and unexpressive.

Violet stared at him, her breath becoming shallow. "What do you intend? That is, what do you wish me to do?"

"I only want good things for you." He smiled, but it was a brittle smile, intended to deceive, no doubt.

"What kinds of good things?"

"You are very inquisitive." He frowned now, narrowing his eyes. "I wish you to live here in the castle as my daughter, to learn your place, to allow me to guide you. A good daughter obeys her father, does she not?"

She wanted to retort that he was not a good father and that

she did not intend to obey him as a daughter would. But he'd already thrown her in the dungeon once, no doubt to instill fear in her that he might do it again. And it had worked.

She hated the fear that crept into her mind. But fear of the dungeon was not the only reason to at least pretend to do as he wished. She needed to be able to roam about the castle in order to look for the record book. And she had the added incentive of wanting to set the people in the dungeon free. In this situation it seemed best to pretend compliance.

"Very well." It was all she could manage to say as her thoughts swirled and she inwardly recoiled from this man who was asking her to relinquish control over her life to him.

He pulled a velvet rope and Violet heard a bell ringing somewhere nearby. The door opened and a middle-aged woman with gray hair came into the room.

"Hagitha will show you to your new lodgings. You will have the run of that floor of the tower. No one is allowed to disturb you in your room except for Hagitha and one other female servant of her choosing. See how generous I can be when you comply with my wishes?"

Violet gave him a tight smile and a slight nod. It was all her sensibilities would allow. She might even have enough freedom to be able to look for the record book, if she wasn't too closely watched.

"You may go," the baron was saying.

"May I ask . . . Will you allow me to write a short missive to my mother and have someone take it to her, just to let her know I am well?"

The baron did not respond for so long that Violet began to wonder if she'd done something terribly wrong in asking. But then he said, "Yes. You may."

"Thank you." Violet turned to see the servant waiting for her.

"Come with me, miss," Hagitha said, nodding deferentially.

As she followed Hagitha, she wondered if Sir Merek and Sir Willmer had been able to escape. The baron apparently did not know anything about that yet, or he wasn't saying if he did.

How despicable the baron was for having his guards beat Sir Merek, bloodying his face and whatever else they had done to him.

Her heart still squeezed every time she remembered how he had looked and sounded, yet his pride would not let him admit he was badly hurt.

They went up one set of steps in the round tower and stopped at a door that Hagitha promptly opened.

Violet went inside to find a bedroom with fine tapestries on the walls and a large canopy bed in the center, its head against the wall between two windows.

"This floor of the tower will be yours," Hagitha said. "There is this room, a solar, and a dressing room there." She pointed to the door at one end of the room. "There is a bell pull by your bed and in the solar. You may ring for me any time of day. I am assigning another serving maid to you to build your fires, bring your meals, and see to anything else you have need of."

"Am I confined to this tower, to my rooms? Am I allowed to leave?"

"I was not told you were confined here." She pressed her

hands together and stared back at Violet, as if waiting for instruction. She didn't smile, but Violet saw what she hoped was compassion in her eyes. Hagitha added, "I will bring you some food, and the master has ordered that some new clothes be made for you. I will accompany the seamstress here later today."

"Thank you."

Hagitha dipped her head in a quick bow and left the room.

Violet put her things down and walked around the rooms, looking into a trunk and finding various woolen blankets and quilts and a pillow. Before she could inspect anything else, a servant arrived with a tray of food.

The young woman set the tray down, then said, "Hagitha wanted me to tell you that she is preparing a bath for you downstairs and will send for you soon."

"I thank you." The girl was already hurrying away, so Violet said quickly, "And what is your name?"

"Lora."

"Thank you, Lora."

She nodded and sank into a quick bow before shutting the door behind her.

Violet sat beside the tray of food, suddenly realizing she was quite hungry. It was amazing how learning you were not about to be killed increased your appetite.

But as soon as she started eating the cured ham, egg custard pie, bread and butter, and fruit pasties, she began to think about the prisoners in the dungeon. They were being fed only once a day, and then they only received frumenty, with no meat, and a hunk of stale bread, no butter.

Tears leaked from her eyes. "God, show me how to help them. And please keep Grandmother safe and well."

Had the men taken Grandmother home as they said they would? She couldn't think what motive the baron could have for not allowing her elderly grandmother to go home, especially if he wished to have Violet's cooperation. She was under no delusion that the baron wanted her love as a daughter for her father, but a man like him? He certainly was scheming something, wanting something from her.

But what?

Wiping the tears away, she told herself it would do no good to cry. She may as well eat the food. She'd have to figure out a way to help the prisoners later. First, she needed to find out just how much freedom she had. Were there guards watching outside her door? Or could she go wherever she liked without being questioned?

So she ate and then quickly wrote a short note with some paper, ink, and a pen she found in her room, explaining to her mother that she was well and living in the castle. She asked her mother to go to Grandmother and let her tell her more about who Violet's birth mother was and why the baron had summoned her, since it seemed too shocking to reveal it in a letter. She did her best to reassure her mother and asked her not to worry, but truthfully, she knew she still would. Since she expected the baron to read the letter, she did not bother to seal it and rang for the servant, who came promptly to take it.

When the servant was gone, she looked for clues to who might have lived in the rooms before her. Could these have been her mother's rooms? Probably not, since she was a servant. But she found no personal items, neither clothing nor a Psalter.

When she was still exploring all the nooks and corners, the servant girl, Lora, came to fetch her for her bath.

The bath made her feel as guilty as the sumptuous breakfast had, but she couldn't deny how good the warm water felt, along with the flowery-smelling soap. When she was done and back in her room, drying her waist-length hair in front of the open window, the seamstress came in to measure her for new clothing.

"I have clothes," Violet told Hagitha, who accompanied the seamstress. "You need only send to my home to fetch my things."

Hagitha did not visibly react to her words. She simply said in a calm voice, "The master wishes you to have all new things. New clothing has been ordered."

"I shall be able to finish one complete outfit by tomorrow morning," the seamstress said. She went about sizing up Violet, moving quickly and giving sharp orders. "Stand here." Then, "Raise your arms." Later, "Turn this way. No, the other way."

She used a string to measure Violet and jotted down her measurements on a piece of slate using a bit of chalk rock.

When she was done, she briefly rubbed her knees as she had been kneeling to get the measurement from Violet's waist to her feet. "I shall return when I have something ready for you to try on, probably tomorrow at first light."

"There is no need to work all night," Violet said.

"Your first dress must be finished quickly. Master's orders."

Violet bit her lip, wanting to protest but knowing that none of them could argue with the "master."

Violet waited a few moments after the seamstress and the servant were gone and then opened the door.

The corridor was empty. She could see both the stairs leading down and the ones continuing up.

She had to find the record book. Their plan to stop the baron depended on it. It was the whole reason Violet was here, the reason she was pretending to be compliant. And the sooner she could find that record book, the sooner she could save everyone from the baron's greed and cruelty.

Sir Merek and Sir Willmer had taken the record book from the dungeon, but had it been returned there? Probably not.

She walked across the corridor and stood looking at the stairs. Would she be more likely to find the record book on a higher floor of this tower or a lower one? She decided to go down the winding stairs.

A small window let in just enough light so that she could see the steps in front of her. She came upon another floor of rooms when she reached the next level, the baron's personal rooms, where she had spoken to him in his solar. But since she heard someone talking, she decided to go back up and see what was beyond her own rooms.

She continued past her floor and up another flight of steps. When she got to the top, she saw a short door. She bent and pushed it open, stooping to fit through.

She climbed a few more steps and found herself on the roof of the tower. The crenellations were at the perfect height for her to look over the edge at the ground below—far, far below. It made her dizzy, so she gazed instead at the treetops that stretched away in the distance.

She looked in the direction of her grandmother's cottage. Was she home safe? Where were Sir Merek and Sir Willmer? Had they been caught, or were they hiding out somewhere?

She went back down a few flights of stairs to the baron's rooms. She stood and listened in the hallway, but this time heard only silence. Violet went through the corridor and tried the first door, but it was locked. She tried the next one, which was also locked. When she tried the third door, to the baron's solar, it opened.

She went inside and searched under the benches and chairs and in the one trunk in the room. It contained a warm bear fur and a wool blanket but nothing else. Since there was nowhere else in the room to hide a book, she tried the door that connected it to the room beside it, but it was locked. So she went out the way she had come and back to the stairs.

At the next level down, she heard voices. She followed them to an open door. Inside were several women, and one was the seamstress who had measured her for her new clothes. All of them were either engaged in sewing or working in pairs folding linens and sheets and putting them away on wooden shelves and in trunks.

"It's Violet," the seamstress said in a hushed voice.

The other women stopped talking and turned to stare at her.

"May we help you with anything?" one of the servants asked with wide eyes and a fake smile.

"No, thank you." Violet turned and left, feeling like an outsider.

What did the servants think of her? She was the daughter of the master, but she did not know her place in the household. Would the servants respect and obey her? Or was she only a prisoner in her room, at the mercy of the baron, just as they all were?

Well, if she was a prisoner, she still hadn't encountered her guard, so she kept going, down to the ground floor of the tower, which led her into another part of the castle. She wandered around, occasionally hearing voices or footsteps and going in the opposite direction to avoid meeting anyone, until she came to the back side of the castle.

In front of her was a door. She opened it and saw the outside world, a sunny day. She could walk through and escape. But escape to where, to what? If she went home or to her grandmother's cottage, the baron would find her. And he might be so angry that he would harm her or her family.

Besides, she wasn't interested in escaping; she needed that record book.

Where might she look next?

A clerk or steward would need to write in it from time to time. There must be a specific room in the castle where they worked.

Violet continued to wander around the castle, not caring very much that she was becoming lost. She found another tower similar to hers and climbed up the stairs.

She went into a room on the second level that was filled with books. Could this be where the steward and clerk worked on the records? Honestly, she wasn't sure what a record book looked like. Was it big? Was it small? Was it bound in leather, was it rolled up like a letter, or were the pages simply folded and tied in the middle with string?

She entered the room cautiously, gazing into the corners to make sure no one was lurking in the shadows. There was indeed a large writing table near the window. On the table was an inkwell and quills, a stack of paper, and two stools drawn up to adjacent sides.

Violet approached the table. A book lay open. Could this be the record book she was looking for?

She leaned over it, seeing rows of numbers and columns with labels. Then she remembered Sir Merek saying that there were two books—the official one that recorded the lawful taxes taken from the people and the true one that showed all of the monies taken, including unlawful taxes.

She heard footsteps. Someone was coming.

Violet scuttled toward a trunk against the opposite wall near the doorway. Raising the lid, she saw it was mostly empty. She stepped into it, lay down, and carefully lowered the lid, leaving only a crack to peek out of.

A man, short and small and definitely not a guard, came into the room. He went straight to the writing table and sat on one of the tall stools. He picked up a quill pen and began studying the book that Violet had just been perusing.

Her heart was beating hard and stealing her breath. There was no chance that she could get out of the trunk and make it to the door without this man seeing her. She would have to wait until he was gone and then steal the book. How long would she be trapped in here?

The door of the room had been left open, so it seemed unlikely the book on the table was the secret one, but she would take it nonetheless. It might prove useful.

She heard voices and the clerk raised his head to look toward the doorway.

"I want her found," the voice, which sounded like the baron's, said loudly and stridently.

"Yes, sir," was the answer.

Footsteps entered the room. It was the baron.

"Lord Dunham." The clerk hopped down from the stool and bowed to the baron.

"Have you seen a young woman wandering about?"

"A young woman, sir?"

"Yes, yes. She has light brown hair and violet-colored eyes. Have you seen her?"

"No, sir." The clerk's voice was gruff and his expression was resolute and confident.

"If you do, escort her to her room in the south tower, then come and report to me."

"Yes, sir."

As soon as the baron turned to leave the room, the clerk's shoulders sank and he let out a sigh. He mumbled to himself as he went back to staring down at his book.

Violet's arm was beginning to cramp, so she carefully let the lid close. Her knees were drawn up to her chest and she curled up in the trunk on top of a musty-smelling blanket.

If she revealed herself to the clerk, he would surely tell the baron. Would the baron have her thrown in the dungeon for nosing around? Also, the baron was looking for her. The longer she remained missing, the more suspicious he would be.

Perhaps it was best if she let the clerk see her so she could get back to her room quickly. It would be easier to steal the book if the baron trusted her.

Yes, that is what she would do. *Please, God, let this work.*

Violet opened the lid of the trunk. As she did, it creaked.

The clerk turned his head as she was emerging. He gasped and fell off his stool.

FIFTEEN

THE PAIN IN MEREK'S HEAD AND RIBS SEEMED TO GROW worse the farther they walked.

He and Sir Willmer concealed themselves in the trees just beyond the stable while it was too dark to see. As dawn approached, Sir Willmer secured two horses, and they rode slowly through the thick trees away from the castle.

Merek was finding it difficult to breathe. Was it only due to the pain, or had a broken rib punctured his lungs? That had happened to a friend of his when he was thrown from his horse. His friend had suffocated to death.

Merek forced himself to take a deep breath. It hurt, but at least the air seemed to go in normally. He would be well in a week or two, after his ribs healed.

"Here's the cottage I told you about." Sir Willmer headed toward a small wattle-and-daub house that was nearly hidden among the trees.

Merek dismounted from his horse but was unable to suppress a groan as he dropped to the ground a little harder than he meant to.

They tied their horses and went inside the hovel that had obviously been abandoned, as squirrels were hiding their nuts in the corners and leaves were all over the floor, spiderwebs in every nook. There were many such houses across England since the Great Pestilence.

The house was devoid of furniture. No doubt people had helped themselves to it after the house was abandoned. But Merek would be well enough. He'd at least have shelter if it rained.

"I'd better get back to the castle before I'm missed," Sir Willmer said. "But I'll bring you some food and whatever I can scrounge without raising suspicion."

"Thank you." Merek felt a moment of guilt for being suspicious of his friend. But only a moment. After all, he hadn't known him long.

"Find out what you can about the maiden Violet and her grandmother," Merek bid him.

"I will."

When Sir Willmer was gone, Merek wondered again if Violet and her grandmother were well. He hated that they'd left them in that filthy dungeon.

He hoped the letter he'd sent by courier had reached the king, though it was very possible that the king would take no notice of such a missive, written by someone unknown to him. It would be much more convincing if he was able to take the baron's secret record book as proof.

Merek did his best to clear a place on the floor, then he lay down. He hadn't realized how tired he was until that moment. He tried to pray, but immediately his words began to slur as he started to fall asleep.

"Father God, my life is in Your hands. Keep Violet, her grandmother, Sir Willmer, and me safe."

Violet emerged from the trunk and hurried toward the clerk, who quickly sprang up off the floor.

"Pardon me. I am Violet."

He stared at her as if seeing a ghost. "How did you—" He stopped and covered his mouth with his hand. "Please don't tell the baron that you were in here."

"I won't tell him you left the door open and that I was in here if you won't."

"Agreed." He swallowed, his throat bobbing. Then he said in a hoarse voice, "Now, will you please go?"

"Thank you," she said and went to the doorway, peeking out.

No one was in sight, so she hurried away, back the way she had come. At least, she was trying to go back the way she had come, but she soon realized she was lost.

The castle was enormous, and a new corridor or staircase or tower appeared every which way she turned. She had no idea how to get back to her tower.

A servant passed her in the corridor.

"Excuse me. Can you tell me how to get back to the south tower?"

The servant woman's eyes were wide as she stared back at her. "I . . . don't know. Who are you?"

"There you are. Don't move." A guard came striding toward her.

The servant immediately hurried away.

"I went wandering around the castle," Violet started explaining to the guard, "and I got lost. Can you help me get back to my room?"

"Come." His voice was gruff and his expression glaring. "This way."

He led her back through the maze of hallways and staircases to her tower. Along the way they encountered another guard, who went to inform the baron that she was found.

When they reached her tower room, she said, "Thank you so much for helping me find my way back."

The guard did not acknowledge her words, just stood blocking the doorway.

Violet did her best to catch her breath—she was finding that the more afraid she was, the more breathless she became—and soon the baron appeared behind the guard.

"You may go," the baron told the guard, who immediately left. "You have been here only a few hours and already I have had to search for you."

"Forgive me. I was so impressed with the castle, so fascinated, that I went exploring. I didn't know I wasn't allowed to leave my room."

He just stared, so she went on.

"I'm afraid I got lost and had to ask for help from a guard.

He kindly led me back here." She smiled, aiming for an innocent expression.

"I did not think you needed to be told not to leave your room," the baron said slowly, "as you would have no need to go elsewhere. You have everything you need here and servants to bring you whatever you desire."

"Yes, and I thank you. It is a very pleasant arrangement."

"There are certain rooms that you are not allowed in," he added.

"I see. Forgive me." She stopped short of promising not to leave her room again.

The baron cleared his throat, still staring hard at her, but he made an attempt at a smile. "And how do you like what you have seen of the castle?"

"I like it very well. It is impressive and quite large."

He stared at her for a few more moments, then said, "I have a guest arriving soon. We will have a feast for him in the Great Hall tomorrow, and I shall expect you to wear your new clothes."

"Of course." Violet nodded.

"In the meantime, if you need anything, ring for a servant."

"Very well."

"Someday soon I shall give you a tour of the castle, if you wish—as long as you don't go off on your own again."

"I would like that very much, thank you," she said, ignoring his admonishment.

"Good day." Abruptly, the baron closed her door and left.

Violet let out a long breath, rubbing her cheeks as she went and lay across her bed.

That had worked out better than she'd imagined; she'd been quite frightened that the baron would punish her. But she was on shaky ground with the baron. She must be careful the next time she left the room. He certainly wouldn't be so forgiving in the future.

Violet was sitting by a bedside with a bowl of water and a cloth. She dipped the cloth in the warm water, then turned to the man on the bed.

Sir Merek gazed up at her. She dabbed at the dried blood in his hair. His eyes were so intent on her, his face so handsome. Next, she dabbed at the blood on his lip. She carefully cleaned the blood away, but his eyes never left her face.

He took hold of her wrist.

"Am I hurting you?" she asked.

"No." He still held her wrist.

She brushed her fingers across his cheek. Then she leaned down and pressed her lips very gently to his.

Violet awoke with a start and a sharp intake of breath. Her heart was thumping hard and fast, and she could still feel Sir Merek's lips touching hers.

Her cheeks began to burn. What made her dream such a thing? Was she depraved? An unmarried maiden having such thoughts about Sir Merek, a knight she barely knew . . . It was unseemly, at the very least.

But she closed her eyes and relived the vivid dream anyway, feeling again the handsome knight's lips as she kissed him.

Thank goodness no one would ever know what she'd dreamed.

"God," she whispered, noticing the bit of sunlight beginning to show through her windows, "please watch over Sir Merek and heal him of his wounds. I pray he was able to escape and is somewhere safe." She sighed. "And if it is wrong to wish I could tend to his wounds, please forgive me." *And forgive me for wanting to kiss him.* She couldn't even say that last prayer out loud.

She drifted off to sleep again, and when she awoke, Lora was setting a tray of food and drink on her bedside table. The seamstress who had measured her the day before was coming in behind her with a dress draped over her arms. Following her was another servant carrying more clothes.

"Good morning, miss," the servants said, one after the other.

"Good morning." Violet sat up and rubbed the sleep from her eyes.

"There is much to do," the seamstress said. "I need you to try on this dress. If it is in any way unsuitable, I will only have a few more hours to alter it. I need to know as quickly as possible."

"It looks marvelous." Violet was already admiring the beautiful silk material, obviously imported from Flanders or some other faraway place, as it was imprinted with colorful flowers and birds.

The seamstress stood looking at her, and Violet realized she was waiting for her to get out of bed.

Violet jumped up and allowed the servants to put the dress over her head, letting it fall down over her underdress that she had slept in.

"Stand on this," the seamstress directed, placing the shortest stool Violet had ever seen on the floor in front of her.

Violet obeyed and the seamstress proceeded to pull at the fabric under her arms and at her waist and place a pin here and there. Then the seamstress went all around the hem of the dress, dragging the stool as she went and sitting on it, pinning wherever the hem seemed to sag too low.

"There. It will be ready in an hour," the seamstress declared. "Take it off."

The servants carefully lifted the dress over Violet's head as Violet said, "Thank you for the clothes. I am very grateful for all the work you have done."

The seamstress did not meet her eye but simply bowed again and hurried out, the dress draped over her arms.

"You must try on these underclothes," the sewing servant said. "Shall I help?" She came toward her as if to take off her underdress.

"No, no. I will do it myself." Violet waited for Lora to leave and the sewing servant to turn around, then she took off her underdress and tried on the fine linen one. It felt so soft next to her skin, she wondered if it was made of silk.

The woman pulled at the sleeves, which were tight on her arms, and inspected the hem. "It fits very well, I think," she said.

"Someone will be here around midday to prepare your hair for the feast tonight."

"Midday? How long will it take?"

"A few hours." The woman stared blankly at Violet, but her eyes were cold and perhaps a bit contemptuous. Did she resent Violet for being so newly installed in the position of the baron's daughter? Yesterday she was just a farmer's daughter. Today she was a pampered maiden who received food at her bedside while seamstresses worked all night to make her a new dress.

Violet could hardly blame the woman if she did feel some contempt for her. She herself had once seen a fine lady on the road riding sidesaddle with several guards and some other elegantly dressed people. When she learned she was the daughter of a duke, she'd felt a pang of envy at the easy, privileged life that lady must live. She'd berated herself for the unkind and selfish emotion, but she couldn't help but wonder what it would be like to have beautiful clothes of silk and colorful embroidery.

The embroidery made her think of her hooded cloak of scarlet. It may not have been fashioned out of imported cloth, but it was made for her by her grandmother and therefore meant more to her than any duchess's gown. Grandmother had embroidered the edge of the ordinary wool hood with tiny vines and flowers. It must have taken her many hours, especially since her eyesight and the dexterity of her fingers were not as they once were.

It was strange to think she would be dining in the Great Hall, in the castle where her birth mother had served. Her poor mother. She must have suffered a great deal as an orphan, forced to become a servant in the household where she would eventually be taken advantage of by the baron.

And now that woman's daughter, Violet, would be sitting for hours while someone arranged and dressed her hair, as if she were going to a ball or being presented to the king. To think that she had once been envious of a duke's daughter. Now all she wanted was to find that secret record book and get out of here.

She said a prayer of thankfulness for her food and sat down at a small table to eat her breakfast. While she ate, she silently prayed for the prisoners in the dungeon and for Sir Merek and Sir Willmer.

Praying for Sir Merek brought back to mind the dream she'd had of him. How real it had seemed, so real that she had to examine herself for what she might do if she were given the opportunity to kiss the handsome young knight. Even if she did kiss him, he was too noble to try anything untoward. After all, he'd had ample opportunity to take advantage of her and hadn't. He had proven himself trustworthy.

Her grandmother had once told her it was not good to go through life without some people you could trust. But Sir Merek wasn't likely to be in her life for very long. She might dream about him and depend on him for now, but their relationship was destined to be quite short-lived. That was something she would need to accept, or her disappointment was likely to be great indeed.

Sixteen

THE SERVANT WHO HAD BEEN DRESSING VIOLET'S HAIR finally handed her a looking glass, then held up a second mirror behind her so she could see the back of her hair.

Violet gasped. Her light brown hair had been transformed, partially piled on top of her head, the rest hanging down in ringlets and braids. And all of it was decorated with tiny flowers and ribbons.

"It's beautiful," she breathed. But just as the sumptuous food, the bath that had been drawn for her, and the dress that the seamstress had sacrificed her sleep for had made Violet feel guilty, her hair made her feel like she was impersonating someone who was born for such luxuries. This was not Violet she was seeing in the mirror, the orphan girl who had vowed to herself that no one else would ever have to suffer because of her.

"It did turn out very well," the woman said. "I haven't had a lot of practice of late. But you have very fetching hair."

Soon after, the seamstress, hollow-eyed, came in to help Violet with her dress. The fine linen underdress, which fit snugly all the way down to her hips, went on first, then the exquisite brocaded gown was placed over it. The seamstress tied the dress on the sides with ribbon, then encircled Violet's waist with an embroidered belt that sat low on her hips and was loosely tied in the front.

The seamstress stood back to look her up and down. "Please don't dribble any food on it." She frowned, a very sour look. "It will be difficult to remove any stains."

Violet's stomach tightened at this admonition. She was so clumsy and often stained her clothes. And she'd heard that wealthy people ate a lot of gravy with their food.

"Your father said he would come himself and escort you."

The seamstress began talking to her assistant as they left the room. Now she was all alone and wondering if the feast would go well for her, or if the baron would yell at her if she soiled her dress, or if she would otherwise feel out of place and unsure what to do. What were the rules of etiquette for noblemen and their feasts? She had no idea.

Violet took a deep breath and blew it out. If she had survived telling the baron the truth and being thrown in the dungeon, then she would survive this night of feasting in the Great Hall.

The baron would be at her door any minute, and Violet suddenly wondered if she looked like him at all. He had dark brown hair and dark eyes, where Violet's hair and eyes were much lighter. His lips were thin while Violet's were full. He was also only slightly taller than Violet. He did have a rather wide face, like hers. Violet had always been aware that her facial structure was different from her adopted family's narrow, long faces.

"Come, my dear." The baron was standing in her doorway, beckoning with his hand, a cold hint of a smile on his lips.

There was nothing to do but advance toward him and follow him down the stairs.

"You look very pleasing, and I believe the viscount won't be able to help but admire your appearance."

"The viscount?"

"He is my guest for the next several days. And he is in want of a wife." Baron Dunham glanced over his shoulder at her.

Might the viscount want to marry her?

It was an overwhelming thought, unsettling her with all the new questions swirling around inside her. And her mind kept going to Sir Merek and how noble and brave he was.

Her grandmother's words came to her. *Love is everything.*

She'd always wanted to marry someone she could love and who would love her in return. Nobility of the heart was much more important than nobility of birth. But would she even have a choice if the baron wanted her to marry the viscount?

She took another deep breath as they reached the doorway to the Great Hall. Several people were already seated at the trestle tables, so Violet kept her eyes focused forward as the baron held out his arm to her.

She placed her hand on his forearm and walked as regally as she could, the baron striding slowly across the large banqueting hall toward the table that was set up on the slightly raised platform at the head of the room.

He seated her next to a young man, then seated himself at the head of the table so that the young man was between her and the baron.

"This gorgeous young lady must be your daughter." The man beside Violet was smiling at her.

"Violet, this is Viscount Eglisfeld. Lord Eglisfeld, this is my daughter, Violet."

Was the viscount handsome? She tried to decide. Truly, he was much younger than she expected a viscount to be. He hardly looked older than she was. His hair was dark blond, and he had a quite prominent nose. His eyes were brown and his lips were full for a man's. He might be considered handsome, but he was no Sir Merek.

Also, she instantly disliked the way he was smiling at her, as if she were something to be approved or disapproved of, the object of this stranger's judgment. Certainly she was not expected, or even allowed, to judge him—at least not openly.

The feast began with a thin soup in individual bowls set before each guest, along with thick slices of buttered and toasted bread. The taste of the soup was quite herby, with flavors she'd never experienced before.

Violet felt preoccupied with the food, trying not to eat too much of each course so as to leave room for the ones following, as well as trying not to dribble any food on her magnificent dress. But when she wasn't focused on the food, she was noticing the immensity of the Great Hall. The ceiling was high with prominent beams, a masculine and woody look, and the stained glass windows displayed the baron's coat of arms in bright red, green, blue, and yellow. They were as beautiful and well-done as the church windows she had seen.

Despite the fact that she knew Baron Dunham was villainous and cruel and took money from the poor, she couldn't help admiring his castle. The size and artistry of it left her in awe, the idea that mere men could create something so magnificent. She'd heard of the cathedrals in London and other large cities on the Continent, had even seen a few drawings in books, and they were supposed to be much larger and grander. But it was difficult to imagine, even for her, and she had a very big imagination, as her mother had often told her.

But she couldn't let anyone see her so awestruck. She was the baron's daughter, and she didn't know how much the baron had told his guests about her background and the fact that he had not known she existed until a few days ago.

"Do you like to dance?" Viscount Eglisfeld asked just as Violet was about to bite into a hunk of roast pheasant perched on the end of her knife. She set the bite of food on her trencher.

"I do. I learned to dance at the market fair, which comes to my village twice a year."

Perhaps she should not have mentioned her village fair. It didn't sound like a very appropriate place for a baron's daughter to learn to dance. But the viscount didn't seem to notice.

"That is good, because the baron tells me that the market fair will be here in a day or two. He will bring the minstrels and troubadours to the castle in the evenings so we can dance." Lord Eglisfeld raised a brow as if he was suggesting something, but what, she did not know.

She did enjoy dancing at the market fair, so she smiled.

Lord Eglisfeld began to speak to the baron of the wine they were drinking. "One does not find such fine wine often, not in England."

"It is from France. I must have my French wine." The baron grinned, then took a sip from his goblet.

With all the conflicts between England and France, Violet was surprised he admitted he imported his wine from France.

Lord Eglisfeld divided his time between talking to the baron on one side and conversing with Violet on his other. Violet endeavored to be polite to the baron's guest, but her thoughts kept going to Sir Merek. Was he safe? Did he have food? Were his injuries healing?

She couldn't help comparing the two men. One was noble and serious, while the other was all smiles and flattery, complimenting both the baron's wine and Violet's beauty—her face and her hair and her dress.

"Tell Violet about your castle in the north," the baron said to Lord Eglisfeld.

"I don't want to boast, but it is the largest castle in Northumbria. The king stays there when he travels in the area. It has five towers, each at least four stories high, and a very large moat surrounds it."

Violet had heard about what the castle residents threw in moats, and she thought it sounded very stinky. But she widened her eyes so that she would appear impressed.

When the baron was talking with the person on his other side, Lord Eglisfeld leaned down close to Violet's ear and said,

"My castle is larger than this one. The Great Hall is slightly smaller, but my keep would rival any castle belonging to King Richard."

Violet had to suppress the nervous laugh that bubbled up in her throat. He reminded her of a small boy flexing his arm and saying, "Look at my muscles."

"I hope you will be able to travel to Northumbria to see it one day."

Violet only smiled and said nothing.

She felt as if she were playing some sort of game, pretending to cooperate with the baron, pretending she was his daughter. And now she was pretending to be impressed by this arrogant viscount.

She only hoped that her pretense would not become reality, that she would not actually be dazzled by this man's interest in her, by his title and his wealth and his knowledge of the world. After all, he'd obviously seen and experienced more than she had ever hoped to. She'd never dreamed of marrying a viscount or any other nobleman. She hated to admit it, but there was a part of her that was enjoying his obvious interest in impressing her.

God, help me guard my heart.

The viscount asked, "Do you like horses and riding?"

"I do, if the horse is not too ornery." She would not tell him that she normally rode a mule.

"Perhaps we could go hunting together while I'm here. Your father says he has the best falcons and hunting dogs."

"Of course, if you like." She was not at all sure she wanted to go hunting with this man, but she would continue with her plan to be agreeable.

Again, her mind turned to Sir Merek. What would Sir Merek do if he was interested in wooing a woman? She suddenly wished her dream of kissing him had been real.

The baron was staring at her with his cold, dark eyes again. She felt herself blush. But he couldn't know she was thinking of Sir Merek and not of the viscount.

The servants brought out another dish of hot meat and gravy—pork this time. It was delicious, but her stomach was becoming too full to eat another bite. She wished she could have a long, cool drink of water from her family's well. The wine was not to her liking, as she had never drunk it before, and it seemed to make her more thirsty instead of less so. She hoped the feast would end soon so she could go up to her room and get a drink from the pitcher of water the servants replenished twice a day.

Finally, when the servants arrived with the last course and were refilling everyone's goblet with wine, Violet saw her chance.

"Father," she said, using the term for the first time to address the baron and feeling a little sick as she did, "may I please retire to my room? I am tired and—"

"Of course." He gave a quick nod.

"And may I escort her to her room, to ensure she gets there safely?" Lord Eglisfeld asked.

"You may." The baron's face was expressionless.

The viscount turned to Violet with a smile and helped her up from the bench.

Violet's stomach flipped as they walked across the Great

Hall together. What were the viscount's intentions? Surely he would not try anything unseemly in her father's castle. Well, if he did, she would make him sorry. She knew where to hit a man to incapacitate him, and then she would run to her room and lock the door.

But the viscount had a respectful look on his face. He offered his arm to her as they reached the stairs, and she placed her hand lightly on his forearm, as if to say, "I know this is the polite thing to do, but I do not need your help to get up the stairs."

"I have very much enjoyed becoming acquainted with you tonight, Violet." He was gazing at her as they walked, and she chanced a quick glance at him.

"Thank you. I enjoyed making your acquaintance as well." She tried to say the words lightly, not wishing to seem to return his interest.

"I hope to see you tomorrow, and indeed, all the days of my visit."

When they reached her door, which did not take long since her tower was next to the Great Hall, he took her hand in his and kissed it. The act sent a shiver up her arm to her shoulder, but not a pleasant one. She pulled her hand free.

"Good evening, Lord Eglisfeld." She quickly pushed the door open, slipped inside, and closed it before he could do anything beyond replying in kind.

Violet locked her door and let out a breath she hadn't realized she'd been holding. "Thank goodness that's over," she whispered.

Only a minute later, Lora came in to help her off with her dress.

"I can manage taking off my clothes," Violet said, "but can you help me take the pins from my hair?"

The servant girl froze. "Are you certain you are allowed to take the pins out? That is, I don't know if Lord Dunham intends for you to wear your hair thusly tomorrow as well."

"Well, Lord Dunham doesn't have to sleep with pins sticking in his head, does he? I think it will be all right to take out the pins and the flowers. I will leave the braids and ribbons."

"Very well, miss."

Lora stood behind Violet while she sat on the stool and released her from the pinned-up mass of hair. Violet gingerly rubbed a couple of sore spots where the pin had been sticking into her scalp.

"Thank you so much." It was well past her normal bedtime, and she yawned. "You may go. I am going to bed now."

Lora left and Violet took off her new clothes and draped them carefully over a trunk, imagining how upset the seamstress would be if she creased the fabric. Then she put on her old underdress, which had been laundered and smelled of fresh lavender, and sank blissfully under the bed linens.

She closed her eyes, shamelessly hoping she would dream of Sir Merek again.

Seventeen

Merek took the things from Sir Willmer's hands, thankful, but at the same time wishing he wasn't so dependent on his new friend.

Merek examined the leather eye patch and tied it around the back of his head. The clothing he had brought was that of a farmer, a skilled laborer, or a shopkeeper—not too rough but not too fine to draw attention.

"I still think you ought to stay here for another week or two," Sir Willmer said. "If someone recognizes you, you might have to fight your way out, and with those broken ribs, you'd be hard-pressed to defend yourself."

Merek believed he could defeat any but the strongest and most skilled guards, but he only grunted and started donning the clothes.

"Are you sure no one saw you take the clothes? And no one suspects you?"

"No one saw me. The baron asked several of the guards if they'd seen you. He asked me, too, but he didn't seem suspicious, just angry that you had escaped."

Merek felt a sense of satisfaction at hearing of the baron's anger.

Sir Willmer nodded. "I'm going, so give me a head start."

"I'll give you an hour or so, then I'll be on my way to the fair."

The clothes Sir Willmer had brought, along with the eye patch, were the perfect disguise. He was hoping Violet would come to the fair, and if she did, he could blend in with the crowd while keeping an eye on her.

Sir Willmer had told him that she was living in the castle now, and that the baron was introducing her to noblemen as his daughter. No doubt he intended to use her for his own profit. He would gain power and leverage with another nobleman by marrying her off to him. And according to the gossip Sir Willmer had gleaned, the baron already had someone in mind for her—Viscount Eglisfeld, who had recently inherited the title from his father.

Violet was spirited and educated, at least enough to write letters to the king. As the daughter of a landed farmer, she'd be expected to marry someone of similar status. But Merek couldn't imagine her being the wife of a farmer. He could, however, imagine her married to a viscount. And he could also imagine her married to . . . him.

Merek had had a lot of time alone, and no doubt that was the reason he'd thought so much about the maiden. He'd probably thought of her too much. After all, she didn't seem to like him, and she certainly had not trusted him.

But that was in the beginning, when she'd first discovered he was in the baron's service. She seemed much more inclined to trust him now, but could her feelings change so much that she could fall in love with him?

Merek had never shied away from a challenge.

He remembered the way she'd looked at him and the inflection in her voice when she saw the blood on his face and asked him about his injuries. He liked to think she wouldn't have behaved that way if she didn't at least feel something for him.

Merek set out for the village. Thankfully he had plenty of money, as Sir Willmer had brought all the coins Merek had saved. They had been tucked in with his belongings before anyone else had a chance to find them.

He'd been growing out his beard, having not shaved in several days, but he knew that alone would not disguise him. So when he was close to the village, Merek pulled the eye patch down over his eye and flipped his hood over his head. He'd also fashioned a wooden staff out of a fallen tree limb and now carried it as part of his disguise, but also to use as a weapon, if necessary.

It was mid-morning, and the market fair was in full array, with sellers hawking goods from every part of England, Wales, Ireland, Scotland, and indeed, all the rest of the world. There were spices from the Far East, fine fabrics from Flanders, and even exotic birds to keep as pets. As the market drew people from several nearby towns, rich and poor alike mingled in the town square where the sellers had set up their booths. Each one was colorful and eye-catching, the better to entice buyers.

There was a festive air about the fair, especially when some minstrels started playing their instruments and singing. An area was cleared next to the fountain in the square, and several couples made their way there and started to dance to the lively music.

Merek had to admit that after four days alone in the little house in the woods, he was glad to be out among people again. And to hear music was even better.

A group of people were making their way along the lane that led down the hill from the castle. Among them was a woman with long, flowing skirts of pale pink and lavender and hair covered with an almost sheer veil fluttering in the breeze. It was Violet.

Beside her was a young man dressed in finery, and the rest of the party were guards and a female servant of middle age, guardians for the baron's daughter.

As they drew closer, he noticed the way the viscount was walking close to Violet, smiling and leaning even nearer to her, and it set his teeth on edge. Was the viscount bothering her? Merek actually felt his teeth grind together.

Time to test out his disguise.

Violet's heart beat to the rhythm of the lute and the pipes being played in the town square below. How delightful to hear music and to contemplate dancing with a partner like Viscount Eglisfeld. She might not be very attracted to him, but at least he was well-dressed and well-mannered, and no doubt he would be a very capable dancer.

When they reached the area of the square where the other

dancers were, Lord Eglisfeld was all smiles as he held out his hand to her.

"Dance with me?" he asked.

She took his hand, and they joined the ring of dancers hopping around in a circle, one of the dances Violet had learned as a girl. She could see a second circle of dancers, the young children from around eight years old to thirteen, reminding Violet of her own childhood.

Little did she know back then that one day she would be wearing a fine silk dress and dancing with a viscount.

Several of the dancers were staring at them. Violet even recognized a woman from her village, a few years Violet's elder, who gave her a big, wide smile.

Violet felt herself blush. After all, she was the daughter of a farmer, and though her family wasn't poor, they weren't wealthy either. She was only an ordinary young woman like anyone else.

But she might as well enjoy the viscount's attentions. Anyone else would. But what would her mother or her brother say if they could see her now? What would Grandmother say?

Her brother would say she had gotten above her raising. Her mother would fret over what people would think of her and what would happen to her, living with the baron. But she liked to think her grandmother would tell her to dance and enjoy herself but to keep her eyes open. She would tell her to "remember that love is everything and you should marry a man who is good and loving and kind."

The dance soon ended with the music. Lord Eglisfeld led her to the side and said, "I love a good cup of ale when I'm attending a fair. Can I bring you a cup as well? Or would you like something else?"

"It is a warm day, and ale sounds good. I thank you."

The viscount went off to fetch their ale, and Violet couldn't help but be surprised at how normally the viscount was behaving, as if he were an ordinary townsperson or villager. But no sooner had she entertained that thought than she saw Lord Eglisfeld bump into a young man possibly fourteen or fifteen years old and yell at him, "Watch where you're walking! You stepped on my foot."

The boy looked sheepish, but when his friend laughed, he turned and the two of them ran away, snickering.

Lord Eglisfeld stared after them, looking disgusted, brushing off the front of his silk brocade waistcoat. He glanced around and she held her breath, hoping he wouldn't send a guard after the boy, who hadn't meant to run into him. Finally, the viscount continued on.

No, this viscount didn't think of himself as an ordinary person. And if he knew she did not consider herself truly to be the baron's daughter, that she'd been raised on a farm and had learned to do the same work as a villein's daughter—milking cows, helping to harvest the wheat and barley, making cheese, and every kind of kitchen work—he might treat her differently.

"Pardon me, my lady."

Violet turned at the sound of the male voice. For a moment, the voice sounded familiar, but when she saw who was speaking—a bearded man with a black leather patch over one eye—she let out a disappointed, "Oh."

The man gallantly bowed to her. Then, with one hand over his heart, he said, "Would you honor me by dancing this next dance with me?"

"Yes." She answered almost before she had time to think. The music was starting again, the viscount was off getting ale, and she did want to dance. Besides, the man's chivalrous manner drew her in.

Soon they were lining up in two rows facing each other. They stepped forward, then away, then together again to clasp hands. And for a moment, their faces were so close that she could see the amber streaks in his blue eye.

There was something so familiar about that blue eye.

And then she realized he reminded her of Sir Merek. But Sir Merek didn't have a patch over one eye and didn't dress as this man did.

As they continued the dance, Violet studied the man's movements and noted his height, his hair color, his face shape. And then she saw the tiny cut on his bottom lip that was nearly healed. It must be him. If the guards recognized him, he would surely be captured and taken back to the dungeon. They would probably beat him again too.

Her heart beat faster. No one else seemed to recognize him, even the guards who were watching her. But she mustn't draw their attention.

She stared into his face as they danced, moving forward and back, alternately spinning and hopping on one foot.

"You are quite a good dancer," Violet said. "Where did you learn the steps?"

"I have been dancing so long, I hardly remember," he said.

"So long? You don't look much older than I am."

She stepped up close as they lifted their hands over their heads. Sir Merek grasped hers in a firm grip, gazing straight into her eyes.

"I am twenty-one," he said quietly, his face only a hand-breadth from hers. The next moment they were stepping apart to the rhythm of the music.

Had he come here to watch over her, as he'd promised he would? Her heart did a little flip inside her chest.

Why was Sir Merek risking his life to be here? Was it only to attend the market fair? Certainly not. He seemed a man of intention and purpose, with sober mind and motives. His disguise was rather good, but if she had recognized him, wouldn't the guards recognize him eventually as well? She could only hope that they would not be expecting to see him here and therefore would not notice him.

"Are you from this town?" he asked.

Was he pretending not to know who she was? He must think she didn't recognize him. Or was he actually not Sir Merek after all?

Had she lost her mind, thinking too much about Sir Merek and imagining he was this stranger with the beard and eye patch?

She stared at him quizzically, not answering. Then she noticed Lord Eglisfeld glaring at them, his arms crossed over his chest, two tin cups of ale sitting just behind him on the lip of the fountain.

"Thank you for the dance," she said quickly, breaking away

from him with a quick backward glance as she hurried over to Lord Eglisfeld.

"There you are," Violet said brightly. "Thank you for the ale." She picked up one of the cups and took a long drink of it. Truly, the only time ale tasted good was when she was hot and very thirsty.

"Who was that man you were dancing with?"

"He didn't tell me his name. He only asked me if I wanted to dance." Violet turned so she could see the dancers and saw that another maiden had taken her place with the man who might be Sir Merek. She noticed he did not step as close to this maiden as he had with her. And she might be imagining it, but his jaw seemed to have hardened. He looked annoyed.

Violet groaned inwardly. She wanted nothing more than to dance with the man with the eye patch and dispel all doubt that he was Sir Merek, but she had to keep Lord Eglisfeld's attention away from him.

But the viscount did not know Sir Merek, did he? He wouldn't recognize him. She just had to keep Lord Eglisfeld from becoming angry enough to set the guards on him.

She suddenly regretted missing the rest of their dance together. Did he know the maiden who was dancing with him now? Did he think she was pretty?

Oh my. I'm jealous.

It was just that silly dream she'd had about kissing him. It had made her mad, moonstruck even.

"You must truly love dancing to dance with a strange man, a

poor man, by the looks of him, with only one eye." Lord Eglisfeld was sneering.

She would have to be careful what she did or said next, but she suddenly didn't want to dance with Lord Eglisfeld anymore.

"He was very polite. I saw no reason why I shouldn't dance with someone who treated me with chivalry and a noble attitude."

"Chivalry and a noble attitude?" Lord Eglisfeld leaned away from her, his brows going up and drawing together at the same time. "You make it sound as if you are in love with this poor one-eyed man."

Violet let out a breath, forcing herself to pause before replying. "If you are so offended by my words and my dancing with another man, you may go and leave my father's guards to watch over me."

Lord Eglisfeld smiled, his expression undergoing a complete change. "Forgive me. I was simply out of sorts seeing you dancing with another man. I had to wait in a line of people to get the ale, you know."

For pity's sake. Heaven forbid the man not find her waiting with bated breath for his return, or that he should have to wait for something.

"I do appreciate you getting it for me, and I am sorry you had to wait to be served." She tried to pretend that she cared.

Certainly Sir Merek would not complain about a little thing like waiting a minute or two for a cup of ale.

She put on a look of placid interest while she sipped her ale, watching Sir Merek dance. If only she could be sure it was him.

Had he recovered from his injuries so quickly? Or did the dancing cause him pain?

The dance ended. He nodded to the young maiden, polite but without smiling, and walked away. As he did so, he wrapped an arm loosely around his side. His ribs were surely still paining him.

"Violet? Did you hear me?"

"Sorry. What did you say?" She quickly turned her full attention to Lord Eglisfeld, who was frowning. "I couldn't hear you. The music was so loud."

"I asked if you would like to dance again."

"Oh yes. Of course." After telling him how much she enjoyed dancing, she probably should not refuse him. She set her cup down on the side of the fountain, but when he held out his hand to her, she shuddered inwardly at having to touch him.

He was harmless, surely. Besides that, the guards were nearby. She had no reason to fear him. And yet she wished she could dance with Sir Merek instead of him. A feeling of resentment toward Lord Eglisfeld suddenly welled up inside her.

First jealousy, now resentment. Was Sir Merek truly the instigator of such emotions? She sighed.

The music began and they started to dance, but she found she was enjoying it less than before. Still, it was good to be among smiling people and to hear the joyful sounds of lively music. To see the sun and to move her body to the sounds. She was soon having a good time again, as long as she did not let herself look around for Sir Merek.

After two more dances, she and Lord Eglisfeld were both a bit out of breath. He found a spot on the side of the fountain for them to sit, and they both drank the rest of their ale.

The viscount called a guard over. "Take these back to the vendor there." He pointed by nodding his head as he handed the guard their two cups.

Violet forced herself not to roll her eyes at his unwillingness to take the cups himself. But perhaps he was afraid she would start dancing with someone else again.

"What? Something amuses you?" Lord Eglisfeld was trying to look into her face.

She leaned away from him without thinking, then smiled. "I'm just very happy to be here at the fair, listening to the music and dancing. And you? Are you enjoying yourself?"

"Of course. I am here with you, and you are a lady fair and gentle. Egads. Your eyes are the most unusual color. Are they violet?"

"They are."

"I suppose that is why your mother named you Violet. I'm surprised I didn't notice the color until just now. I think of myself as being very observant."

Violet acknowledged his words by nodding, her gaze wandering over the crowd in front of them, but she didn't see Sir Merek. Had he left?

Lord Eglisfeld said, "My own father died a year ago. I was his heir, but I do have two older sisters. They're married, and I have the full run of my castle. I'm anxious to get back there."

Violet nodded politely, still letting her gaze wander. Was

that Sir Merek over by the blacksmith's booth? No, that man did not have an eye patch, and on second look, he was too short to be Sir Merek.

"I have a large bailey inside my castle yard that would serve very well for dancing in good weather. I can send for musicians and singers."

"I see." Violet smiled and nodded. Was he only bragging, or did he have a purpose for these boasts? Why was he so eager to impress her? Did he wish to marry her?

Violet's throat tightened. Perhaps she might accept him as a husband if he was less petty and boastful and more . . . more like Sir Merek.

No, she would not wish to marry Lord Eglisfeld. After all, if he was interested in her, it was only because she was the baron's daughter. But how could she discourage his thoughts about her as a wife? She could be rude to him, but that might make the baron angry.

If only she could get her grandmother's advice. She was quite sure she could not love Lord Eglisfeld the way she wished to love her husband. She wanted to respect and admire her husband, and the only way she could do that was if he was a good man, noble-hearted and chivalrous.

Someone like Sir Merek, or at least the kind of man she believed Sir Merek was.

As if her thoughts about him conjured him up, she saw him standing next to a spice merchant's booth. Their eyes met, but he didn't turn away. He was watching over her, just as he'd said he would. She smiled at him.

Lord Eglisfeld started to turn his head in the direction she was looking.

Violet stood up quickly. "Let's dance. We must take advantage of the music while we can, after all."

Thankfully, he seemed to forget about trying to see who she was smiling at, but he also seemed to take her enthusiasm as an invitation for him to get closer to her, because he put his hand on her upper back and leaned in.

His voice was uncomfortably close to her ear. "It is good to see a woman so happy to dance and make merry the way you do."

Violet shuddered, trying not to show her aversion. She quickened her pace, almost trotting toward the other dancers, forcing him to drop his hand from her back.

She was glad it was another fast dance in which they linked arms in a circle and danced all together. She was enjoying herself, but she also wished she could get away from the viscount and speak to Sir Merek.

When the dance was over, Baron Dunham was standing next to the fountain, watching them. There was a satisfied look on his face. Violet felt a little sick wondering if he was set on her marrying Lord Eglisfeld.

She and the viscount walked over to where the baron was standing.

"Is the fair to your liking?" the baron asked, looking at Lord Eglisfeld and ignoring Violet.

"Yes, your daughter and I are enjoying the dancing very much," the viscount said.

"Good. I shall have the minstrels attend our feast tonight

and you can dance there as well." The baron began to speak to the viscount in a lower voice, obviously not including Violet in the conversation.

"I shall return in a moment," Violet said. "I want to look at the silk scarves."

The baron gave a curt nod and said, "Here." He took a small purse from his belt and placed it in her hand. "Buy something for yourself."

"Thank you."

He turned away from her before the purse even touched the palm of her hand and was already talking to the viscount again.

Violet walked away quickly. Her heart seemed to lift her off the ground. She was free!

She hurried through the rows of sellers until she was sure the baron and viscount could no longer see her. Then she stopped to catch her breath, a nervous wave washing over her at having escaped the two men, and hopefully the guards as well.

She began to wander from booth to booth, slowly taking in the wares. She came to a woman selling hot cross buns that were smeared with a sweet glaze and bought one, eating it as she walked.

Standing at a booth of saddles and saddlebags, she glanced around, looking for any sign of guards who might be following her or watching her. She stood out a bit, with her colorful silk dress, but among the booths and with the crowd of people mingling around her, it seemed she had lost sight of the guards.

Even though she wanted to, she would not look for Sir Merek. He would approach her if it was safe to do so.

She should buy a scarf or two. She went to the nearest booth selling silk scarves and veils and began to look through them.

She picked one out for herself, even though she rarely covered her head, and whenever she did wear a scarf, it usually ended up becoming unknotted and falling off. It was the same with shawls, which weren't as comfortable to wear as her favorite red cloak. But she picked out a scarf that she thought her mother would like, as well as a shawl for her grandmother. She was paying the seller for them when she became aware of someone standing beside her.

"Is the lady enjoying the fair?"

Sir Merek gazed at her from under his hood.

Eighteen

"I am indeed." Violet's heart beat fast at being so close to him. She lowered her voice to a whisper. "And who are you supposed to be?"

"I am a farmer, of course." He gave her a smile. "You may call me Andrew."

"I didn't want to bring attention to you," she whispered, "lest the guards notice you."

"Am I so recognizable?"

"I recognized you."

"They only knew me a short time, so I don't think they will realize it is me, as long as they don't get too close. But I came to see if you were well. I hope the baron is treating you well."

"Yes, I have my own room, but I am not allowed to leave it without being accompanied. However, I did go wandering around the castle by myself the first day there and found a room where a clerk was writing numbers in a book. I even saw the book he was writing in, but I am not sure if it was the official

206

record book that is shown to the king, or the one that reflects the monies he has stolen."

Sir Merek nodded. "Don't risk getting caught. I am working on a plan to get inside the castle so that I can search for it."

"That is much too risky. Please don't try it. You will be caught."

They had moved away from the booth when they started talking and were standing in a somewhat hidden corner, sheltered by merchants' tents and a large awning covering one of the seller's booths.

"I don't want you endangering yourself," Sir Merek said, as if it were an order.

"You would be endangering yourself much more than I would be."

She could see the set of his jaw. The only way to keep him from endangering himself and searching for the book was for her to find it herself.

Merek could see that Violet was concerned about his safety, and he felt slightly offended. Did she not trust him to find the book without getting caught? But then, he had already gotten caught once.

He wanted so much to protect her, almost as a way to make up for how he had failed to protect his brothers, Delia, and even his father, who'd been murdered on his own estate. But he wished to protect her not only because she was an innocent maiden, but also because he had started to think of her as much more.

Violet was different from other maidens. She was brave

and brutally honest, standing up to the baron and risking being thrown into the dungeon. She was also quite alluring, the way her eyes flashed purple in the light, her perfect nose, her teeth and lips . . .

But he needed to remember why he was here.

"I would prefer it if you did not look for the book, but I also know that you likely will not listen to me."

She lifted her delicate brows, as if to say, "You are right about that."

"So if you find the book, send me word by Sir Willmer. He is still at the castle doing his duties. And if you cannot find Sir Willmer, you can place a note in the hollow of the old stump at the back of the stables. Sir Willmer and I will check it twice a day."

"Very well." She nodded, and he noted the strong-willed expression.

"If you ever need me for anything, just send word and I will come," Merek said. "Do you feel safe in the castle? If the baron ever does anything to mistreat you, I want you to tell me right away."

"He is rather cold, but he has given me clothing and food, and there are servants tending to my needs. He did not like it when I left my room and he couldn't find me, but he did not punish me."

"Does he know you were in the clerk's room and saw the record book?"

"No. The clerk saw me, but he was very fearful of the baron finding out that he had left the room unattended, so we agreed that neither of us would tell anyone."

"Where was this room located?"

"I am not certain, as I was lost when I came upon it, but I believe it is in the tower farthest to the east."

"To the east?"

"Yes."

"You are so familiar with direction?"

"I am." She lifted her chin a notch. "My father told me I have a good sense of direction. As long as one knows where the sun comes up and goes down, it is not hard."

He smiled, impressed.

"But I should not have told you that. Now you will try to get into the castle and find it."

"I would have found a way into the castle and looked for it even if you had not told me. This way I have a better chance."

"Well, if you get caught, hopefully I can save you from getting killed, now that I'm the baron's daughter."

"And because you're the baron's daughter, you will have to marry as the baron wishes. Is he planning to marry you to the viscount?"

Her face clouded over. "I think so. But I won't marry him."

"He is wealthy, and he seems less cruel—and less ugly—than most noblemen I've met."

"Are you trying to convince me to marry him? Well, perhaps I will."

Merek's gut twisted. Would Violet marry the viscount to spite him?

"I'm not trying to convince you to marry him, just wondering why you are so sure you would not."

"I don't think he is very kindhearted. I have a sense about people. I can tell a lot from their expressions, the look in their eyes, the things they say and the way they treat others."

"Discernment. I suppose you could tell right away that I was a good man." He put his tongue in his cheek.

"I couldn't, because you were working for the baron, and neither the baron nor his men are good. But you have since redeemed yourself."

Merek smiled. "Then perhaps the reason you don't want to marry the viscount is because of me."

"Arrogant." Violet shook her head at his presumptuous statement.

"Your viscount will be looking for you, and so will your father's guards. But remember what I said about the stump and Sir Willmer."

She was still staring at him with lowered brows, but he thought he saw a hint of a smile at the corners of her mouth and in her eyes.

He smiled and said, "Enjoy the fair."

He moved away from her, pulling his hood down farther as he walked away. He remembered her look of disapproval, her accusation of arrogance, and he couldn't help smiling. She was a spirited one, but she was too clever to marry the viscount just to spite him. He hoped.

Violet huffed out a breath as she watched Sir Merek leave. He sounded as presumptive as Robert, who thought she would surely want to marry him for his farm, even though he'd offered her nothing in the way of love. But Sir Merek had smiled when he spoke, and she was fairly certain he was only jesting. And unlike Robert, he had mentioned nothing of marriage.

Most maidens believed it wisest to marry a man who had the most property or money or material goods. If she were like most maidens, she'd have married Robert Mercer, who owned enough land to have tenants, and now she'd marry Viscount Eglisfeld, with his castle and his wealth. But her grandmother had taught her that it was almost as difficult to live without love as it was to live without necessities like food and shelter.

Perhaps the reason Sir Merek's jest bothered her so much was because it was embarrassing how close to the truth he was. She hadn't been able to stop thinking about him for days, and when she compared him to Lord Eglisfeld, she much preferred Sir Merek.

Violet wanted to marry a good man whom she could love and respect, and who would love and respect her. Remembering all her grandmother's advice, she was determined to do just that and not settle for less.

Violet ate hot fried pasties and her favorite—buns filled with meat and pickled cabbage—drank water from the town well, and danced a few more times with Lord Eglisfeld. But he was becoming less and less inclined to keep a decent distance from her, touching her shoulder or her arm or her hand every chance he got, and so she excused herself when she had a chance and spent more time wandering through the sellers' booths, looking at their wares, wishing Sir Merek would appear by her side again.

Soon she began to grow tired and wished for a nap before the inevitable feast and dancing in the evening at the castle. So she told Lord Eglisfeld she was going back to the castle to her room to lie down and that she would see him later in the Great Hall.

"I shall accompany you." He turned and called a guard over, demanding that he escort them back to the castle, "for the lady's safety."

Once they were back inside the castle, Violet parted quickly from the viscount so that he would not try to hold her hand or kiss her. After their last dance, he'd leaned in quite close, staring at her mouth. He'd almost had her pinned against the fountain, but she slipped out sideways, rudely nudging him aside.

Did he think he could force a kiss on her, and in public? She didn't feel the need to be polite to such men.

She took off her lovely silk dress and lay across her bed, reliving the day. She just wanted her thoughts to be quiet and to get some rest, but her mind kept going through all the possible scenarios, thinking of how her life might be if she married Lord Eglisfeld, if the baron cast her off and she went back home, if she married Robert Mercer, but most often her mind wandered to what her life would be like if she married Sir Merek.

Which was ridiculous. He had not asked her to marry him, nor was he likely to. He was a knight, the son of an earl, and after he exposed Baron Dunham to the king as a thief, he would find a new position, a new war or battle to join. And Violet would go back to her life with her mother and brother, baking for her neighbors, milking cows, and helping with the harvests.

But someday, when Sir Merek had the means to marry, he

would marry a woman from a highborn family, or at least some-one with a fortune.

While she was daydreaming, the seamstress came to her room to fit her for a new dress. She had dark smudges under her eyes. How much had the poor woman slept, if at all?

"Truly, I am sorry the baron has asked you to make another dress for me," Violet said. "The one I have is more than sufficient for the feast tonight."

The seamstress gave her a cold look. "The baron is the mas-ter here, and he has ordered a second dress. Now let us pull it over your head."

Violet obeyed, feeling sorry for the woman, even if she was a bit rude. She felt even sorrier for the assistant, who tripped over her own feet in coming forward to help, drawing a sharp reprimand from the seamstress, but the poor thing was so tired she could hardly stay upright.

So this was what it was like to be rich and have servants to order about. The wealthy disregarded anyone's needs and wishes but their own. No wonder Jesus said that it was harder for the rich man to get to heaven than for a camel to go through the eye of a needle. But then He'd said that nothing was impossible for God. Perhaps it was not impossible, even for Baron Dunham?

But that was too much for her to think about just now.

Once they had tried the dress on her and the seamstress had plucked and pinched at it from every side and seam, the dress was declared too large at the waist. "But I am not sure there is enough time to take it in." The seamstress blinked as if holding back tears.

"No, no, it is good," Violet insisted. "Indeed, it is. I shall eat so much at the feast that it will be snug before it's over. Please. Besides, the baron is the last person who will notice such a thing. The dress is perfect as it is, truly."

The seamstress had a pained look on her face, but finally she nodded. "Very well. We did our best." She sighed. Her assistant was so worn down, she hardly reacted.

"It is very beautiful. Thank you very much. You are very talented."

The seamstress froze and her eyes widened slightly. She mumbled, "My pleasure," as she turned to leave.

The servant who had prepared her hair the day before worked hurriedly to arrange it again. A few minutes into her frenzied plaiting and pin-sticking, Lora came to the door.

"The master is asking for Violet. He said he is waiting for her to begin the feast."

"Oh dear," the servant who was working on her hair said.

"It looks very well," Lora said timidly.

"There." The servant stabbed her head with one last pin.

"I'm coming." Violet hurried from the room, calling, "Thank you!" to the hairdresser.

The Great Hall was even more festive than it had been the night before. Every face was bright and smiling as the musicians were busy getting ready on the small balcony that jutted out from the wall.

Violet hurried over to the dais and was helped up onto the platform by a guard. She went and sat in her place beside Lord Eglisfeld, whose face was quite red.

"It looks as if you got too much sun," Violet said without thinking. "Perhaps the baron has some soothing lotions for you."

The viscount gazed at her with a strange expression. He opened his mouth to speak, but the baron interrupted him.

"My daughter is here. Good." The baron motioned to the musicians in the minstrels' gallery. They immediately began to play and sing a ballad that had been a favorite of Violet's when she was a child.

Despite all she'd eaten at the fair that morning, her stomach growled when the servants brought out the first course. All the dancing must have made her hungry.

Thankfully, Lord Eglisfeld seemed in a less talkative mood than usual, and when he did speak, he talked more with Baron Dunham than with her. Violet was able to relax and enjoy the music and glance around at the rest of the guests.

The guards and knights were quite festive already, loud, boisterous, and eager to laugh.

The food came out more quickly than the evening before, and soon Violet had eaten as much as she could and was glad for the bit of extra room in her dress, just as she'd predicted.

The minstrels were playing the livelier songs now, and Lord Eglisfeld turned to her. "Will you dance with me?"

"I am quite tired after being in the sun most of the day," Violet said.

"I think I have done something to offend you," Lord Eglisfeld said. "Will you tell me what I did?"

"You have not offended me." Violet could see the baron giving her a look, watching her interaction with the viscount.

"I know you enjoy dancing. It must be me you do not enjoy."

"I do not mean to upset you. Nothing is wrong—I am just tired. I will dance with you one or two dances, but then I must retire."

Truthfully, it was more her mind that was tired than her body.

After Violet danced with Lord Eglisfeld to two songs, she bid him a good night and walked toward the stairs. The viscount ran after her.

"You need to let me escort you to your room," he said, half out of breath.

"Very well." Violet hurried up the stairs, staying at least two steps ahead of him, and when she reached her room, she said brightly, "Thank you. Good night." Then she quickly added, "I hope your sunburn will not pain you tonight. I shall see you in the morning."

But in her effort not to make him feel snubbed, she was too slow to avoid his taking her hand and kissing it.

"Good night, fairest Violet. I look forward to seeing you tomorrow."

She smiled and slipped into her room, quickly closing the door. She locked it with the key and took off her outer dress, then went and poured herself a cup of water, drinking the whole thing in one long drink.

What an eventful day it had been. Her mind felt exhausted but restless at the same time.

She wandered to her window and gazed out at the bright full moon. No one seemed to be out. No one was working at the blacksmith's stall or at the stable, as they were probably all home asleep in their beds or at the feast in the Great Hall.

Then she caught sight of someone pacing slowly into and out of the shadows beside the stable. From the rough clothing and the way he walked and held himself, she was almost certain it was Sir Merek.

Did she dare go and speak to him? She found her old dress that she'd come to the castle in, put on her red hooded cloak, and quietly left her room.

NINETEEN

MEREK HAD STAYED IN TOWN FOR THE REST OF THE DAY, keeping an eye on Violet, watching the viscount and making sure he did not do anything untoward. His face had heated whenever the man gave Violet that arrogant smirk of his.

Merek could see that Lord Eglisfeld was confident he could have Violet if he wanted her, and having observed the way the baron looked at Violet when she told him she was his daughter, he couldn't imagine the man felt any protective feelings that a father would naturally have. In fact, Merek had known other noblemen who were the same; it was not uncommon.

Violet had called Merek arrogant. Perhaps he deserved it, as he'd never been known for his humility, but he did hope she had begun to see him as a good and noble knight, at least. She certainly seemed to smile at Merek a lot more than at the viscount.

It was evening now, and the musicians and singers had made the trip up the hill to the castle. Merek sneaked inside the castle wall and waited outside for Sir Willmer to be released from his duties so they could talk about their plan. He stood in the empty courtyard, in the shadows of the stable, listening to the muffled sounds of music coming from the Great Hall.

What was Violet doing now? Was she dancing with the viscount? No doubt the soldiers and knights were getting drunk off the baron's strong spirits, which he made through a process called distilling. Merek wondered if he made it for the purpose of keeping his soldiers loyal to him, for there were few people in England who knew how to make the strong distilled wine. The baron's soldiers were so enamored with the drink that they lived for the next feast when it would be served.

Merek never saw the baron drink it or serve it to his guests, only to the guards.

In Merek's opinion, the distilled wine tasted bad and made those who drank it behave like children, picking fights and saying and doing foolish things. Besides that, they all got sick, not only that night but the next day too. Merek preferred the much milder ale and wine, and water from a fresh, cold spring was even better.

As he lingered, he let his mind dwell on Violet and how pretty she had looked as she picked out scarves. He'd listened to her chatter on with the seller, a woman who had complimented her, making Violet blush. She'd told the woman she was buying for her mother and grandmother, telling the woman their favorite colors, searching carefully through all the various scarves that Merek would have said looked all about the same.

He knew she must be dancing with Lord Eglisfeld at this

very moment, as the minstrels were playing some quick and merry music perfect for dancing, and he hated to admit it, but it made him jealous, wishing he was inside dancing with her. But he would not let this emotion get the better of him. Indeed, he would not allow this passing fancy for the maiden to control him. He'd seen a few men taken over by their obsession with a woman who did little besides bedevil them and make their life a misery.

His own father, for example. The woman he'd married after Merek's mother died had not only tried to turn him against his own children but actually had him murdered.

Merek would never allow that to happen to him. At least he knew Violet was not that kind of woman.

He remembered the last time he'd seen his brother Edwin and his sister, Delia, and her husband, Strachleigh. Edwin and Strachleigh had been eager to give him advice on choosing a spouse, even though he'd told them he was far from being ready to marry. After all, he was only twenty-one and had no permanent home or means of supporting a wife.

"Marry a kindhearted maiden who has sincere affection for you," Edwin had said.

"Marry a woman who is morally good and has a heart to care for the poor," Strachleigh had said.

He felt certain that Violet was indeed a morally good person, and she probably cared for the poor more than anyone he'd ever met—standing up for them against the baron and taking them food. But as far as whether she possessed sincere affection for him, he had no way of knowing.

Indeed, she might end up marrying Viscount Eglisfeld, especially if the baron had his way.

Merek's blood had boiled every time Eglisfeld touched Violet—when they were dancing, when he was handing her a cup of ale, when he held out his arm to her.

Merek didn't know the viscount personally, had never met him, but he knew his type. He was pompous and arrogant, cared for no one but himself, and felt, as a man of noble birth, he was entitled to mistreat the lowborn.

He was pacing slowly, making sure to keep an eye—and an ear—open to anyone who might be nearby. Someone left the castle, their dark red cloak catching the light of the moon. Now that person was coming toward him.

It was a woman, and he knew almost instantly that it was Violet.

His first instinct was to go to her, but he forced himself to wait in the shadows. It wouldn't be good for either of them if they were seen together.

"Are you all right?" he asked when she came closer.

"I am well. And you? Have your ribs healed?" She had taken off her hood and he could see her face in the moonlight.

"I am well enough."

"Does it still pain you?"

"I've gotten accustomed to the pain."

She winced.

"Is the baron still treating you well?"

"Yes, so far. I still believe he wants me to marry Lord Eglisfeld, but the viscount doesn't know anything about me, that I grew up on a farm, that the baron only just discovered my existence a few days ago. Not that any of that matters, because I am determined not to marry him, regardless."

A door creaked open, and a guard emerged from the castle.

Merek and Violet hurried to step farther into the shadows. They plastered themselves against the wall of the stable, and Violet pressed herself against his shoulder, her eyes wide.

The guard walked a few steps from the castle and stood on the grass of the courtyard. The man lifted his tunic, drew down his breeches, and started to relieve himself. Merek realized what he was doing, but too late to block Violet's view of him.

Violet turned her face away. He wanted to tell her that the guards weren't allowed to do that, that it was against the rules to urinate anywhere except the outhouses on the other side of the soldiers' barracks, but neither of them dared to make a sound.

Truthfully, it wasn't uncommon for men to relieve themselves on the side of the road, in plain view. Some hardly cared who saw them, so it probably wasn't the first time Violet had seen a man urinating. Still, he hated that he hadn't been able to shield her. She was a sweet, innocent maiden. Anyone could see that. No doubt Viscount Eglisfeld saw it, too, and that was why he wanted her for his wife.

With both the baron and the viscount pressuring her to marry, how could she escape their will? With Merek's help, that was how.

When the guard was finished, he turned and went back inside.

"He's gone now," Merek whispered. She was still hiding her

face against his shoulder, and he could smell the light fragrance of her hair, like flowers. He liked how soft she felt as she leaned against him, her hands resting against his upper arm as she lifted her face. Her eyes met his. They could hear the minstrels playing a lively dance tune.

He gazed at her exquisite moonlit face, wishing he could kiss her lips. If she continued to look at him like that and lean on him . . .

"Are you out here waiting for someone?" she asked in a whisper that sent a warm sensation through him.

He wasn't sure he liked being so vulnerable to her beauty and her sweet, innocent eyes, her hoarse whisper, and yet she made him feel alive and invincible, tenderhearted and protective. He had never felt this way before. He had avoided women, mostly, on principle and to keep himself from temptation. He didn't want to be like those men who took advantage of young maidens who would do anything they wanted after a few compliments and an hour or two of attention.

Merek despised men like that. He would never allow himself to do such things. But with Violet, everything was different. She made him want to conquer the world and hand it to her on a silver charger.

He very much feared he was losing his heart to this maiden, and in this moment he wasn't even sorry, especially if she felt the same for him.

"I'm waiting for Sir Willmer, but he has guard duty. It could be hours before he is able to come."

He watched her draw in a long breath, then let it out slowly.

The music coming from the castle made him long to dance with her again. "Shall we dance?"

She smiled and nodded. "I would like to dance with you."

The music was a bit slower now. They stayed in the shadow of the stable and locked arms, his left arm with her right arm, standing side by side. They moved in rhythm with the music, taking two steps to the left, then two steps to the right, then unlocking arms and spinning around each other, changing places, then locking arms again and stepping two steps to the left, two to the right, then spinning.

Violet stumbled, as if the last spin made her a bit dizzy. He slid an arm around her, steadying her. She just stood there gazing into his eyes, not pulling away.

"When you were in the dungeon, I was so worried about you," she whispered. "I wanted to tend your wounds and make sure you were all right."

His heart beat hard against his chest.

"I'm glad you are not seriously injured."

"You are very kind," he said, wondering why his words sounded so simple, almost childlike. Indeed, he didn't want to talk at all, only to stare into her eyes, drinking in the honest, tender look in their depths. Her violet eyes sparkled in the moonlight, and then he realized it was because there were tears swimming on the surface.

"Thank you for always helping me and watching over me, for being so brave and good." She blinked and the tears dissipated.

"It is my duty as a knight. But it is not only that. You, Violet, are worth protecting. You make me want to protect you."

Again, he felt as if his words sounded clumsy and inadequate. But the way she was gazing up at him, her hand pressed against his chest, reassured him.

Was it his imagination, or was she leaning closer? Her gaze dropped to his mouth. Her breathing was shallow, her lips slightly parted.

He put his other arm around her, very gently, and pulled her ever so slightly closer. She didn't protest but slid her other hand around his back.

His heart seemed to have moved to his throat now, and he couldn't help staring at her mouth, those full lips that seemed to beckon him. He leaned even closer. He shouldn't be doing this . . .

She leaned in the rest of the way and pressed her lips to his.

His insides melted as his arms tightened around her. He barely contained the moan that rose into his throat as her lips moved against his in an inexperienced way, as if she didn't quite know what to do.

He kissed her, his heart soaring out of his chest. She wanted him as much as he wanted her.

A strange, possessive feeling crashed over him like a wave of the sea. She was his now, and he would hold her forever.

TWENTY

VIOLET COULD HARDLY BELIEVE SHE WAS KISSING SIR
Merek—and he was kissing her back. It was a glorious feeling,
and terrifying at the same time. Was she in love with him? Was
he in love with her? Where would they go from here? But it felt
so good she couldn't stop, didn't want the kiss to ever end.

"Sir Merek?"

Violet jumped, pulling away, as Sir Merek with one motion
placed his body between hers and the voice.

"It's me, Sir Willmer." The whispered voice materialized into
Sir Willmer, coming out from behind the stable. "Who is with
you?"

Violet's cheeks were burning. She expected Sir Merek to
push her away, but he still had one arm firmly around her waist
as he stepped back, bringing his shoulder around as he stood
beside her.

"Sir Willmer. I didn't expect you for a few more hours."

"Everyone's duty is shorter tonight, so no one misses out on the feast."

She couldn't help reveling in the way Sir Merek was holding her so close to his side, the way he seemed a bit scattered, his breathing coming faster than normal. But her face was hot as she wondered what Sir Willmer must be thinking of them. Did they both think her shameless, coming out here in the dark to be alone with Sir Merek? But somehow she didn't really care. Sir Merek had kissed her! Her heart skipped a few beats as she could still feel the sensation of his lips on hers. Could it be that he loved her?

She should not get so caught up in these kinds of thoughts. He couldn't marry her.

And in that moment her heart crashed at her feet, her chest hollow.

"I should go," she whispered. "Before someone realizes I'm gone."

Sir Merek turned to face her, putting his back toward his friend. "Don't forget about the stump behind the stables, to send me word if you need anything."

"I won't forget." She took a step away from him.

"I will be watching out for you." He touched her cheek with the backs of his fingers, sending a delicious shiver across her shoulders.

"Fare well." *I love you.*

She turned and hurried away, feeling his gaze on her, entering the castle without looking back.

She quietly hurried up the steps of her tower and thankfully did not encounter anyone, as music was still coming from the Great Hall.

When she was in her room and had locked the door, her hands trembled as she took off her cloak and her dress and went to bed.

She lay awake a long time, alternately smiling and reliving the kiss and asking God if she had done something foolish.

The next morning Violet waited in her room for instructions, but none came. She broke her fast in her room and amused herself with reading a book she had taken from a bookshelf in the room adjacent to hers. She'd owned very few books in her life. All of hers were at her home and out of reach, and it was exciting to be able to read new books she'd never even heard of before.

Violet had always longed to learn all about the world, to read the romances of King Arthur and his knights, and to learn other languages, but hiring a tutor had seemed foolish to her father, who said he was fully capable of teaching her how to read and write English himself, and what else could she need to know?

Never would Violet have demanded more than her father deemed good. She was grateful just to be called their daughter and to have her basic needs provided. The fact that her father bought her a book once a year when he went to London made her feel as if God had been more gracious to her than to anyone she knew.

As she was reading, lying across her bed and thinking she

was passing a most pleasant day, she was startled by a knock on the door. She opened it to the baron.

"Good day," she said formally, still unsure what to call him.

"Violet. I have some excellent news for you."

She felt her stomach sink, dreading what he would say. "Yes? What news?"

"The viscount, Lord Eglisfeld, wishes to have you for his wife. He is willing to overlook the fact that you did not enjoy the privileges of a baron's daughter until recently, understanding the ambiguities of your birth, and will not hold that against you. You are to be wed in a week or so, whenever his mother is able to make the trip here."

Violet felt sick. Should she pretend to go along with him?

Never in her life had she pretended so much, and it gave her a sense of self-loathing.

"I do not think I want to marry the viscount. I have known him so little time and—"

"Did you think you had a choice in the matter? And why would you, a girl raised on a farm by people who were not your real family, think you were above marrying a viscount?" The baron's face was hard, his jaw set, his eyes cold. "You will marry him."

Violet's thoughts clouded as her breathing grew faster and shallower. How dare he treat her as if her feelings did not matter, as if she had no say in whom she married?

"I will not marry him."

"You will marry him, or I will have your grandmother and everyone you love executed."

Violet felt the blood drain from her face. *O God, please don't let him hurt Grandmother or Mother.*

She took a step back, lowering her head, trying to breathe through the feeling that she was about to faint. She prayed silently, *Help me, God.*

"You will murder my family if I don't marry the viscount?"

"I will."

"Then I will marry him." She felt defeated as she said the words, but she would not endanger those she loved for anything, not even to save herself from a marriage she didn't want.

"I am glad you are able to see reason. Sometimes a person must sacrifice what they want in the moment for something even better."

Was that supposed to be some kind of fatherly wisdom? "The way you sacrificed my mother?"

"I didn't sacrifice her; she ran away. She could have had everything, but she gave up a life of luxury, choosing to let you grow up in poverty and among strangers." The look on the baron's face brought to mind only one word: *savage.*

She could argue with him that she grew up among good people, people far better than him, people who taught her right from wrong and loved her. And love was better than any luxury. Love was everything.

But he wouldn't understand, and she refused to argue with him.

"I shall tell the viscount the good news. We will have a feast tomorrow to celebrate. Today we will go hunting, as I have acquired a new falconer. Have you ever hunted with falcons?"

She forced herself to answer his question. "I have never hunted at all." Only noblemen were allowed to hunt deer, and usually even they had to have permission from the king. She wouldn't tell him that everyone snared hares and other small animals, even though they were also disallowed for ordinary people.

"We will be mainly hunting deer, but if that proves unfruitful, we will see what the falcons can do."

Her heart was so heavy, she wasn't sure if she could stay on a horse, especially if they forced her to ride sidesaddle.

"I think you will enjoy hunting. Spirited young women ordinarily do." He gave her a small smile, as if he expected her to rejoice in his tepid compliment.

She would go hunting, she would pretend to acquiesce to his demands, but she would not simper and smile and pretend to be happy with what he no doubt considered to be the excellent life he was providing for her, taking her hunting like a noblewoman and marrying her off to a rich viscount.

"You will have to wear your old dress for hunting."

"Very well."

"Be ready in an hour. You will be sent for."

Violet bowed, lowering her head. When she looked up, the baron was gone.

She closed the door, as he had left it open, and went to her window. She stared out at the guards and servants going about their duties below her. Her gaze lingered on the place where she and Sir Merek had danced in the shadows and where they'd shared a kiss.

Would she ever kiss him again? What would he think when he discovered she'd agreed to marry Viscount Eglisfeld?

Sir Merek's kiss had been real. She'd felt the way he reacted when their lips touched, the tightening of his arms around her; his slight, quick intake of breath; the way he moved his lips against hers. There was nothing fake about it. So even if she never kissed him again, even if she had to marry Lord Eglisfeld, at least she would know what it was like to share a real kiss and to not pretend.

A tear slipped down her cheek and she swiped it away. She had to be strong, and if she had to marry Viscount Eglisfeld to save her grandmother and the rest of her family, then she would do it. But until then she would pray for God to make a way of escape.

A man was walking across the courtyard with a falcon perched on his gloved hand. He had a black patch over one eye. If she wasn't mistaken, it was Sir Merek.

Her heart leapt inside her at seeing him. Was Sir Merek the baron's new falconer?

She would have to be careful not to speak to him in a familiar way, but if he went on the hunt with them, at least she would get to see him. But then her cheeks heated at the thought of him seeing her with the viscount.

She pressed her hands to her cheeks. If only she could be alone with him and explain. But there seemed little chance of that.

Merek helped the master of hounds by putting the hunting dogs on leashes. Then he spent some time walking up and down the bailey with the falcon, talking to her and giving her commands.

Merek had managed to secure the position of falconer that very morning. The previous falconer had died a month ago, and no regular handler had been hired. Merek had experience training falcons. In fact, he'd been told he had a natural way with the birds, and as he had spent some time with this falcon before, helping with her care and training, it was the perfect way for him to get close to the castle and watch over Violet.

So far no one had recognized him or even stared hard at him. The eye patch, the beard, and his rough clothing seemed to be all he needed to go unnoticed.

The night before, when Sir Willmer had come upon Merek and Violet when they were kissing, he'd wanted to strangle his friend for causing their kiss to end prematurely. The way she looked at him, the affection in her eyes, was the same way he was feeling. He'd wondered if she might be enticed by the viscount's wealth and position into marrying him, but then he'd reminded himself that Violet was the last person to be swayed by such things. No one so intent on thwarting the baron's greed would choose a husband based on riches.

The only problem was that she might not be allowed to choose. The baron could force her to marry Viscount Eglisfeld, but Merek had made up his mind about Violet and he was not about to give her up. It was his nature to fight for what he wanted, and right now Violet needed someone to fight for her.

The men began to assemble, the hunting party consisting of the baron, Lord Eglisfeld, the viscount's beady-eyed uncle Lord Cosworth, who was a landowner in Derbyshire, and last of all, Violet, who came striding out to meet them.

The grooms already had the horses saddled and ready. If Violet noticed him, she did not let on, but spoke to the men as they greeted her.

Lord Eglisfeld seemed particularly eager. He even spoke into her ear, smiling as if he might try to kiss her as he bent his head toward her, but Violet only nodded, avoided eye contact with him, and sidestepped toward her horse.

Surprisingly, the viscount did not appear offended. He was still smiling as he helped Violet onto her horse.

At least the man was not being aggressive or belligerent with Violet. *If the baron forced her to marry him* . . . As soon as the thought went through his mind, his hand clenched into a fist. He would do whatever he needed to do to prevent her from having to wed this man.

There was no knowing how the viscount might treat her once they were married. Merek had known quite a few highborn men who abused their wives, or at least neglected and ignored them in favor of other more illicit company. Sometimes it was the wife who mistreated her husband, but he had seen it more the other way around. He also had seen enough of Violet's actions and decisions to know she had a good and honest heart.

Merek mounted his horse with the falcon still perched on his arm, and the master of hounds set out on foot with a few of the grooms who helped train the dogs, each holding two or three of the dogs' leashes. Meanwhile, Merek kept the falcon's head covered, and she hardly moved as she rode on Merek's wrist, which was protected from her sharp claws by a leather glove.

He found himself longing to set the bird free. Nothing should be controlled to the extent that this bird was, and Merek couldn't help but feel pity for her.

The dogs, on the other hand, couldn't seem to keep still in their eagerness to begin the hunt, barking and straining at the ropes tying them to their human.

He forced himself not to look too much in Violet's direction. She was riding sidesaddle, which was the custom for nobles, but often ladies dispensed with this unsafe way of riding. He happened to know that if a lady did not wear an underdress, which was narrower, the skirts of their outer gowns were generous enough to cover their legs. Therefore, most people did not object to a lady riding astraddle. But someone, probably the baron, must have insisted on it. Ridiculous in a hunt, when horses were forced to gallop at high speeds as they chased deer.

Of course, Merek could say nothing to protest it, but Lord Eglisfeld could. But instead of thinking of Violet's safety, he seemed full of himself, grinning and staring at Violet, paying no attention to where he was going, his poor horse forced to walk through thornbushes.

It wasn't long before the dogs caught the scent of something. The tracker said he wasn't sure if it was a boar or a deer, as he had seen signs of both.

They loosed the hounds, and off they went, baying, barking, and running with so much energy that the horses were hard-pressed to keep up with them.

The riders gave chase, with Violet bringing up the rear. He was glad she was not letting her horse go fast enough to keep pace with the others, partly because it was dangerous to go after a wild boar. With their tusks, they could gore the stoutest of men, and they were very aggressive. They often turned and charged straight toward those hunting them, fervid in their rage to kill their would-be killers.

The viscount slowed his horse and called to her, "They're leaving us!"

"I can't go any faster," Violet called back. "You go on ahead."

As the viscount drew nearer, he said with a slightly disgusted look, "No wonder. You're riding sidesaddle. You can't ride fast enough like that."

Merek said, "I can keep a watch over the lady if you want to catch up to the others."

He could see the conflicting emotions on the man's face. Finally, Lord Eglisfeld said, looking at Violet, "Do you mind if I go ahead? This man can make sure you don't get lost, and I'll come back and find you."

"Of course. Go and join the hunt."

The viscount turned his horse around and galloped away.

Some of the dog handlers were nearby, quite far behind their hounds, alternately running and walking after them as the underbrush allowed. But Violet slowed her horse so much that the men on foot soon outpaced them.

"It seems we are alone," she said, smiling rather shyly at him. Once she started talking, she spoke quickly, almost tripping over her words. "I'm glad, because I wanted to explain that the baron told me the viscount wants to marry me. I said I would not marry him, but the baron said if I didn't marry the viscount, he would execute my grandmother and mother and everyone I loved. I had to agree to marry him to save them."

By the time she finished speaking, their horses were walking side by side, quite close, and Merek's blood was boiling.

So the baron thought he could bully Violet into marrying the viscount? He had expected that from the baron, but it still raised his temperature.

Challenge accepted.

"When does he expect this marriage to take place?"

"When the viscount's mother arrives, in a week or so. I had to say yes. I couldn't let him hurt my family."

"You did the right thing. But don't worry. I will do whatever I have to do to stop it from taking place. Do you trust me?"

And as he gazed into her eyes, her expression changed from abject worry to profound gratitude, and he knew he would indeed do anything to save her and her family.

Twenty-One

Violet had been horrified at the thought that Lord Eglisfeld might say something in front of Sir Merek about her agreeing to be his wife before she had a chance to explain the circumstances to him. Now she felt almost weak with relief and gratefulness that Sir Merek not only wasn't angry but was pledging to stop the wedding.

Hope bloomed inside her. But just as quickly she realized the viscount or the baron could come riding back toward them at any moment. "It could be dangerous for you if anyone sees you talking to me," she said quietly. "I don't want to draw attention to you."

"I meant to tell you sooner, but I sent your letter to the king several days ago," he said without replying to her fears, "and I added my own letter confirming what you said."

"Thank you. I hope something comes of it, that the king will read it and act on our behalf."

"I've been pondering it, and I think you should wait until we have heard from the king before you endanger yourself again looking for the book."

"I don't think the baron would do anything to me."

"But he might do something to your grandmother or your mother."

"That is true." Her heart sank at the thought.

Violet became aware of crashing sounds, as of a large animal running through the underbrush, getting closer.

The baying of the hounds was also closer. Whatever the dogs were chasing, it was coming toward her and Sir Merek.

Merek guessed it was a wild boar just before it came into view, charging at great speed toward them, veering at the last moment so that it brushed against Violet's horse's leg. Had it gored the horse with its sharp tusks?

Her horse screamed and reared up on its hind legs, coming down hard, then kicking its back legs as if trying to kill the wild pig.

In the blink of an eye, Violet disappeared on the other side of her horse.

Merek dismounted so fast he upset the falcon as he raced around Violet's horse.

The wild boar had stopped and was facing them. He snorted, then charged straight toward Violet, who was lying on the ground, unmoving.

Merek snatched the hood off the falcon's head, sending her

flying into the air just as the wild boar lurched forward, running toward Violet's defenseless body.

Merek unsheathed his long knife.

The falcon screeched as she flew at the wild boar, getting a talon into the boar's eye before being slung off. But the falcon had slowed the boar, and Merek used the distraction to lunge forward and jump onto its back.

The boar squealed but kept running for Violet, who suddenly lifted her head and cried out.

Merek reached under the boar's neck and stabbed with the knife, jerking the blade back and up.

The animal's squeal ceased as it plowed headfirst into the ground, throwing Merek off.

Merek landed on his side and jumped to his feet, clutching the bloody knife. He held his blade at the ready, but the boar didn't move.

He turned and ran to Violet while the hunting party galloped up and surrounded them. "Are you hurt?"

She was sitting up, propped on one hand. "I hit my head, but I am well. Thank you." Her eyes were trained on his face.

He gently brushed a bit of dirt from her temple.

She reached up and touched his hand, then whispered, "You must go. Now."

"Violet!" the viscount shouted.

Merek backed away as the viscount dismounted and knelt in front of her.

As a servant, he was nearly invisible, but then the baron shouted, "Who killed this boar?"

Someone pointed at Merek. "The new falconer, my lord."

Merek ducked his head, but not before the baron fixed him with a keen eye.

"Thank you, falconer, for saving my daughter from the wild boar." The tone of the baron's voice sounded insincere.

"It was my duty, sir," Merek said, trying to disguise his voice and accent. He kept his head down.

"Won't you be my honored guest at the feast later today?"

"If you wish it." Merek bowed, praying his beard and eye patch and the unkempt condition of his hair would fool the baron. But the baron was paying a bit too much attention to him.

Out of the corner of his eye, he saw the viscount lifting Violet to her feet. He wanted to tell her she should be careful not to fall asleep for the next few hours. Men much hardier than she had succumbed to a head injury when they fell asleep too soon afterward and could not be awakened.

But the viscount was helping her onto her horse, promising her that they would ride slowly and urging her to ride astride. He even gave her his knife so she could split her underdress part of the way up.

At least the man had a knife and was thinking of her. But then Merek noticed the baron watching him, so he backed away and told the master of the hounds, "I'm going to look for my falcon. She should be nearby."

He hurried away, calling the falcon as he went, but his mind was on Violet. He wanted to go with her, to see her safely back and watch over her.

Unfortunately, he shouldn't go back to the castle, not until he had acquired a new disguise.

He looked over his shoulder to see the men preparing the dead boar to be carried home. How fortunate it was that he'd been able to save Violet from being attacked and gored by the animal. *Thank You, God.*

Merek had always been quick in his pride to take credit for the good things that happened. But he was realizing, more and more, that good things often happened by the grace of God. After all, how else was it that he happened to be on this hunt today? For that matter, how else had he ended up at Baron Dunham's castle, and how was it that he and Sir Willmer had been the ones sent to fetch Violet?

He thanked God for all these things. And he thanked God for Violet. He didn't want to imagine his life without her.

He was becoming as sentimental as his brothers Berenger and Gerard.

Or perhaps he was beginning to understand why a man might give up his homeland, as Gerard had done, or give up lands and a castle, as Berenger had done, so that he could marry the woman with whom he'd fallen in love.

Merek hid behind a tree and watched the baron walk over to the guards. He interrupted their work with the wild boar, as they were lashing it to a sapling pole. The baron said something in a low voice, and one man turned his head and the others cut their eyes in the direction Merek had just gone.

He waited, holding his breath. The men stopped what they were doing and started toward him.

Merek turned and hurried through the thickest part of the forest. He had only the slightest lead on them, and they would eventually catch up.

He came upon two ancient stacks of stones, with a long flat stone placed across the top like a table. On the other side of this was a recessed place in the side of the hill that Merek had discovered going to and from the little hovel where he'd been staying.

Merek ignored the pain in his ribs and dove under the raised rock. He slid on his hip a few feet down the hill. He dropped down under the rock outcropping and hid himself by pressing his back against the rocky wall, visible from only one angle, and only if the person looked directly at him.

He hated hiding there, waiting for them to pass him by. He'd rather confront them and fight, but he had no weapon other than his knife.

As soon as the sounds of their trampling through the underbrush faded in the distance, he came out of his hiding place and quickly headed toward his little hovel in the woods, trying to think of another way to disguise himself to get back into the castle.

Violet examined the bruise just above her eyebrow in the looking glass. But instead of remembering the fall, she remembered the way Sir Merek had brushed the dirt away, his fingers as gentle as the look on his face.

She sighed.

But the next moment she thought of how she was to marry

Lord Eglisfeld, and her stomach churned. She prayed Sir Merek would find a way to save her.

A knock came at her door. She hadn't locked it, so the door opened. Grandmother stood there with the baron beside her.

Violet rose, her eyes on her grandmother's face, trying to read her expression. She smiled, and Violet embraced her and urged her to come into her room.

Finally, she looked past her grandmother at the baron, who was still standing in the doorway. His eyes met hers and he said, "Just a reminder that you are marrying Viscount Eglisfeld." Then he closed the door and was gone.

Evil man.

"I'm so glad to see you," Violet said, squeezing her grandmother's hand.

"I know what he meant," Grandmother said, eyeing Violet with a sober look. "He told me that you must marry the viscount or he will kill your mother and me. But I don't want you to worry about that." Her grandmother shook her finger at Violet. "I know you and Sir Merek can escape, and I have lived my life. Besides that, he won't risk killing someone from a landholding family."

"Of course he would risk it." Violet felt the prickling heat in her face, hysterical words coming from a place of fear deep inside. "He is an evil man who does as he pleases. He's entitled, in his mind, to whatever he wants." She said these words in a loud whisper, her breathing coming faster with every word.

"Calm yourself, my dear." Grandmother laid a hand on her shoulder. "It does no one any good to worry and fret."

"I know, but I don't know how to stop." Violet felt the tears of outrage and frustration flood her eyes.

"You are just like me, Violet."

"How can you say that? You're so calm, and I'm so afraid."

"I was just the same as you until I learned three things: that most problems work themselves out, that most of what we worry about never comes to pass, and that God is trustworthy. He is working all things for our good even when we don't see it or understand it."

Violet wiped the tears away as quickly as they leaked out. *God, give me faith like my grandmother's, faith like a child's, faith as a mustard seed that nevertheless can move mountains.*

"It is difficult to see it now. Sometimes we have to wait a long time to see the good, I know." Grandmother patted Violet's shoulder.

"I do want to believe that everything will be well, but I cannot let the baron hurt you or Mother if I can prevent it."

Grandmother stared at the floor as if deep in thought. "When I was young, it was not so easy to trust God and not worry. I made mistakes, thinking I knew what was best for me. But I discovered that I could think I knew what was best and be very, very wrong."

"When? What happened?"

"When your grandfather asked to marry me, I didn't ask God if he was the right man for me. I was afraid it might be my best and last offer, because I was twenty-four—so very old, you know." She rolled her eyes. "So I said yes. I told myself your grandfather was an upright and decent man, and he said he loved me and that he would always care for me. He was very insistent that he was a good man." Grandmother shook her head. "Never trust a man who feels the need to constantly tell you that he is good. But I told God, 'See? He loves me, and I am ready to be married. He may not be exactly what I wanted, but he is good enough.'"

Grandmother sighed. "That is the one and only time I have ever told God that I knew better than He did. Trusting my wisdom instead of God's did not work out very well."

"I'm sorry Grandfather was not a very worthy husband."

"You probably heard your mother or me say that he hated farming and that he went traveling with some minstrels and troubadours once and we didn't see him for a year and a half. Your mother was twelve when he left."

"I remember being told that."

"Yes, well, we were just as well off when he wasn't here as when he was. He broke my heart too many times to count. Every time I thought he was going to do better, to care for me and for his children, he would disappear."

Grandmother's voice was very quiet now, her head hanging low. "He died when your mother was fifteen. He was walking along the road and just fell over dead, they say. I hardly mourned him. Instead, I thanked God that the consequences of my sin of not asking for God's leading, of thinking I knew what was best for me, had finally come to an end."

"I'm so sorry." Violet kept her arm around her grandmother and squeezed her hand. How had her grandmother learned anything good from such a horrible situation? From having a husband who treated her badly, who would not even work his own farm so he could provide for his family? "You did not deserve that."

"It was not a question of whether I deserved it as much as it was the natural consequence of my decision to marry a bad man."

"But you didn't know he was a bad man."

"No, I didn't. But I also didn't ask God if I should marry him. I was afraid God would say no, so I didn't ask."

God, may I never be afraid to ask You for wisdom.

"But I tell you all that to say that everything worked out well for me. My children and I were always fed. I was strong enough to work the farm myself, along with my two brothers, and your mother was always a hard worker as well. Have you ever seen her pick peas? She is so quick and efficient, and she can never stand to see a dirty dish. She always has to wash it. Yes, we always had enough, not only for ourselves but enough to share with others less fortunate than we were.

"I did go to work at the castle when my brothers took over the farmwork, and your mother was married by then. And that is what led to you becoming part of our family. So I am not sorry things happened the way they did. I wouldn't have missed knowing your birth mother, or being your grandmother, for anything."

"I am so grateful for you and for my mother and father for taking me in."

"You are a blessing to your mother. Never doubt that."

"I don't feel like a blessing, especially the last several days. My mother is tormented by worry for me, I have no doubt."

"Well, try not to fret too much about that." Grandmother squeezed her hand. "She needs to trust God. Perhaps this is how she will learn to release her fears."

Her grandmother was always so full of hope and trust. *God, help me be more like her.*

"And what is this bruise on your forehead?" Grandmother's expression clouded as she noticed the small scrape and purple bruise.

Violet told her about the hunt and how she fell from her horse and how Sir Merek saved her from the wild boar.

"That Sir Merek is very admirable." Grandmother smiled, her brows rising. "A very courageous and handsome knight."

Violet blushed, thinking about their kiss. She didn't regret kissing him, but she wasn't brave enough to talk about it. Besides, she didn't know if anything would come of it, as Sir Merek had never told her how he felt about her. She did like to think that his actions proved he cared.

She and her grandmother spent the rest of the afternoon and evening and the next day talking and eating the food that was brought to them. No one sent for them for the better part of two days.

In the late afternoon, as the sun was waning, a servant came and said, "The viscount's mother is arriving just now and there will be a feast tonight in the Great Hall. Your and your grandmother's presence are required."

Violet's stomach sank. She had agreed to marry the viscount when his mother was able to travel here. And now she was here.

TWENTY-TWO

THE NEXT DAY, WHEN MEREK MADE IT BACK TO THE CASTLE to check the tree stump behind the stable, he found a note from Sir Willmer.

The viscount's mother arrived today.

Merek clenched his fists. He would have to take whatever action was necessary to stop this wedding, and he would have to do it now.

Earlier he'd buried his eye patch in the ground and discarded his clothing, then put on some new clothes from the pile Sir Willmer had brought him. He'd also trimmed his short beard into a goatee and practiced speaking in a Welsh accent.

As soon as night began to fall, Merek pulled his hood—this one more of a huntsman's dull green, tight-fitting liripipe—down over his forehead and headed across the bailey toward the castle.

Would the baron have already forced Violet to marry the viscount? Well, if it wasn't consummated—a revolting thought—then it didn't count in the eyes of the Church. But either way, Merek would still rescue her.

Hopefully the wedding ceremony would not take place until the next morning. That would give Merek more time to stop the wedding, find the record book, and escape the castle with Violet.

He'd always loved a challenge, but Violet's life and family depended on his success in carrying out this quest. Determination flowed through his veins like liquid fire. He would save her—or die trying.

He heard the celebratory music as he neared the castle. No one was guarding the entrance, so he opened the door and went inside.

The tables were crowded with knights and guards eating and laughing and shouting, while the table on the dais was filled with well-dressed guests. Besides Violet and her grandmother, he saw an older woman who was most likely the viscount's mother.

The music died down and the baron stood, lifting his cup high in the air.

The room quieted.

"Give a cheer to Viscount Eglisfeld, who is to be married tomorrow morning to my daughter, Violet."

Merek felt a wave of relief. The crowd did as he asked, some stomping the floor as they lifted their cups and shouted their approval of the coming nuptials.

Merek searched the room for Sir Willmer but didn't see him. Never mind. He would look for the record book without him.

Merek tried to see Violet's face. He could only see her profile, but her grandmother looked well, although she didn't wear her usual smile. No doubt the baron had brought her grandmother to the castle to remind them both of what would happen if Violet refused to marry the viscount.

Merek quietly left the Great Hall and the sickening celebration of a marriage that would be forced on Violet for the baron's benefit. He probably wanted to secure the influence of the viscount with the king and to solidify his hold over his region.

Merek went toward the east tower where Violet had told him she found the clerk and the open record book.

It wasn't likely that the secret record book was there, but he might as well look. Besides, if he could get both the official record book as well as the secret one to show the king, the better his case against the baron would be.

He found the easternmost tower and went up, searching every room that wasn't locked. Fortunately no people were around; they were all either at the feast or helping with it. He had been through the first two floors when he discovered a locked door. It had a little round knob that slid from side to side in a metal lock mechanism with a keyhole.

He had not encountered anyone on the way here, neither in the halls nor on the stairs, so he went to the iron sconce on the wall where candles were placed and took hold of it and gave it a hard, swift tug. It gave way and came off in his hands, lit candle and all.

He took out the candle and used the iron sconce as a hammer, slamming it down on the door's little round knob. The knob broke off but the lock held fast, so he still could not open the door. He hit the metal slide once, twice, and it bent and broke and the door swung open.

He only hoped all the guards were at the feast in the Great Hall, unable to hear all the noise he had just made. Merek quickly went inside still holding the candle, which was the only light inside the dark room besides the bit of light coming through the window's murky glass panes.

An open ledger lay on the table near the window. It was pointless to try to peruse it now, though it was possible it was the official record book. Certainly the secret one was elsewhere, protected under lock and key.

He saw no other record books in the room, at least no open ones, so Merek closed it and stuffed it inside his tunic, holding it under his arm.

He left and headed back toward the tower where both the baron and Violet had their private rooms.

He was getting close to the Great Hall now. The music had stopped, but the guests were still milling about, laughing and talking. He hid inside a doorway and watched as people emerged through the Great Hall's open door.

He carefully checked each face. There. Sir Willmer was leaving, turning the opposite way from the rest of the crowd, coming toward Merek's hiding place.

Merek held his breath, waiting, and when Sir Willmer walked by, Merek reached out and grabbed his arm.

Sir Willmer raised his fist, then recognition dawned on his face. They both ducked into an open room and shut the door. They were inside the laundry and linens storage room.

"I found a record book, and I think it might be the official one," Merek said quietly as he showed him the book. "I need to hide it somewhere and then search for the real one."

He and Sir Willmer found a trunk that was filled with folded bed linens, hid the book under several layers, then closed the trunk.

Merek said, "I had thought to search the baron's bedroom, but he's probably on his way there now. I'll have to wait until he has time to fall asleep."

"That won't be long," Sir Willmer whispered. "One of the kitchen servants and I managed to sneak some sleep herbs into the last goblet of wine the baron drank."

"Sleep herbs?"

"An old healer woman sold them to me. I tested them out. Trust me, they work. The baron should fall asleep as soon as his head hits his pillow."

"Perfect." Merek's spirits lifted.

"And I stole the key to his bedchamber from the head house servant." Sir Willmer held up the iron key.

Merek shook his head, feeling his smile spreading across his face. "Let's go."

Violet and her grandmother had finally been allowed to leave the Great Hall and the feast.

Back in her room, Violet knelt by her bed in the dark while Grandmother slept. She alternately prayed silently and in barely audible whispers, pouring her heart out to the God who saves.

"God, I need You to show me what to do. I don't want to marry the viscount. I know very little about him, but what I do know makes me think it would be difficult to respect him, and I would very much like to be able to respect my husband. But that's not the biggest reason I don't want to marry Lord Eglisfeld."

Violet sighed. God already knew her thoughts; nothing was hidden from Him. But she felt it was helpful and good to speak the truth anyway.

"I don't want to marry Lord Eglisfeld because I love Sir Merek. He is straightforward and speaks his mind. He is a bit arrogant about his own abilities and knowledge, and he can be irritating, but he is a good man. He is not afraid to stand up to the baron. He's courageous and believes in doing what's right."

Violet tried to think of another man of her acquaintance who was so courageous, who would risk his own life to protect hers. Perhaps her father would have. But she knew her brother wouldn't, and she didn't believe Robert Mercer would either.

She loved Sir Merek. There was something about him, the way he seemed to understand what she was thinking when he looked into her eyes. And she hoped he felt the same about her, but it could be that he was only protecting her because it was the right thing to do, not because he loved her. Sir Willmer had pledged to protect her from harm as well and he hardly knew her. He seemed to be a good and noble man, like Sir Merek, but she didn't feel for him the way she did for Sir Merek.

What would it be like to be married to Sir Merek? They would have disagreements and would get angry with each other, she knew, but they would always forgive and resolve their conflicts. She could imagine them learning more and more about each other with time, falling more in love, helping each other, raising children together.

"God, forgive me for pondering things that may never be. Please show me what to do, for I do not want to endanger anyone for selfish reasons, especially the family who so generously took me in and provided for me."

Her grandmother had told her not to marry the viscount to save her or Violet's mother, but how could she live with herself if the baron harmed her family?

And what about Sir Merek? She had a bad feeling that the baron had recognized him after he saved her from the wild boar. He'd stayed behind and said something to the guards who were readying the animal to be carried back to the castle. Was he telling them to capture Sir Merek? Even now he might be locked in the dungeon. Or worse.

But she couldn't let herself think like that. Sir Merek would want her to believe in his strength and cunning to survive.

"God, only You know everything. Only You can help us. Show us where to find the record book and help us get it to King Richard so we can get his help in stopping the baron. Help us save the people from the baron's robbing and thievery. And please keep Sir Merek safe, God, wherever he is."

Since it seemed most likely that the baron would keep his secret record book close to him, she decided to go look in the baron's bedchamber. There were a dozen other places he could hide it, but she felt drawn to go look there. Though it was late, he might still be in the Great Hall. The men often stayed behind after the women retired.

But then she opened her door and realized that all was quiet. Had everyone left the feast and gone to bed? It was a risk she would have to take. She knew the baron's bedroom was on the floor directly below her own, so Violet put on her scarlet cloak over her white underdress, hoping it would help conceal her in the dark halls of the castle.

She listened to her grandmother's soft snores to reassure herself that she was sleeping soundly, then opened her door again as quietly as possible and slipped out into the corridor.

She didn't see anyone about, so she closed the door and went toward the stairs.

Violet started down, listening hard and straining her eyes in the darkness. She trod carefully, unable to see her feet or the steps, except when she was directly beside a window. She heard a few faint sounds from far below, probably servants working. But there was no sound from above.

She arrived at the floor below hers and saw the same set of doors that were on her own floor. She went and stood in front of the door that she believed was his bedchamber, a faint light shining at the crack at the bottom.

She heard some light scuffling noises, a grunt, then the light went out, leaving her feet once again in darkness.

She stood waiting. How long might it take the baron to go to sleep? Did she dare try to explore his other rooms now? Perhaps she should go back up to her room and wait until he'd had time to fall asleep.

Footsteps, very quiet, were coming up the stairs behind her.

Violet glanced around, but there was nowhere to hide. She ran as quietly as she could in her bare feet around to the other side of the round tower and tried to open the door to the solar, but it was locked. Plastering herself against the wall, she didn't move, praying for her breathing to slow down and not give her away.

Even though she could hardly see anything, she kept her eyes wide open, searching for any movement. A barely visible outline of a man came into view. He was coming toward her.

She did her best to calm her breathing, terrified her loud breaths would reveal her presence.

But there was something familiar about the stealthy way the man was moving, slowly coming closer and closer.

"Sir Merek?" she whispered.

"Violet?"

She reached out and touched his arm, moving away from the wall.

He pulled her toward him, then whispered in her ear, "Are you looking for the record book?"

"Yes," she whispered back.

She tried to read the look on his face. Despite the darkness, she was so close to him, and with the barest light coming from the window several feet away, she thought his expression was a bit hard and displeased. But if he could look for the book, why couldn't she? It was far less dangerous for her than for him. And she would have told him so if she weren't worried about someone hearing them.

Sir Merek reached for the door behind her and saw for himself that it was locked.

Violet motioned with her hand for him to follow her and moved noiselessly down the corridor, farther away from the baron's door. As she came to an open window with moonlight streaming in, Sir Merek stopped her with a hand on her shoulder, looking at her questioningly.

She whispered, "I was praying and the thought came to me that I should come to the baron's room and see if I could find the record book."

He leaned in and whispered in her hair, "I was doing the same. Sir Willmer stole the key to the baron's bedroom, and now Sir Willmer is watching the base of the tower to make sure no guards come up the stairs." His breath fanned her ear, sending a warm sensation down her neck and across her shoulders. She closed her eyes and thought of kissing him again.

When she opened her eyes, he was staring at her, a strange look on his face. Slowly, he reached up and lifted a lock of hair from her shoulder, letting his fingers slide through it.

As she had been ready for bed, her hair was unpinned and spread over her shoulders.

Twisting the lock of hair loosely through his fingers, he brushed her cheek with his thumb. "You are so beautiful," he said in a serious whisper. "Beautiful and brave, and any man would be fortunate indeed to marry you. But please don't marry the viscount tomorrow."

"I have no intention of . . . that is, I will try not to, but I must keep my grandmother and mother safe."

He stared intently into her eyes. She'd seen him looking fierce, so often serious and sober, always courageous, but now he had a tender look about his eyes and mouth, making her heart melt inside her.

Could it be that she, Violet, had inspired such tenderness in this noble knight?

A crease formed between his eyes and another on his forehead, in a look of pain. A small sound escaped his throat, a cross between a sigh and a groan, just before he leaned down and captured her lips with his, wrapping his arm around her lower back while his other hand, still tangled in her hair, cupped the back of her neck. He kissed her as insistently as their first kiss had been gentle and sweet. She held on and tried to memorize every heart-stopping moment.

He pulled away just as suddenly and looked as if he was about to speak. He kissed her cheek instead, his lips moving up to her temple, lingering against her skin. Then he hugged her tightly to his chest, burying his face in her hair. His arms quaked for a moment as he held her close.

Her heart soared at his fervency. How glorious to be held by Sir Merek, a man so noble and brave, so chivalrous and strong, to be kissed so passionately.

"Forgive me," he said, letting her go.

She stumbled backward at being released so suddenly. He took hold of her shoulders to steady her.

"Forgive me," he said again. "You looked so beautiful, and I was so grateful at seeing you alive and, well . . . I have no excuse."

Violet slid her arms around him and buried her face in his

chest. She couldn't bear it. It was too much happiness, too much joy, to have this powerful knight humbly asking her forgiveness, telling her she was beautiful. Sir Merek was too proud to be so vulnerable with her unless he felt as much as she did.

He held her gently, and she felt him lay his cheek against the top of her head.

After several moments, Violet sighed, and they each moved a tiny step back. He took her hand in his as she turned and started back around the curved corridor toward the baron's bedchamber door. She leaned toward Sir Merek, her lips quite close to his ear, and whispered, "He was awake a few minutes ago."

"It's all right," he whispered back, his breath on her ear sending delicious shivers across her shoulders. "He'll be asleep now."

Dizzy from the sensations spreading through her, Violet only nodded, trusting that Sir Merek knew what he was doing.

Sir Merek stuck the key in the keyhole. He worked with it for several moments, wriggling it, making a bit of noise as he did so. Finally, there was a *click* and the door opened.

The room was very dark. Sir Merek took hold of her hand as they went inside.

Twenty-Three

Merek had no right to kiss Violet—again. She was so comely, so strong and yet vulnerable, and when he could see in her eyes that she wanted to kiss him, too, he couldn't think of a good enough reason not to.

And though he wanted to send her back to the safety of her room, he knew her well enough to know that she wouldn't go without a fight.

He led her inside the dark room. "Wait here," he whispered and went toward the outline of a window, which he could just make out as his eyes adjusted. He bumped into something—a stool perhaps—but finally arrived at the window. He fumbled with the latch and managed to open the shutters, letting in a bit of moonlight. It was enough to see that they were in a sort of dressing room, sometimes called a wardrobe, which was rather bare for the private apartment of a baron.

"I thought this was the baron's bedchamber." Violet's whisper was barely audible. "But it must be that room," she said, pointing to another door.

Merek nodded. "We may as well look in here first."

Violet started rummaging around inside a trunk. Merek went to inspect a table and another trunk against the opposite wall. When they had finished searching the relatively bare room, Merek and Violet came together again and he whispered, "He's probably keeping it in his bedroom, under his bed, perhaps."

Violet nodded as Merek took her hand in his and rubbed the back of it with his thumb.

She closed her eyes, and the way she looked, he wondered if he'd died and gone to heaven, remembering their kiss. Was she doing the same? But he could not kiss her again, no matter how much he wanted to. They had to find the book and get out of here before they were caught.

Merek started toward the door that Violet thought led to the baron's bedroom.

"Be careful," she said.

She was so beautiful, with the pale moonlight glinting off her eyes. How delicate, how perfect her features were.

He stared at men all day every day whose faces and manners were often boorish, but he had seen his share of fair maidens, from servant girls to dukes' daughters, even foreign princesses and heiresses. But none of them compared to Violet's fierce beauty, at once delicate and determined. Her character made her more beautiful still.

"All will be well. But if you hear anything, or if the baron awakens, I want you to run back to your room and lock the door."

"But I can't leave you here."

"You can and you must. I have weapons to defend myself. I

am a knight. Do not worry about me. Promise me." He squeezed her shoulder.

"Very well, I promise."

"Good. Now stay behind me."

She didn't look as if she liked him telling her what to do, but she said nothing. Truly, if she were a man, Merek would befriend her and want to keep her as an ally. She would be someone he could trust and depend on to be chivalrous and noble and brave. But she was not a man, and he was glad she was a woman; he wanted to keep her even closer.

But he was getting distracted again. He pushed those thoughts away.

He tried the door to what they presumed was the baron's bedchamber. It opened easily, and Merek put his eye to the slightly open door and peeked inside.

He could see a bit of moonlight through the open window on the back wall, revealing the outlines of the objects in the room, including a bed with its head against the wall.

Merek pushed the door open enough for him to walk through. It made a slight creaking noise.

He froze and held his breath, his mind going to the long knife he had strapped to his outer thigh. He stared hard at the bed, watching for any movement.

The large canopied bed was just the kind you might expect to see in a baron's bedroom. The curtains were drawn back and fastened with cords at the posts to let the cooler night air in. As he watched and listened, Merek heard heavy breathing mixed with light snores.

His eyes fastened on a trunk that sat against the wall next to the bed. Could the record book be in there? There was another trunk against the wall nearest the door, but he guessed that the baron would want the book closer to him. And with that in mind, Merek wanted to look under his bed first, as there was just enough space underneath the heavy wooden bed for a flat metal strongbox.

Merek trod lightly, and he was halfway across the room when he realized Violet was right behind him. Hadn't he told her to wait for him? He was considering whether to risk whispering to her to go back when she went straight to the trunk near the door and opened it.

He ranted silently at her, but that was a waste of time. She reminded him of himself.

He went to the bed and silently knelt beside it, listening all the while for any sign that the baron was waking up. But his heavy breathing was proof that he was sleeping soundly. No doubt his sleep was made heavier by how much wine he had drunk, as well as the herbal concoction Sir Willmer had supplied.

Merek leaned down and stuck his arm under the bed, carefully feeling around. His hand came in contact with something long, and he soon realized it was a sword. He kept feeling around, but there was nothing else except spiderwebs.

He got up off the floor and looked back at Violet. She was still rummaging through the trunk. Merek walked around to the other side of the baron's bed and knelt down again, running his hand under the bed, feeling around until his hand touched something hard and smooth, like a metal box.

His heart beat harder as he took hold of it and pulled.

The ensuing scraping sound caused him to stop and wait to make sure the baron was still sleeping, then more carefully he slipped his fingers underneath the box and pulled it out noiselessly.

He tried to open it but it was locked. He put the box in his lap and used the key Sir Willmer had given him, but it did not work.

A man entered the room, startling Violet, causing her to drop the lid of the trunk she was searching through. It made a muffled sound as it hit something soft that must have been in the way. Otherwise it would have been much louder.

The man was the same height and build as Sir Willmer, but Merek couldn't see his face in the dark room so he wasn't sure.

The baron snuffled, as if waking up, as the man whispered something to Violet. Violet pointed toward Merek and then motioned frantically to him.

Merek slipped the key back in his pocket and stood up with the metal strongbox in his arms, hurrying to Violet, seeing with relief that it was Sir Willmer.

Sir Willmer motioned to them as he backed out of the door amid sounds from the bed that the baron was stirring, turning over in the bed, snuffling some more, then going silent.

Once they were in the adjacent room, Violet carefully closed the door to the baron's bedroom.

"Sir Goring is on his way here," Sir Willmer whispered. "A servant said he saw a strange man enter the castle. Sir Goring went to get another guard. He'll be here any minute."

Merek made sure to lock the door behind them as they hurried out of the room and then raced up the stairs behind Violet and Sir Willmer.

They could hear the guards' heavy footsteps and deep voices below them. Then Violet stopped at the next floor, and Merek and Sir Willmer followed her. She opened a door and motioned for them to come in, then closed the door behind them.

"You can hide in there," she whispered quickly, pointing to a wooden cabinet against the wall.

Merek glanced at her bed, seeing a gray-haired woman lying there—Violet's grandmother. Meanwhile, Sir Willmer had crossed the room and opened the door of the tall cupboard and climbed inside.

Merek stopped and turned to Violet. "Hiding is for cowards." It didn't sit well with him to be hiding so much.

"Please," Violet begged, clasping her hands in front of her. "You must. They will be here any moment."

He relented and stepped in beside Sir Willmer, letting her close them inside.

"Did you find the record book?" Sir Willmer whispered.

"I hope so. I found this strongbox under the baron's bed, but I couldn't get it open."

He didn't like this one bit. But the truth was, he had only a knife, and those guards would have swords. He'd still gladly fight, even outnumbered and without a sword, but he knew it was more prudent to hide.

He stood motionlessly waiting, wondering if he'd once again

stolen the secret record book. Would he be able to keep it this time and get it into the hands of King Richard?

He wondered if Violet was safe in her room. The urge to fight was almost overwhelming. Certainly, if the guards started to harass Violet, Merek would throw down the strongbox and come out slinging his knife.

Violet's heart was beating in her ears as she threw off her cloak and jumped into bed, scrambling to get her legs under the covers. They would know she had not been lying in bed, though, when they saw how hard she was breathing.

"What is the matter?" Grandmother said, waking up next to her and half sitting up.

"All is well," Violet whispered to her. "I heard some footsteps and voices, that's all."

"Why are you breathing so hard?" Grandmother said. "Are you sick?"

"No, no. All is well." She wanted to tell her grandmother what was happening, but it was probably safer for her if she didn't know.

Grandmother lay back against her pillow. "I hear them now," she whispered. "Who do you think it is, and what do you think they are doing this late at night?"

"We hardly care, as long as they don't come up to our room, eh?"

"If you say so, my dear," Grandmother mumbled, but she obviously suspected Violet knew more than she was telling.

"Just in case." Violet leapt out of bed and locked the door, then got back into bed and closed her eyes.

She listened to the muffled footsteps and voices, barely audible now. But moments later, someone knocked on her door.

Violet tried to sound sleepy. "Who is there?"

"Mrs. Cooper," the head house servant said.

Violet got up, threw her cloak back on over her underdress, and opened the door. "Yes? What time is it?" Violet kept her eyes half closed, noticing the guard behind Mrs. Cooper.

"It is after three o'clock," Mrs. Cooper said. "But the baron insists that I check on you. Are you well, Miss Violet?"

"I was asleep." She tried to look grumpy and rubbed her eyes with the heel of her hand.

"Of course, my dear, but the baron wishes a guard be allowed to search your room. You don't mind, do you?"

"My grandmother is asleep," Violet whispered. "Can you not come back in the morning?"

"I'm afraid the baron says we must."

"Very well, but I assure you, there is nothing to see but two women trying to sleep." Violet opened the door wide. "What are you searching for?"

"You have not seen a strange man, have you?" the guard asked.

"A man? No, of course not. Did you not observe that my door was locked? And I have been asleep. Please, can you go now? Tomorrow is my wedding day, and I desperately need to rest." Violet sniffed. "I get so weepy when I don't get enough sleep."

She let her voice rise in pitch. She wasn't even pretending as she started to cry.

"So you have seen no strange man?"

"No." Violet infused her voice with anger this time.

The guard made a point of sticking his head in the room and looking around. "Very well. Forgive us for disturbing you."

Violet pulled her red cloak closer about her neck but said nothing.

The guard and the house servant both bowed to her, and she shut the door and locked it again.

She went to the cupboard and opened the door. "They're gone," she whispered, "but I think you both should stay here for a while. They're still looking for 'a strange man' someone saw entering the castle."

"And they won't stop looking once the baron discovers this is missing," Sir Merek said, holding up the metal box.

Sir Willmer found Violet's hairpins and started working at the lock with them, bending one into a hook as he poked and prodded the lock.

"I see I cannot fall asleep around here," Grandmother said, sitting up and watching them from the bed, "or I will miss something important." She was actually smiling.

Finally, they heard a *click* and the box opened. Sir Merek lifted out a record book and immediately opened it.

"This has to be the one we were looking for." Violet couldn't hide her excitement. "Let me take the strongbox and put it back under the baron's bed."

"And I'll go get the other record book so we can compare the two," Sir Willmer said. He was already leaving before anyone could protest, opening Violet's bedroom door and looking out, then shutting it behind him.

"I'll go with you," Sir Merek said to Violet.

She tucked the record book under the covers in the bed with Grandmother and left with the box.

As soon as they opened the door, they heard voices below, including Baron Dunham yelling and cursing, his words slurred and angry. Violet shut the door and turned to Sir Merek. "You should hide."

"Perhaps the men will leave and we'll have our chance to put the box back," Merek said.

"They must have discovered it's missing. That's probably what the baron is yelling about."

Sir Merek let out an aggressive sigh. He knew she was right.

They were still discussing what to do when the door opened and Sir Willmer came in.

Violet locked the door, weak with gratitude that it was Sir Willmer and not someone else.

Sir Willmer reached under his shirt and pulled out another record book.

"Can you light a candle?" Sir Merek asked, looking up at her. "But don't take it near the window."

Violet hurried to light the candle in the candlestick by her bed, using an ember from the fireplace. Then she knelt beside Sir Merek and set the candle on the floor, but with their bodies blocking it so that the light wouldn't show under the door.

After comparing some dates and various numbers and notations, Sir Merek said, "We have what we need to prove to the king that the baron is taking unlawful taxes, that his men are robbing the people. It should be enough to at least get the king's attention."

Just then they heard voices outside Violet's door. Her heart jumped inside her.

"Hide!" she whispered urgently.

"You locked the door," Sir Merek said, not moving.

"Yes, but I'm sure the baron has a key. If he suspects—"

"I'm tired of hiding," Sir Merek growled. "I'm ready to fight this unjust, evil man and his followers."

"I agree. But we need to get these books to the king." Sir Willmer glanced anxiously at the window.

"You can't escape now," Violet said. "Wait until the commotion has died down a bit. Then you can sneak away."

Sir Merek's scowl deepened when she said "sneak away." He was sick of sneaking, too, apparently. But didn't he realize that if he tried to fight now, he'd be killed? He had no sword, and he and Sir Willmer were woefully outnumbered.

"You need to stay alive," Violet said, feeling her emotion rising, almost choking her. "Just stay alive and get these books to the king."

Sir Merek met her gaze and his expression softened. He reached out and brushed her cheek with his fingers. "Don't worry," he whispered.

His touch made tears sting her eyes. She couldn't *not* worry. But her throat was too constricted to allow her to speak as she fought back the tears.

Sir Willmer was staring at them, so Sir Merek let his hand drop, then blew out the candle.

The two knights went to the window and looked out. Violet followed suit.

A few guards were running toward the castle from the barracks. Sir Merek turned to Sir Willmer. "You can walk out of Violet's room, as long as no one sees, unless you think the baron suspects you."

"He doesn't, that I know of." Sir Willmer went to the door and listened. Then he came back over to Violet and Sir Merek. "But we need a plan."

As the two knights talked, Violet interrupted them. "Please don't forget that I'm supposed to wed the viscount in the morning. I need to get out of here before that happens." She couldn't marry one man when she was in love with another.

Sir Merek took hold of her arm. "We'll make a rope out of bedsheets or whatever we can find, and I will use it to go out the window with the record books. Sir Willmer will go out and create a distraction for Sir Goring and the guards."

"I'll tell the guards that a servant saw a strange man coming out of the eastern tower with a book under his arm, then ducking into a nearby room to hide," Sir Willmer said. "As soon as the guards are gone, I'll come and take you and your grandmother out of the castle before the guards can come back."

Sir Merek said, "I'll be waiting in the stable, and we'll take four horses and travel to London."

Violet nodded, relieved. She only hoped this plan worked.

TWENTY-FOUR

MEREK WATCHED SIR WILLMER SLIP OUT. VIOLET CLOSED the door noiselessly behind him just as dawn was breaking.

Merek climbed up to the window, holding on to the rope they had made from ripping her blanket into strips. It was tied to her bedpost, and he lowered himself down the outside of the tower. When he was several feet from the ground, he jumped. As he'd instructed, Violet untied the makeshift rope and tossed it down. He threw it behind a bush and hurried through the bailey with the two record books strapped to his sides.

Merek went to the stable and watched the door of the castle, waiting for Violet. She and her grandmother and Sir Willmer should be only minutes behind him. But the longer he waited, the tenser he grew, his hand tightening on the handle of his knife. The sun was getting closer and closer to the horizon, casting more and more light into the brightening sky.

Where were they?

Violet prayed silently as she watched Sir Merek lower himself down by the rope they had made, drop safely to the ground, then make it to the stable without being seen.

"Come, child. Sir Willmer will be back any moment now." Grandmother had gathered up their things and tied them into a bundle, with Violet's red cloak draped over her arm.

"Let me take that." Violet put the bundle under her arm, but when she tried to take the red cloak, her grandmother drew back.

"I will wear it. It's a chilly morning." She smiled as if they were on their way to the market.

Violet shook her head at her feisty grandmother.

"Come. Let us join your Sir Merek."

Violet opened her mouth to say he wasn't *her* Sir Merek, but instead she went to the door, listening for Sir Willmer. She didn't hear anything but left the door unlocked as they waited.

When some minutes had gone by, Violet's stomach twisted into a knot. "Something's wrong. He should have been here by now." She ran to the window and looked out. No one was outside. Sir Merek should be in the stable waiting for them, saddling the horses. But her heart sank more and more with each passing moment.

"We will go meet Sir Merek. Come." Violet opened the door and started out, with Grandmother just behind her, then heard footsteps coming up from the floor below.

She and Grandmother hurried back into her room and closed the door. Violet hid the bundle in the closet just as a knock came at the door. Then the door opened. It was the baron.

"You are up very early." The baron's eyes were red, with dark half-moons underneath. "Excited about your wedding, no doubt."

"Of course," Violet answered.

"You look as if you're going somewhere." He glared at her with cold eyes.

"I was about to go down and ask for breakfast. Grandmother and I are hungry."

"All you need do is pull the bell for the servant."

"I didn't want to disturb anyone so early in the morning." She forced herself not to think about her real motive and objective. She had to pretend nothing was amiss.

The baron took a step toward her, pointing his finger at her nose. "You will marry the viscount, and you will do so this morning." He turned to the guard behind him. "Go to Lord Eglisfeld's room and tell him that the wedding is to be in one hour." He turned back to Violet and said, "And I will wait with the bride until he comes."

Violet's stomach sank to her toes. How would she get out of here? Their plans were ruined.

If she tried to run, the baron would capture her. Perhaps she could beg the viscount to release her from their marriage agreement and even ask him to help her flee from her overbearing father. It seemed unlikely, but she had no other choice at this moment. Lord Eglisfeld did not seem to her to be very chivalrous or noble, but surely he wouldn't want to marry someone who didn't want to marry him.

God, please, please help us.

The baron motioned for two more guards to accompany him into Violet's room, then he shut the door.

"Violet needs to change her dress before the wedding," Grandmother stated in a matter-of-fact voice.

"This dress she is wearing is not suitable at all for a wedding, is it?" The baron was still glaring at Violet. He waved his hand at the guards. "Search the room."

The guards looked under her bed, then in the trunks against the walls, then searched the tall cupboard in the adjacent room.

Violet tried not to let her mind go to where they had hidden the strongbox, putting it inside the latrine that was connected to Violet's dressing room.

"Why was your door unlocked?" the baron asked her suddenly.

"I leave it unlocked most of the time. So many servants come in and out. Should I keep it locked? Am I not safe here?"

He seemed to be studying her, his cold, dead eyes going through her like an arrow. After a long silence, he finally spoke.

"Soon you will be married to Viscount Eglisfeld. Does that not please you? You should count yourself quite fortunate to be marrying a viscount."

"I count myself fortunate to have been raised by good people, to have a godly grandmother who loves me." And to have chivalrous and noble knights such as Sir Merek and Sir Willmer who cared about her and, most of all, cared about justice and protecting the poor from evil men intent on harming them for their own profit.

But of course she couldn't say any of that. If she hoped to

get out of this, she would have to force herself not to antagonize the baron.

"But I am giving you a chance for greatness, to have wealth, to see your children raised in luxury and prominence, children of a viscount. Or do you fancy someone else? A knight, perhaps?"

Did the baron know something about her and Sir Merek? Could he have been told about them? By whom? She supposed someone could have seen them kissing in the dark by the stable or talking by the merchants' tents in the market. And where was Sir Willmer? Why had he not come back for her and her grandmother?

O God, please help me.

There was a loud knock on the door. The baron opened it and found the viscount standing there, slightly out of breath.

"I was told the wedding is to be in an hour, but my mother . . . She will not like being awakened so early."

"Forgive us," the baron said with a sneaky smile. "Violet is so anxious to be married. She wanted to have the wedding as soon as possible."

Violet cleared her throat. "The truth is, I would greatly wish to have someone dress my hair for the occasion, and that will take at least two hours."

The viscount was looking from Violet to the baron and back again, his expression becoming more exasperated. He obviously had just gotten out of bed; his hair was uncombed, and he was not fully dressed, wearing only hose and a long shirt that was open at the throat. And she couldn't help wishing it was Sir Merek standing there, about to marry her.

"Baron?" The viscount put one hand on his hip while he held his other hand out, palm up. "I don't understand. Now the wedding is to be in two hours?"

"Women can be so fickle." The baron put a hand on Lord Eglisfeld's arm and turned him around, steering him toward the door. "Do you think your mother can be ready in two hours? We will meet in the chapel and . . ."

The baron's voice trailed off as he steered the viscount away. But unfortunately, the guards stayed in her room.

Sir Merek must be wondering what had happened to her. Had Sir Willmer been captured?

A sudden thought made her heart seize up. What if Sir Merek thought she had changed her mind and wanted to marry Lord Eglisfeld? Surely he wouldn't think that, but her breath was coming faster and her hands were shaking.

Footsteps were coming up the stairs. Moments later, the baron was back.

"I will send the servant to do your hair. You will be ready and in the chapel in two hours. Do you understand?"

Violet couldn't speak, so she nodded. She just had to pretend compliance and then she could figure out how to escape. She had to get to Sir Merek.

The baron motioned for the guards to go with him. He shut the door and Violet put her ear up to it.

"No one is to go in or out except the female servants . . . ready for the wedding . . . understand?"

So the guards would be standing outside her door. She had to find a way past them. She couldn't marry the viscount.

Merek hated inaction more than anything. But the plan was for Violet to come to him, and he had been waiting for what seemed like an hour. Had she been caught trying to leave? Had Sir Willmer not been able to create a distraction and get her out of there?

At least a dozen things could have gone wrong. And though he knew Violet was a capable woman, he couldn't stand there and do nothing.

He pulled his hood low over his forehead and went toward the back of the castle. He picked up an armload of firewood and carried it into the kitchen, dropping it in the box where the firewood was kept beside the oven and the giant fireplace that had to accommodate all the cauldrons needed to cook the food for the entire castle.

"Who are you?" a servant girl asked.

"John. I was hired to keep the firewood supplied and . . ."

She was already walking away, too busy to listen to his explanation. They were all frantically running to and fro, getting breakfast ready for the household, as well as preparing another feast, this time for the wedding.

Merek went back to the woodpile and picked up another small armload of wood. Then he passed through the kitchen and entered the castle, keeping his head down. And at the moment he still had both record books, the real one and the fake one, strapped to his middle.

Perhaps he should have taken the time to find a good hiding place for them outside the castle.

Two guards were standing at the bottom of the steps leading

up the tower to Violet's room. He passed by them and went toward the chapel.

Viscount Eglisfeld was standing outside the door speaking to an older woman, probably his mother. Merek took his time, walking slowly past them with his armload of wood, even though a servant bearing firewood would be out of place there.

"The wedding should take place in a few minutes. Just be patient," the viscount said in an irritable tone.

"I hope so. You know my leg pains me when I have to stand too long."

Merek passed by the mother and son and took a meandering route back to the corridor that led to the chapel. He slipped into an open door—an empty bedroom—close enough to the chapel that he could hear what the viscount and his mother were saying to each other.

"I will go and see what is taking her so long." The viscount walked past Merek's hiding spot, where he stood with a crack in the door just wide enough that he could see who was passing by.

The viscount called out, "There you are, Violet. I was just coming to look for you."

"She is here." The baron's voice was strident. "Let the wedding begin. The priest is in the chapel?"

"Lord Eglisfeld." Violet's voice sounded breathless.

Merek's heart stopped beating at hearing Violet say that man's name.

"Please forgive me," Violet went on, "but I don't wish to marry you."

Merek's heart started beating again.

"What do you mean?" Lord Eglisfeld had backed up a couple of steps and was now in Merek's view. He looked both shocked and slightly angry. "Your father wishes it. Why would you not want to marry me?"

"The very idea that this girl would not wish to marry my son," the viscount's mother said forcefully. "What is the matter with her? Is she soft in the head?"

"Violet." The baron's voice carried a stern warning. "Lord Eglisfeld, she is a spoiled child and is only testing me. It is her way of getting her revenge on me. She does wish to marry you, I assure you."

"No, I don't," Violet said from the corridor, just out of Merek's view.

"Excuse us, Lord Eglisfeld and my lady."

Merek heard a rustling sound and imagined the baron taking Violet by the arm and leading her away so that the viscount couldn't hear what he would say to her.

Merek stepped behind the door just as it opened and the baron brought Violet into the room where he was hiding.

Twenty-Five

Violet had no choice but to let the baron lead her by the arm. He took her into a room and closed the door.

The baron leaned in close, so close that his nose was almost touching hers.

"You think because you're my daughter that I won't kill you if you make me angry enough, but I will." His voice was a low snarl. "Your only purpose is to serve me, and if you refuse, I will have no further use for you. And I will kill your mother and grandmother in front of you first, unless you go now and beg the viscount for his forgiveness and tell him that you were only trying to spite me. You will tell him most emphatically that you do want to marry him, and you will marry him now, this very hour."

As if to prove his words, he pressed a knife point to her throat.

Violet held her breath as the knife point pricked her skin.

What was she to do? She couldn't let him harm her mother and grandmother. But at least the viscount knew she didn't want to marry him. He wouldn't force her to marry him, would he?

"I am willing to kill you," the baron said.

"And I am willing to kill you."

Violet gasped as Sir Merek appeared behind the baron.

The baron's face changed. He was still holding her arm in his viselike grip, but she took a step back, leaning away from him.

Sir Merek held a knife to the baron's side. In fact, it looked as if he had already sunk the point of the knife into his flesh.

The baron suddenly turned and slashed with his knife at Sir Merek's throat. Sir Merek ducked and the baron's knife sliced a red line across his forehead.

Violet screamed, unaware she had done it until the door opened and a guard stepped into the room.

The baron bent forward. His knife clattered on the floor just before he fell, slowly, first to his knees and then to his side. As he did, Sir Merek pulled his knife blade free from the baron's body.

A dark red stain bloomed on the baron's clothes high up on his side, almost under his arm.

"Kill them," the baron rasped to the guard.

The guard drew his sword but then stopped short, looking from Sir Merek, who held his knife pointed at the guard, to Violet and back again.

The viscount came into the room, nudging the guard aside. "What has happened? Violet? What happened here?"

"The baron is trying to force me to marry you so he can have more influence with the king. He's stealing from the people, taking unlawful taxes."

"But what happened to him? Violet!"

"This man saved me from the baron," she said, pointing to Sir Merek. "The baron was trying to kill me."

"You there," the viscount said, pointing to a guard in the hall. "Go find a healer, quickly, and the head house servant. Tell them the baron is wounded and needs attention."

The baron was gasping now, holding a hand to his side. The blood was flowing through his fingers, more blood than Violet had ever seen before. She felt so light-headed suddenly that she had to take deep breaths, her eyes closed.

When she opened them, the guards grabbed Sir Merek, and thankfully, he dropped his knife and did not put up a fight.

"Don't hurt him," Violet demanded, surprising herself with how vehemently she spoke. "He was only protecting me."

"The baron was trying to kill you?" Lord Eglisfeld scrunched his face, his mouth hanging open. "He would not try to kill his daughter. For shame, telling such a lie about your father, even as he is bleeding in front of you."

The baron was indeed still bleeding. He seemed to have lost consciousness, his eyes closed and his hand falling away from the wound and lying limply on the floor.

"Take him to his bed," the viscount instructed the guards.

Violet moved out of the way as they lifted him awkwardly and carried him out.

"Who is this man?" the viscount demanded, pointing at Sir Merek.

"He is the man who saved me from the baron."

"I don't believe you. How can you continue to say such a thing?" The viscount stared at her again, open-mouthed.

"It is the truth! The baron did not even know he had a daughter until a few days before you came. He cares nothing for me. He was only using me to get the king's favor through you."

The viscount's face looked pinched. "I thought you were such a sweet, comely maiden. I thought you would make me a good wife. Now I know not what to think of you." He looked at the guards, who were waiting for instruction. "Take this man to the dungeon and take the baron's daughter to her room and guard the entire floor. Don't let her leave. I shall make sure the baron is being properly cared for."

He gave Violet one last accusatory glance before turning to go.

The guards took Sir Merek away and then nudged her toward her room, though they did not take her by the arm or handle her roughly. And by the looks of the guards' expressions, none of them were particularly upset that the baron was severely injured, possibly even dying. Sir Goring, however, was not among them.

The viscount continued up the stairs of the tower while Violet and her grandmother were escorted to Violet's bedroom.

"What will happen to Sir Merek?" Violet whispered to Grandmother when they were alone.

"Perhaps your friend Sir Willmer will help him escape the dungeon."

"Yes, Sir Willmer . . ." Where was Sir Willmer?

In the meantime, Violet would beg the viscount to listen to

her. She would explain everything to him and tell him they had the evidence they needed to convince the king of the baron's wrongdoing. But Lord Eglisfeld was neither the brightest nor the noblest man. Perhaps she should consider that he might even be as evil as the baron.

Violet recalled the way the baron had crumpled to the floor, the ashen look on his face, the blood coming from his wound. So much blood. It reminded her of when her father killed a hog by slitting its throat, then hung it up to let the blood drain out.

She felt sick again.

But she was so grateful for Sir Merek. She could still feel the baron's knife pricking her skin. She had been afraid to swallow or even breathe with the knife at her throat.

Tears flooded her eyes, and she pressed her fingers to her lips to keep them from trembling.

"My poor girl." Grandmother pulled her into an embrace, letting her put her head on her shoulder. "Don't worry, child. All will be well."

Would all be well? Perhaps she shouldn't think of the worst that could happen, but somehow her mind always went there, to the worst possible outcome. But she would choose to believe as her grandmother instructed and she would not worry.

"Even if something bad happens," Grandmother went on in a soothing voice, "God is with us. He will be near, and we can trust that He hears our prayers."

Thank You, God. I believe that You will work all things together for our good. But doubt immediately assaulted her mind. There were so many bad things that could happen. And how was

Grandmother comforted by the thought that even if something bad happened, God was with them? *God, forgive me. I do believe. Help my unbelief.*

Merek could still smell the blood from the baron's wound, which had run down his knife handle onto Merek's hand. He was not sorry he had stabbed him. The baron had given him little choice but to defend himself.

Truthfully, it would be better for the people of the entire region if he died. *God, forgive me if it's a sin to think like that.*

He was a knight, and it was his purpose to right wrongs, to see that justice was served, and to protect the innocent. He was only doing his duty. Besides, Baron Dunham would have killed Violet and Merek, too, if he had not stabbed him.

The knife blade had gone quite deep, and he'd stabbed upward toward the heart. The amount of bleeding seemed to indicate he'd struck an important blood vein.

It was a sobering, even sickening thought that he had taken a man's life.

He sat on the bench in the dungeon staring at his hands. But at least Violet was safe and unhurt. *Thank You, God.*

He touched the back of his hand to the cut on his forehead. It was already crusted over, barely anything at all. But if he had not ducked, the baron would have sliced his throat.

That thought made him feel considerably better about injuring the baron.

And when he remembered how the baron had been holding

a knife to Violet's throat and threatening to kill her, telling her that even though she was his daughter, she was nothing to him, he felt better still.

If the viscount did as the law mandated, he would have to take Merek to the king to be tried in the king's court for murdering the baron if he died, since Merek was the son of an earl. Merek welcomed such an outcome since he needed to get to the king anyway.

It was possible the viscount would have Merek killed and marry Violet against her will, but he seemed too cowardly for such a bold undertaking. Even so, Violet was still in danger, and he needed to get out of this dungeon and escape to London with her.

How he was to escape this time was still as much a mystery as what had happened to Sir Willmer.

A knock came at Violet's door.

Violet opened it to Viscount Eglisfeld. He looked so grim, almost angry, that Violet didn't dare speak but waited for him to break the silence.

"Your father is dead. The healer said he likely bled to death."

Violet felt the weight of the ominous words. But she couldn't deny that it was a relief to know he could not retaliate against Sir Merek or her. She prayed silently, *Forgive me, God, if it is a sin, but I am thankful that he cannot hurt anyone now.*

"Do you have no tears for your father?"

"Father? He took advantage of the mother who birthed me,

threatened to kill my grandmother and mother if I did not marry you, and tried to kill me. He is not my father. My father, the man who cared and provided for me, died years ago. I shed many tears for him. But the baron . . . I only regret that he attacked Sir Merek, thereby bringing about his own death."

The viscount stared at her for a few moments, then said, "I am not sure if I believe you. But at least now I know the name of the man who murdered Baron Dunham. Sir Merek, did you say?"

Had she committed a terrible error?

"Tell me about this Sir Merek. Who is his family? Where is he from?"

She suddenly realized the viscount couldn't harm him because of his noble blood. "His brother is the Earl of Dericott. Since he is from a noble family, you cannot condemn him or carry out any kind of punishment against him."

"Then I shall take him to King Richard and let the king's court decide his fate."

"You should be thanking Sir Merek for saving Violet from the baron." Grandmother spoke up from behind Violet. "He is a good and chivalrous knight who cares about what is right."

"Perhaps he is and perhaps he isn't. It will be for the court to decide." The viscount looked smug, but then his expression changed as he focused on Violet again. He let out a deep sigh. "If I find that you had nothing to do with killing the baron, I might still be willing to marry you."

It suddenly occurred to Violet that if the king believed she was the baron's daughter, she might very well be granted owner-ship over all the baron's property—although she might not, since she was a woman. But if the king made her the heir, the viscount could very well gain it all if he married her.

"How magnanimous of you." Violet rolled her eyes.

"That sounded hostile . . . I do not understand you, Violet." He shook his head slowly, as if deeply disappointed in her. "I thought you were docile. Spirited, yes, but your attitude toward your own father shows a coldness I have rarely seen in a woman."

Violet was tempted to say something to prove just how hostile and cold she could be, but she refrained. After all, her fate and Sir Merek's were in his hands for the moment.

"May I at least visit Sir Merek to express my gratitude for his coming to my rescue?"

"No, you may not. He is in the dungeon. That is no place for a woman."

"And yet the baron had me and my grandmother locked in the dungeon."

"The baron would not have done such a thing."

"He most certainly did," Grandmother said. "If you don't believe us, ask his guards."

"I shall ask the guards," the viscount said in a sulky tone, reminding her of a child.

With that he left the room.

TWENTY-SIX

"IF SIR WILLMER CAN FREE SIR MEREK FROM THE DUN-
geon," Grandmother was saying softly, "I can distract the guards
long enough for you to get away."

Violet shook her head. "What would make you think of such
a thing? I do not want you to put yourself in danger."

"I may be an old woman, but I want to do something to help."

"I appreciate that, but . . ." Violet sighed. She loved her
grandmother so much. How fortunate she was that she'd been
able to grow up with such a wonderful woman to influence and
encourage her, especially when she thought of how she might
have grown up in this very castle with the baron. If her birth
mother had stayed here with him, Violet might have grown up
seeing her father mistreat her mother. She would have experienced his duplicity and deceit and inevitable abuse of her, his own
daughter. What kind of person would she have become?

Thank You, God, that my birth mother took me away from the baron.

"We shall see what happens," Violet told her grandmother. If for some reason the baron's men seemed intent on punishing Sir Merek for killing their master, she would try to rescue Sir Merek from the dungeon herself.

"I am so glad you have had Sir Willmer and Sir Merek to help you these last few weeks. Especially Sir Merek." Grandmother gave her a side glance, a secret smile on her lips.

If Violet hadn't been so worried about Merek being in the dungeon and Lord Eglisfeld's intentions, she might have giggled and told her grandmother everything.

"You are insinuating that I think more of Sir Merek than I should. I know he is a knight and the son of an earl, but—"

"I think only that Sir Merek looks at you with love in his eyes, and I hope the two of you will be wed someday. That is all." Grandmother folded her hands in her lap, as calm and unworried as she usually was.

Hearing her own thoughts expressed aloud by her grandmother was a bit unnerving.

Just then a servant came to the door bearing a tray of food. When she left, Violet realized there was no guard at her door.

Perhaps it was silly to even consider it, but Violet desperately wanted to go to the dungeon and see if Sir Merek was all right. And if there was no guard, why should she not? The stairs to the dungeon were not very far from the ground floor of her tower.

"Grandmother," she whispered, "will you be all right while I go down to the dungeon to see Sir Merek?"

"Of course, child. Don't worry about me. Just go. If you are able to get away, leave straight from the dungeon and go all the way to the king. No one will harm me. I am only an old woman." She smiled and winked.

"I don't expect to be able to set him free, as I don't have a key, but I thought I might as well go down there while there's no guard at the door."

"Yes, go on while you have a chance," she whispered urgently, then kissed Violet's cheek.

Violet kissed her grandmother's soft cheek and hurried out the door.

She carefully made her way down the stairs, but when she was nearly at the bottom, she stopped at the sight of a guard. At the same time, he looked up and met her gaze. It was Sir Willmer.

He looked around, then started up the stairs to meet her.

Merek opened his eyes. Where was he? Oh yes, the dungeon.

"Sir Merek?"

The urgent whisper made him jump up from the bench where he'd been sleeping. "Violet." He breathed her name as he saw her standing in front of his door.

"I found Sir Willmer." She was smiling as his friend came into view beside her.

He wasted no time but started working at the lock with a key. "I'm sorry I wasn't able to help Violet escape this morning. The baron started asking me questions about you, if I knew where you were, how long I'd known you, threatening to kill me if I knew something I wasn't telling him, and then he ordered me to search the barracks for your belongings."

"It is all right. I know you did your best," Merek said, realizing he'd come a long way from the time when he would have wondered if he could trust Sir Willmer. But if Sir Willmer was caught helping him escape the dungeon, it wouldn't be the baron who would have him killed. "What do you know of this Viscount Eglisfeld?"

"Very little. His guards don't seem especially loyal or in awe of him, but he also strikes me as a petty man. He might execute you just out of spite, then cover it up and deny it, especially if he suspects there is something between you and . . ." He let his sentence trail off, but Merek knew what he meant.

"I agree, and I don't want to put my head in a noose."

The lock suddenly gave the telltale *click* and swung open.

"Let's get you both out of here." Sir Willmer led the way toward the rough-hewn stone steps.

"You are coming with us, are you not?" Merek said to him as Violet slipped her arm through his.

Violet suddenly stopped. "I can't leave my grandmother. She's still in my room in the tower."

"Let me fetch her," Sir Willmer said. "Then we'll meet you at the stable."

They quickly made it up the dungeon steps, and despite the danger and uncertainty ahead, Merek reveled in the way Violet clung to his arm and pressed closely to his side on the narrow steps.

Sir Willmer opened the door at the top, looked cautiously around, then motioned for them to follow him.

They hurried toward the tower steps but heard footsteps almost immediately. They slipped into the nearest room, which happened to be where the servants were sorting and folding the clean linens. They stopped what they were doing and stared.

"Pardon us, my dears," Sir Willmer said with a charming smile.

The female servants smiled back. This was a side of him Merek had not seen before.

"We are only in need of a few moments of your time," Sir Willmer said. "Could you hide my friends under your laundry?"

One of the servants motioned Violet and Merek into the corner of the room. They sat on the floor, and she covered them with a sheet, then piled more on top of them.

Violet was facing Merek, quite close, and he formed a pocket of air with his arms, holding the sheets away from their faces. They both stayed perfectly still.

He could hear voices. More than one man had entered the room.

"We're looking for the baron's daughter." The voice was muffled because of the sheets over their heads, but Merek could make out the words.

"Haven't seen her," Sir Willmer said, "but I'll help you look. You lovely ladies haven't seen the baron's daughter, have you?"

"No, not today."

"No."

"No, Sir Willmer."

Merek could imagine the smiles on their faces when Willmer called them "lovely ladies." What a charmer. Luckily for Sir Willmer, he had never tried to turn that charm on Violet.

A few moments later, he felt a tap on his shoulder. "They're gone," a female voice said.

Merek threw off the linens and he and Violet stood up. All the guards had left, including Sir Willmer.

"Thank you for your help," Violet said quietly, nodding to each of the women in turn.

"Yes, thank you for hiding us. Hopefully we can return your kindness someday."

One woman looked doubtful but smiled anyway.

"We hope you are able to get away," one young woman said.

"I knew your mother," an older woman said, looking at Violet. "I hope the baron doesn't mistreat you."

Had they not heard about the baron's death? He and Violet exchanged a look.

"The baron has died," Violet explained quietly. "But all will be well if we can get away from the viscount. Thank you again."

The women gazed at each other with wide eyes, perhaps in disbelief.

Merek took hold of her hand and went to the door. He listened, and when he didn't hear anything, he opened the door.

They slipped out into the corridor and started forward, but once again he heard footsteps coming their way. He ducked into another room, but this one was empty. He waited for the footsteps to go by, then went out again. They made it nearly to the other side of the castle by ducking into empty rooms, avoiding the guards. It seemed a miracle that they hadn't been seen. And the whole time Violet kept hold of his hand, sometimes also holding on to his arm with her other hand.

They neared the side door of the castle closest to the stable. Up ahead and standing inside a small alcove against the wall was Violet's grandmother.

Violet gasped when she saw her. But her grandmother suddenly unfurled the red cloak Merek had seen Violet wear many times and put it on.

Once again, they heard footsteps. Violet's grandmother smiled, winked at Merek and Violet as she threw the hood of the cloak over her head, and hurried toward the sound of the footsteps.

"She's leading the guards away from us," Violet said in a horrified whisper.

Merek and Violet moved forward just in time to see Violet's grandmother open the door and rush out, the guards a dozen or so steps behind her.

"Stop!" a guard shouted.

When Merek reached the door, the guards were chasing the red cloak as the old woman ran in the opposite direction from the stable.

He pulled Violet by the hand toward the stable. She made a strangled sound but kept going, all the while looking over her shoulder at her grandmother.

They soon reached the stable, going from late-day sunshine into the dimly lit horse barn, but Merek knew his way around and went straight to the horse Violet had been riding. He led the horse out, then let Violet take charge of saddling her while he went to get his own horse.

He wondered where all the stable boys were but was grateful they were alone and would be able to get away unnoticed.

By the time they had saddled their horses and Merek had helped Violet to mount, only a few minutes had passed. He untied the strap that had been holding the record books to his body, pulled them out of his shirt, and handed them to Violet.

"Take these to the king. I will catch up to you if I'm able."

"What? No! Get on your horse."

"I need to make sure your grandmother is safe first."

She bit her lip, a look of torment on her face.

"It will be all right. You need to get those record books to the king."

When they were near the doorway to the stable, he had an uneasy feeling. All was quiet and there was no one in view. He moved cautiously, approaching the doorway with Violet and her horse just behind him. As he stepped out, something slammed into the side of his head.

Merek turned to face the assault, but he was hit from the other side and knocked to the ground.

Violet screamed. At least half a dozen guards wearing the viscount's colors were all around them. They grabbed Violet and pulled her off her horse.

The viscount's men held Merek down with a knee in his back, quickly tying his hands behind him.

"If you hurt her, I'll kill you," Merek said, straining but unable to see what they were doing to Violet. "I'll kill you, I tell you." He could hardly see for the rage clouding his vision. He struggled, but whoever was holding him down was too heavy, and with his hands tied, he could do little besides rage internally.

God, help her.

Twenty-Seven

Violet screamed as a guard struck Sir Merek's head with the handle of a sword, knocking him to the ground.

Violet tried to get her horse to charge into the guards to get them away from Sir Merek. She kicked at the man who had hit Sir Merek, but another guard grabbed her and pulled her off the horse.

As she fell, she dropped the record books on the ground. A guard grabbed her arms and held them behind her before she could pick them up. She had to get those books!

"Violet. You disappoint me." The viscount was walking toward her.

"Let us go. We have done nothing wrong." Violet longed to choke him as she struggled to break free from the guard.

Her heart ached to protect Sir Merek, to demand that the viscount not harm him, but her thoughts were also on her grandmother. "Where is my grandmother? You had better not have harmed her."

"You are hardly in a position to make demands." Lord Eglisfeld looked at her with raised brows and a feigned expression of pity.

"Where is she?"

"What was she doing wearing your scarlet cloak? Was she trying to lead my men away so you and this murderer could escape justice?"

"My grandmother is a free woman and does as she sees fit. And Sir Merek is no murderer. He is a knight who was defending me and himself from the baron."

"I don't know whether to believe anything you say." Lord Eglisfeld's bottom lip actually quivered. Was he trying to make her pity him? "I wanted to marry you, Violet. Now I wonder if you would murder me in my sleep."

Violet rolled her eyes heavenward. The man was ridiculous. But then she remembered the record books. Those books were their best hope of saving themselves.

"I have proof. Look." She turned her head and saw them on the dirt. *Thank You, God.*

Sir Merek was watching her while the guards hauled him to his feet, then started binding his hands behind his back. Blood was once again oozing from a wound to his head. She silently cried out to God to protect him. In the meantime, she had to keep a clear head and do her best to get the viscount to see reason.

"Those two record books there. See? We were taking

them to the king to prove that the baron was stealing from the people. He was keeping one book for the king's stewards and the other one is the true one. It shows how much money he was taking."

"You are so quick to judge and condemn your own father." The viscount shook his head slowly at her.

"No, it is not like that." How frustrating to be so misunderstood by this man! The Holy Writ said not to judge or you would be judged by the same measure. Violet tried to adhere to that. "I am not judging the baron. I am trying to defend my people from him. He was harming them, taking what they needed to survive, what was unlawful for him to take."

Viscount Eglisfeld raised his brows at her.

Why did she feel like she was talking to a boulder?

"If you will just look at the books, you will see that what I am saying is true."

He sighed. "Sir Goring has suggested executing you and Sir Merek now, along with your friend, Sir Willmer, who was seen helping you free Sir Merek."

She looked back at Sir Merek. He was still several yards away, the guards standing around him, holding on to him. Was he badly hurt? His silence was worrisome.

Sir Goring was standing at the viscount's side, glaring, his cold, dead eyes reminding her of Baron Dunham's.

Then she caught sight of the guards pushing and shoving a man whose face was bloody, his hands bound behind his back. It was Sir Willmer.

"How dare you let your guards abuse an honest knight

like Sir Willmer. You will answer to the king for your guards' crimes. And you cannot lawfully execute us without a trial in the king's court. I am the daughter of a baron, Sir Merek is the son of an earl, and Sir Willmer—"

"I won't have you executed, so calm down." The viscount frowned. "I know the law as well as you do. But I must say that this visit here has ended in great disappointment."

The viscount was now confirming that her instincts about him were correct. He was a petty, ridiculous man, and being married to him would have been dreadful and demoralizing. She felt sorry for whoever did marry him.

"The baron was my friend," he went on. "He was even like a second father to me."

How could anyone see the baron as either a friend or a father? Either the viscount was lying or he had felt a sort of kinship with the man because their natures were so similar.

A third possibility was that the viscount was just very gullible and hadn't spent enough time with the baron to know his true nature.

She could see he was not inclined to do anything for her, so she tried a different tactic.

"Forgive me for seeming unfeeling toward the baron. I am horrified that he came to such a terrible end. I am sorry it had to happen that way, but you saw the baron's knife on the floor after he fell. You can see even now where he pricked the skin on my neck." She lifted her head to show him. "If Sir Merek could have avoided killing him, he certainly would have, but he had to protect me. I am very sorry that you have lost your friend, but just as you had feelings for the baron, you must have had feelings for me as well. Please, allow me to defend myself. Allow me to take those record books to the king."

"I have said I will not execute you." He sounded miffed and let out an exaggerated sigh. Lord Eglisfeld nodded to a guard. "Go and pick up those books and bring them to me."

The guard did so, handing them to the viscount. He looked disgusted at the dirt covering them and shook them off.

"I am a fair and just person," he said with a haughty look. "I always do what is right. I shall take these books to the king as your only evidence to support your claims and let him determine the truth."

"I thank you," Violet said. "And if you allow your guards to harm Sir Merek or Sir Willmer further, I do not think the king will take it lightly. He may punish you when he sees them looking as if they've been mistreated."

The viscount's expression shifted a couple of times before he finally snapped his fingers and said to his guards, "Take Sir Merek and Sir Willmer to the dungeon, but see that no harm comes to them. I want them fit to see the king when we arrive."

He turned back to Violet. "What am I to do with you and your grandmother? I do not trust you, and so I'm afraid you shall have to spend the night in the dungeon."

Violet said nothing, but she could have told him that she didn't mind. After all, she'd be closer to Sir Merek, and there were much better men in the dungeon than in the castle above it.

Violet hugged her grandmother. "Thank you for trying to help us."

Grandmother sat on the bench in the same cell where they'd been kept before. She was still wearing Violet's cloak.

"I will fix it for you," Grandmother said, looking at the tear. The guard had ripped it, thinking she was Violet, when he caught hold of it and yanked her back.

Violet hugged her grandmother again. "I'm not worried about the cloak, only about you."

Sir Merek and Sir Willmer were in two cells nearby. Thankfully, their spirits were high. Sir Willmer even sang a song and laughed, as if the beating the guards had given him had brought out his gregarious side. Sometimes Violet didn't understand men.

The next day the guards came and took them out. Violet was placed on a horse, her grandmother held by a guard next to her. What was going to happen to her? Would she be going with them to see the king?

When the viscount came out of the castle, all his servants were with him. "We are starting on our trip to London," the viscount said to her with a sour look.

Sir Willmer and Sir Merek were also being brought out, their hands bound, but with jaunty looks on their faces. Sir Willmer, thankfully, did not look the worse for his beating. He'd even been given water to wash the blood from his face, and though

Sir Merek had appeared a bit dazed after the blow he'd suffered, today he showed no signs of it.

Her eyes drank in the sight of Sir Merek. He still had the scratch on his forehead from the baron's knife, which was a good thing since it would help to prove the baron had been trying to kill them. She also saw the bruise above his eye where the guard had struck him. His eyes met hers and he gave her a slight smile, as if to say, "All will be well."

The two knights were on their horses, each man's hands tied in front of him to the pommel of his saddle.

Violet was thankful her hands had not been tied, but she was also a little offended that they didn't see her as a threat or think she posed an escape risk.

Her grandmother was still standing with a guard, so Violet looked imploringly at the viscount and said, "Please don't hurt my grandmother."

"She is free to go. I assume she can get herself home." The viscount frowned.

Violet let out a breath of relief. *Thank You, God.*

Grandmother lifted her chin. "Of course I can." She winked at Violet, smiled, and said, looking from Violet to Sir Merek, "I shall be happily awaiting your triumphant return."

They all started walking toward the castle gate, and Violet said, "I pray you get home safely, and please tell Mother that we are all well and that I shall be home soon."

"Of course, my dear."

Outside the castle gate, they turned in opposite directions and bid each other fare well.

The journey to London was long and tiring. Worst of all, she never had an opportunity to speak to Sir Merek privately. She was thankful he seemed perfectly calm, surprising her when he didn't argue or try to fight the guards.

The viscount spoke to her occasionally. His conversation was often annoying, though.

It was Sir Merek she wanted to speak to. How she wished they could be alone together, even for a few minutes. But she had to content herself with praying for him and praying for favor with the king.

She kept her hope strong by thanking God for what He had done for them, for His continuous protection, and for what He was going to do.

Merek was glad when he saw the White Tower of the Tower of London castle compound in the distance. He only hoped the viscount had sent someone ahead to tell the king they were coming.

He kept a close eye on Violet. The viscount conversed with her, but thankfully he was being neither aggressive nor amorous toward her. And he saw Violet many times turn her head away from the viscount with a look of mild disgust.

Merek and Sir Willmer were taken to a cell in the White Tower. He didn't know how long they would be there, nor where they'd taken Violet, and that gnawed at him. He was surprised when, the next morning, the guards let them out of their cells, then allowed them to bathe and put on fresh clothes. Soon someone came and told them they were being taken to see the king.

Before he knew it, he was being ushered into a large open room. It was not the same room where he and his brothers had been tried, and there were not dozens of courtiers around, all talking and milling about. Even the king's advisors were not there. Only King Richard was present, sitting on a large throne at the other end of the room, with a few guards around him.

Violet was led in and his heart lifted at seeing her safe and unharmed, and the way she looked at him made him wish he could kiss her.

She was led to stand beside him and Sir Willmer, while Viscount Eglisfeld and Sir Goring stood to one side, looking on.

The sight of those two men sent heat into his face. He was being falsely accused all over again, just like five years ago, and he wanted to demand justice and call down holy fire on his accusers. He forced himself to say a quick, silent prayer instead.

"Viscount Eglisfeld," the king said without preamble, "I suppose you have an explanation for why two of my knights and this noblewoman are standing before me after spending the night imprisoned in the White Tower."

"Yes, Your Grace," the viscount said, bowing to the king. "I shall explain the whole of the affair." And he set about telling how Baron Dunham had pledged his daughter, Violet, in marriage to the viscount, but she had refused him. When the baron had taken her into a room to speak privately with her, the baron was stabbed and subsequently died. His guards had found the baron bleeding on the floor, with Violet and Sir Merek standing over him.

"So Baron Dunham is dead?"

"Yes, Your Grace, I regret to tell you that he is."

The king turned his attention toward Merek, Sir Willmer, and Violet.

"Is this true?" the king asked. "Did it happen as the viscount said?"

Violet and Sir Willmer both looked to Merek, so he answered. "Yes, Your Grace. But the baron was holding a knife to Violet's throat. When I tried to protect her, he went to slash me across the neck, but I ducked. As you can see, he cut me across my forehead."

"And then you stabbed him?"

"Yes, Your Grace."

"Your Grace, if I may," Violet said. Her voice shook just a bit, the only sign that she was anxious about having to talk to the king of England.

"Violet, is it? I have been told that you are from the village of Burwelle and that you recently discovered that Baron Dunham was your father. Is that correct?"

"Yes, Your Grace. That is all true."

"You may speak."

"I have the evidence to prove that Baron Dunham was taking money unlawfully from his people. Lord Eglisfeld is holding the baron's record books, which will prove what I say is true."

The king said, "Bring me the books."

The king waved a hand, and a guard took them from the viscount and gave them to the king.

"Those are two record books for the same time period. One is the baron's official book he would have shown to you or to your representative, and the other is an accounting of all the monies he was taking from the people, far above what he was lawfully allowed to take."

Violet looked so brave and strong. If she loved him, he'd think himself the most fortunate man in the world.

The king took the books and opened them side by side in his lap. He bent over them while everyone else was quiet. Hardly a sound was heard besides the king turning pages or mumbling under his breath.

A few minutes went by before the king lifted his head. "Thank you for providing these." He nodded to Violet. "I also received your letter. And I am very gratified that you were able to find two good knights to help you in this matter." He nodded to Merek and Sir Willmer. "Sir Merek of Dericott, I am pleased to see you, though your integrity has yet again landed you in trouble."

"So it seems, Your Grace." Merek felt the tension flow from his limbs. *Thank You, God.*

"You and your friend—Sir Willmer, is it?—seem to have taken care of the matter with very little trouble to myself. I am grateful to you both. And I wish to express my gratitude by granting you a reward. I am open to suggestions of what you think might be appropriate. But first, this young lady, Violet, as the only heir of Baron Dunham, should inherit all his property and his title and become Baroness Dunham. I believe, from her letter and the courage she has shown, she shall be a much more noble and righteous leader for the people of the region. What say you?"

Violet was smiling quite broadly now. "I say thank you, Your Grace. I am very grateful, and I shall do my utmost for my people."

"And you, Sir Merek? What may I do for you?"

"I would be most humbled and grateful to be allowed to marry the baroness, if she will accept me."

The viscount made a sound like he had swallowed his tongue, then coughed.

"Well, well." The king was ignoring the viscount, still focused on Merek, and he smiled for the first time. Then he looked at Violet. "And how do you wish to respond to Sir Merek's proposal, Baroness?"

"I say yes. If it pleases the king, I am very happy to marry Sir Merek." She smiled at Merek, and he was sure he would remember this moment for the rest of his life.

"It is settled, then. But I should like to bestow on Sir Merek a new title as well. You shall be a viscount. But what shall be your name? Perhaps the name of a village near the castle."

"Burwelle?" Violet's village was the first name that came to his mind.

"Viscount Burwelle. That is very English-sounding, is it not? Does it suit you, Sir Merek?"

"It suits me very well." Merek hardly cared what he was called, as long as he was marrying Violet and she was happy. Although he had to admit, he liked the idea of having a title.

The king turned to Sir Willmer. "You have served the viscount and his soon-to-be bride very well, a credit to your king, your country, and your knighthood. What may I do for you?"

"If it pleases the king," Sir Willmer said, "I should very much like an estate of my own near my mother's family's ancestral home, Eldwick Manor. Since my uncle died a year ago without an heir, the house has been taken over by a group of outlaws, and his villeins and the people of the region have been harassed and mistreated."

"Say no more. The house and the land are yours, whatever belonged to your uncle. And I shall create for you a barony. You shall be Baron Eldwick. Does that suit?"

"Yes, Your Grace. You are most gracious and generous."

"As for you . . ." King Richard turned to Viscount Eglisfeld. "I hope you can make amends to Baroness Dunham, the Viscount Burwelle, and Baron Eldwick for treating them so ill, binding their hands and taking them prisoner and disbelieving their good word."

Viscount Eglisfeld's cheeks went pale, and he cleared his throat, looking down.

"No amends are necessary," Merek said, "as long as Viscount Eglisfeld agrees to always treat everyone fairly."

Eglisfeld's face was now as red as a November sunset, but he said nothing.

"Lord Eglisfeld?" the king prompted.

"Yes, sir, yes, of course, Your Grace."

"As for you, Sir Goring, there is a mention in Sir Merek— Lord Burwelle's letter of you killing innocent guards and others on Baron Dunham's behalf. Therefore, I shall imprison you to give time to allow the family members of the people you killed, as well as any witnesses, to come forward and accuse you in court. If no one comes forward, you shall be released in six months' time." He motioned to his guards, who went forward and took the red-faced Sir Goring from the room.

The king, looking wise and in control, said, "You may go, Lord Eglisfeld."

"Thank you, Your Grace." Eglisfeld backed out of the room, bowing as he went.

"And I hope you three will stay and be my guests tonight. We will have a feast and I shall announce your new titles."

"Yes, of course," they all said.

Merek was gratified that the king was inviting them to be his guests, but even more pleasing was the way Violet was looking at him and moving closer to him.

It was a good day indeed. Not only was he not being beheaded, but he was now a viscount and soon would be the husband of the most beautiful, courageous, exciting woman in England.

At the feast that night, the king said to Merek and Violet, "You will want to have a wedding in your village surrounded by your family, I assume."

Merek nodded and Violet smiled.

"But I want to honor the Raynsford family in a special way for all the good that you have done for England, for exposing injustice and standing up to the evil in the world. So before you have your family wedding celebration, and even though the banns have not been cried, I should very much like for you to do me the honor of getting married tomorrow in the chapel here."

Merek looked at Violet. Her eyes were wide as she stared back at him.

"We do not have to if you're not ready," he whispered in her ear, enjoying the smell of her hair, like flowers in springtime.

"The queen and I would enjoy being your witnesses, and then you can be married in your own church when you return home."

"I should like to have the king as our witness," Violet said quietly, breaking eye contact with him, as if she was suddenly feeling shy.

So the next day Merek and Violet were joined in marriage by the chaplain of the Tower of London in the Chapel Royal of St. Peter ad Vincula. It was a small ceremony attended by King Richard and Queen Anne.

When it was over, the king and queen bid them to be happy and prosperous and left.

As soon as they were alone, Merek caressed Violet's cheek, and she slipped her arms around him, pressing her face to his shoulder. But soon enough they were kissing, and Merek could think of nothing but his beautiful bride and this moment with her. Nothing had ever existed before, and nothing existed after.

Violet pulled away and whispered breathlessly, "I'm so glad the baron sent you to fetch me that day."

"You didn't seem very pleased. In fact, I was fairly certain you hated me."

"But I don't hate you now."

"You don't?" He kissed the tip of her nose.

"No."

He kissed her forehead. "I don't hate you either. In fact, I love you, and I intend to love you in good times and bad times, till death."

When he looked into her eyes, they were swimming in tears.

"What's wrong?"

"Nothing is wrong. I am just so happy. I love you."

They kissed again, and he felt his sometimes cold, angry heart expanding in his chest, truly warm and happy and content for the first time in his life.

Epilogue

VIOLET WAITED AT THE TOP OF THE TOWER OF THE CASTLE that belonged to her now—her and her new husband—as she watched for Merek to come riding through the castle gate.

"There he is!" Violet cried as Merek's sister, Delia, Lady Strachleigh, waited beside her.

Soon Merek saw them and waved back, then rode his horse to the stable.

They both hurried down the steps to see him. By the time they made their way to the front door of the castle, Merek was being greeted by his brothers, each one of them smiling and clapping him on the back.

Violet and Merek had been married in the king's chapel at the Tower of London two months before, but they had decided to restate their vows before their families in a ceremony at Bilborough Cathedral, and though his brothers and his sister had arrived earlier, Merek had not been home to receive them. He had been helping Sir Willmer finish apprehending the outlaws who had taken over his uncle's—and now his—lands and castle.

Merek caught sight of Violet and pushed past his brothers, running the last few steps to reach her.

Her heart soared as he embraced her and lifted her feet off the ground.

She reveled in his smile and let him kiss her, even though so many people were watching them, since she had missed his kisses horribly for the two weeks that he'd been gone.

"I love you," he said as soon as the kiss ended.

"I love you too." She sighed happily, then said, "But we have guests. The queen of Montciel is here with her husband, your brother, Prince Gerard." She tried to direct him to the people standing behind him, waiting to talk to him.

"What do I care for queens and brothers when you are here?" He kissed her again.

Violet pushed him away, laughing. Thankfully, the queen was tending to her baby in another room and could not have heard his impolite words.

Merek kept his arm around Violet while he allowed his brothers and Delia to command some of his attention. Charles, Merek's closest brother in age, congratulated him on cleaning up Sir Willmer's estate.

"We heard you ran off the rabble from the land," Charles said, "and that is very well and good, but the real feat is what Violet did."

"Is that so?" Merek said, raising his brows at his younger brother.

"Yes. She has tamed our hotheaded brother."

Everyone laughed.

"She is the real conqueror," Berenger added.

Gerard said, "I am impressed."

Merek took their jests with a calm look and a half frown. "She is no one you would want to cross, Charles." He playfully pointed his finger at him.

The midsummer sun was sinking low as they all sat together in the Great Hall, which Violet had quickly refurbished with new tapestries and banners to replace the baron's, even devising a new coat of arms with the addition of a lion on a blue background from the Dericott coat of arms.

With her mother, grandmother, brother, and all of Merek's family on hand to witness it, they would be married in their own cathedral on the morrow. But as everyone ate, drank, talked, and laughed, Violet sighed, greatly content, as she laid a hand on her lower belly and smiled at the secret she would reveal to Merek tonight.

Her grandmother was the only person she had told, and she caught Violet's eye from across the table and gave her a teary-eyed wink, reading her thoughts.

Violet winked back.

Her mother had a worried look on her face, and Violet heard her tell Theo, "I hope they can afford all this food and drink."

Violet shook her head but couldn't help smiling, joyfully reminding herself that now she would be able to take care of her mother to repay her for the kindness she had shown her.

Merek leaned over and whispered in her ear, "Can we retire to bed now?"

Violet answered, "Yes. I have something to tell you."

Merek looked slightly surprised, but he took her hand and led her from the room, wishing everyone a pleasant night.

As they climbed the stairs, often pausing for a kiss, Violet whispered, "I cannot wait to tell you any longer."

"What?" His look was tender and curious. "What is it, my love?"

"No one knows except Grandmother, as I talked with her for confirmation, but I am with child."

Merek's breath rushed out of him, and he pressed his forehead to hers. He opened his mouth but couldn't speak. A moment later, he was hugging her close.

"That is the best news I have ever received." He spoke into her hair, then kissed her cheek, then her lips.

He was hugging her again, and she suspected he was trying to blink away a few tears. Finally, he picked her up and carried her the rest of the way up the stairs while she laughed, her own tears starting to leak out.

The next morning, as they prepared themselves for their wedding, Violet said, "I love your family, your sister and your brothers and their wives. I only wish they didn't all live so far away."

"Well, I love them, too, but I think it's a good thing they don't live with us. We wouldn't always wish them to be underfoot."

Violet laughed and shook her head at him.

"You are my wife," he said in his serious voice as he closed the gap between them and put his arms around her. "You are the best thing that has ever come into my life. And our child will be the next best."

"Love is everything," Violet whispered back, tracing her finger over his cheek. "Grandmother was right when she said I would marry a knight someday."

"But you didn't marry a knight; you married a viscount."

"A knight and a viscount." Violet sighed contentedly. "I once thought that my ideal husband would be handsome and brave and would be like David, singing and playing music."

Merek frowned.

"I know you don't sing or play music, but I realize that's not important. I also wanted my husband to love me more than anything."

Merek's face took on a satisfied expression. "And he does."

Violet smiled. "You love me very well, and love is everything."

ACKNOWLEDGMENTS

I WANT TO THANK MY WONDERFUL PUBLISHER, AMANDA Bostic, my editors, Lizzie Poteet, Kimberly Carlton, and Julie Breihan, Kerri Potts, and all the other people at Thomas Nelson and HarperCollins who made this book the best it could be and make sure it is seen by as many people as possible. I am very grateful to you!

I always want to thank my agent, Natasha Kern, who goes above and beyond professionally and has been a great friend and supporter. Thank you so much for all you do. You do it well!

My friend and writing accountability partner, Anne Marie Costello Brehm, really helped me get this book finished in a timely manner, so thank you!

I'm so grateful for my husband, Aaron, who helped me brainstorm and talk out my story at various stages of the plotting and writing of it. And thanks to my daughters Faith and Grace for always being willing to weigh in with their opinions and a listening ear. I love you!

Thanks also to all the wonderful librarians and teachers who recommend my books to their patrons and students. You are greatly appreciated!

Discussion Questions

1. Why did Violet initially not trust Sir Merek? Do you think this was justified? Why or why not?
2. If Violet were making a list of pros and cons for marrying Robert Mercer, what might the pros have been? The cons?
3. What had happened in Merek's past that may have been an underlying cause for him not trusting people and for too quickly reacting with anger and suspicion?
4. What had Merek's priest taught him about controlling his anger? What would you consider to be your greatest fault? Have you ever taken steps to try to overcome it?
5. Violet had a horror of causing her family trouble, desperately wanting to be a blessing and not a curse to her mother and grandmother. Could her mother's death have caused her to feel this way? How does childhood

trauma affect our thinking? Has it ever affected your
thinking? How?

6. Violet marveled at how different her mother and
grandmother were, since her mother often seemed
consumed with fear and worry, while her grandmother
always seemed at peace. How did her grandmother say
she had learned to overcome worry?

7. Violet's grandmother said, "Love is everything." What
did she mean by that? Do you think it would be harder
to live without luxuries like nice clothes, new cars, and a
big house, or without love?

8. Violet believed God told her that He was holding her,
her mother, and her grandmother in the palm of His
hand. Violet wondered if that meant that God would
protect her from being thrown in the dungeon, but she
concluded that it meant God was with her even if she
was thrown in the dungeon. Do you believe God holds
you in His hand? What does that mean to you?

9. We all face difficult things that can cause us to worry.
How do you overcome worry and anxiety? First Peter
5:7 (NIV) says, "Cast all your anxiety on him [God]
because he cares for you." What does it look like to cast
all your anxiety on God?

10. When she was choosing to marry her husband, what
was Violet's grandmother's reason for being too afraid to
ask God for wisdom? Have you ever been afraid to ask
God for wisdom? How did that turn out?

11. What were some of Merek's strategies for overcoming his anger problem? Do you think he will be able to change his reputation as the angry, ill-tempered brother? What part has humility played in the changes Merek has made?

LOOKING FOR MORE
GREAT READS?
LOOK NO FURTHER!

THOMAS NELSON

Since 1798

Visit us online to learn more:
tnzfiction.com

Or scan the below code and sign up to receive email updates
on new releases, giveaways, book deals, and more:

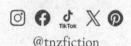

@tnzfiction

From the Publisher

GREAT BOOKS

ARE EVEN BETTER WHEN THEY'RE SHARED!

Help other readers find this one:

- Post a review at your favorite online bookseller

- Post a picture on a social media account and share why you enjoyed it

- Send a note to a friend who would also love it—or better yet, give them a copy

Thanks for reading!

ABOUT THE AUTHOR

MELANIE DICKERSON IS A *NEW YORK TIMES* BESTSELLING author and two-time Christy Award winner. Melanie spends her time daydreaming, researching the most fascinating historical time periods, and writing and editing her happily-ever-afters.

Visit her online at MelanieDickerson.com
Facebook: @MelanieDickersonBooks
X: @MelanieAuthor
Instagram: @melaniedickerson123